THE CONTI TRILOGY – BOOK 3
THE CARTEL WANT CARLO DEAD.
THEY WANT TO MAKE AN EXAMPLE.
THIS TIME: NO LOOSE ENDS.

THEN THERE WAS ONE

BRUCE HEWETT

HEWETTWRITES.COM

Published by Grigson Publishing

grigsonpublishing.com

ISBN: 978-0-6456593-4-4

Cover design, illustration and interior formatting:
Mark Thomas / Coverness.com

Again, I must thank Rod Grigson for his inspiration and patience in guiding me through the writing of the trilogy over the past three years. My writing has continued to improve with his input.

A special thanks to my wife, Bev, who has tolerated me being locked away for hours at a time in my study, my fingers pounding away on my keyboard. The trilogy is at an end, and normal transmission can be resumed.

Cheers to all those who have bought my book and enjoyed reading the tale of the Conti Brothers. Thanks for your continued support throughout the journey.

CHAPTER 1

The driver of the Ford SUV with maximum window tinting looked in his rear-view mirror as the passenger side rear door opened. He turned and seemed to pause before acknowledging the oddly dressed, unknown person with a nod. She was shabbily dressed in a heavy, dusty, black, woollen overcoat despite the hot, humid weather of the Columbian capital Bogota and carried what looked to be a metallic crutch. She wore a dirty, dark brown, fur-lined aviator hat with goggles hanging around her neck. Her face was streaked with dirt, and the driver's nose twitched upon detecting a strong odour from the woman.

"Ma'am, my instructions are to take you to level one of the Plaza la Centriale Shopping Centre underground carpark and signal for our contact in the centre security to turn off the CCTV upon our arrival," informed the driver. "I will await your return for 60 minutes and return you to the embassy."

"Thank you, driver," responded the passenger in a distinctively English accent, causing the driver to take another look at his passenger in the rear-view mirror.

The US Marine Corps guard raised the boom gate allowing the vehicle to exit the US Embassy and merge with the heavy Saturday afternoon traffic. A large crowd was expected to attend the election rally of incumbent President Xavier Torres at the Casa de Nariño, the Presidential Palace. Cuban President Cortes was reportedly in attendance to support the re-election of the anti-US Government of President Torres.

The shopping centre lay en route, only a short walk to the Casa de Nariño. As the SUV entered the shopping centre's underground carpark, the driver slowed the vehicle and flicked his headlights with three long, followed by three short illuminations. The boom gate lifted without the driver needing to take a ticket.

"That's taken care of the CCTV for five minutes, ma'am," noted the black-suited driver in his Texan drawl. "I'll park nearby to the elevators so you can make a quick exit from the centre and will await your safe return in the allocated time."

"Thank you, driver," the woman replied as she held the crutch and reached for the door handle.

When the driver pulled to a stop and gave the thumbs up to his passenger, she slid off the rear seat and shuffled toward the elevator. Mumbling to herself, with her head down, she hobbled with the aid of the metallic crutch nestled under her right armpit. At the entrance to the elevator, people stood aside and screwed up their faces at the smell as they invited her to enter the elevator and ride solo to the upper levels.

Exiting the elevator at the street level, the woman cut a path through the shoppers, who quickly moved out of the path of the strange woman. She approached the Plaza's street exit and was swept up in the crowd, excitedly heading towards the Presidential Palace with Columbian flags.

The two-story, flat-topped Palace was constructed in cream-coloured bricks with many tall, narrow, rectangular windows overlooking the plaza in front of the building. A spear-topped grilled-metal fence separated the growing crowd from the military band and presidential dais. The square outside the palace fence was surrounded by government buildings that overlooked the palace grounds.

On entry to the public square, the hobbling woman approached the gathering crowd from the rear. She headed down a narrow laneway to the rear of the building facing towards the palace. The building though smaller than the palace, was a mirror image of the palace's design. Two-story, flat-topped, with multiple windows facing onto the public square below.

Screened from people heading down the laneway towards the palace by a dumpster at the rear of the building, the woman extracted a security pass from her pocket. She tapped the pass on the scanner, and the door leading into the kitchen area clicked open. On entry, she stopped and listened for the sound of any movement. Not detecting any activity, the woman picked up her crutch and quickly bound up a staircase to the door leading to the rooftop. She cautiously opened the door, just enough to give her a view of the rooftop. With no movement evident after a few minutes, she approached the leading edge of the building that overlooked the palace and stationed herself behind a large, raised skylight.

Now hidden from view from anyone else accessing the rooftop, she removed her heavy padded coat and lay it on the ground atop the white pebbly surface. She unscrewed the top of her aluminium crutch, extracting her specially designed sniper rifle, which she set up on a bipod with the barrel pointing through the concrete balustrades overlooking the palace grounds.

In the distance, the band began to play, and the crowd, in a festive mood, began to cheer as various dignitaries moved up onto the dais and took their seats. The woman sniper lay prone on the ground and peered through the telescopic sight, and started the process of identifying her target seated on the dais with the VIP's.

There you are Senor Munoz. Your cocaine cartel will shortly be without a leader.

After acknowledging the Cuban President to the crowd's applause, President Torres commenced an anti-American tirade accompanied by the burning of American flags in the crowd and chants of "death to the capitalists."

The sniper checked the wind direction and strength, then began to calm her body, allowing her heart rate to slow in preparation for the shot of 210 metres. She lined up the target on her site and went through her ritual.

Take a deep breath, slowly exhale, and gently squeeze the trigger.

The deadly leaden 0.5 calibre bullet was sent on its journey at 853 metres/second.

In a fraction of a second, the target's head exploded like a watermelon being smashed with a sledgehammer. The now headless body occupied the chair on the stage, bringing shrieks and screams from those on the dais. Security guards leapt onto the dais and provided an umbrella of protection around the VIPs as they were led away from the unknown danger. Military personnel with guns raised began to scan the crowd that quickly started to flee in panic from the square.

Job done. Let's get out of here.

Keeping low, the sniper peered over the edge of the building and noted the attention of the military personnel starting to focus on her building. Her pulse quickened as she put on her coat and scanned her surroundings for anything she may have left behind. Keeping low, she picked up the expended round, placing it in the left side pocket of her coat. She checked her watch – *thirty minutes to reach the rendezvous.* The sniper's rifle was replaced in the crutch, and she moved rapidly to the staircase to exit the building.

At the exit from the kitchen, she slightly opened the door and saw people streaming away from the area. She quickly exited the building and emerged from behind the dumpster as uniformed military and plain clothes security personnel arrived on the scene, looking to access the building. They ran down the length of the building, checking each door opening out onto the rear of the building.

As a plain-clothed, gun-toting security officer approached the woman, she reached into her left side coat pocket and removed a small bottle of gin. She rested on her crutch and unscrewed the bottle throwing the top at the feet of the officer as she took a swig from the bottle.

I don't want him to get too close and see through my disguise.

"Disgusting," he stated as he sucked in his breath as the odour from her body reached his nostrils. The officer stepped back as she spat on the ground next to his boot and, with a mumble, started moving down the alleyway from the building towards the palace square.

"All clear. All the access doors are locked," reported a fellow officer. "We have the building surrounded so no one can get out."

"What's this?" The officer said as he stooped down. "It's a fucking shell case.

Right, where that crazy woman was standing near the dumpster. Where is that bitch?"

She placed the gin bottle back in her coat and felt around with her hand as she got away. *Shit, I dropped the shell case back at the dumpster. What a stupid mistake. I better get a move on.* The woman began to pick up the pace in response to a shout she heard coming from behind her.

"Which way did she go?" The officer yelled as he led several fellow officers into the rapidly emptying palace square. "You two go that way. You two are coming with me towards the shopping centre. I want to question her. We can't let her get away."

The sniper continued to move quickly along with the crowd fleeing the shooting scene and heading towards the shopping centre. She now neglected to hobble in her haste to reach the safety of the entrance to the Plaza and the waiting transport.

I'm nearly at the Plaza. I'll be safe once I'm inside. I can disappear into the crowd and get down to the Embassy car.

She felt the cool air as she entered the centre, and her eyes quickly scanned the entrance foyer. A large crowd began forming in front of the huge TV screens suspended above the escalators leading to the upper levels. The first announcements of a shooting at the Presidential Palace were being broadcast.

The announcement of the shooting was a trigger to create a wave of movement amongst the shoppers towards the centre's exit. Not wanting to risk being caught waiting for an elevator, the sniper identified the entrance to the stairs leading down to the carpark and quickly entered the staircase and closed the door behind her.

*

The two officers entered the Plaza, and their eyes began to scan the shoppers surging past them towards the exit.

"I think I saw her, sir, that black coat," said the officer to his commander. "She's headed towards the carpark staircase."

The commander started calling into his radio for backup at the centre, "suspect has entered the Plaza la Centriale Shopping Centre, and I need the building sealed off *rapido*."

With guns drawn, the two officers cautiously entered the stairwell and yelled at people to get out of the way as they descended the stairs. They opened the entrance to level one and tentatively looked in opposite directions as they scanned the area for their quarry.

"There's some movement near that black Ford SUV, sir," noted the officer as he started to edge towards the vehicle.

*

"You cut it fine, ma'am. They are just about to turn the CCTV back off for our exit," noted the driver as he reached for the ignition key. "I think you have drawn a crowd by the look of those two guys approaching us with guns raised."

In the back seat, the sniper dropped the crutch onto the rear storage area along with her outward clothing and covered the load with a blanket. The driver was surprised by what he saw with the disguise removed. She was an attractive woman around thirty, about six feet tall, of slim build, well-tanned, with penetrating blue eyes and long, jet-black hair pulled tightly back into a ponytail.

Wow, I wouldn't mind getting to know her.

As the officers approached the car, she exited the back seat, "I won't be long. I need to pick up a few things in the pharmacy."

"Did you see an old woman go past?" the officer asked.

"Sorry, I don't speak Spanish," the woman replied as she reached into her pocket and presented the officer with an ID for the US Embassy.

"Pardon, madam," the officer replied in English, lowering his gun. "You better get out of her now, as the building will shortly be locked down."

He watched as the woman got back into the vehicle, and the driver immediately fired up the V8 engine and accelerated towards the exit. The officer was surprised as the boom gate opened without inserting a card-*perks of the diplomatic corps.*

"I'll go and get onto security to see if we can track her down on the CCTV," replied the junior officer.

"Good idea," the senior officer replied. "I'll speak with the general to shut down the area surrounding the Plaza. She can't have gotten too far."

*

On the return to the Embassy, the sniper was escorted to the Drug Enforcement Administration (DEA) offices for a de-briefing on the mission.

"Nice shooting Miss Emmett-Jones," said Agent Andy Carter admiringly.

"I made a stupid rookie error that nearly cost me and the operation," replied a rather glum Penny Emmett-Jones. "I took a bottle of gin out of my coat pocket to make me look like a drunk. However, removing the bottle caused the empty shell case to fall to the ground. I covered it with my foot, but when I moved away to get to the pickup point, the officer saw it and gave chase."

"Apart from the shell casing, everything went to plan," responded Agent Carter. "The site and distance for taking the shot were perfect, and your disguise was very clever, getting you to and from the palace square with your weapon. Don't be too hard on yourself. A mistake like that could have happened to anyone. You don't fancy a bit of dinner tonight to celebrate your success?"

"Maybe another time. I want to return to my hotel and unwind," Penny replied as she stood to terminate the meeting.

He is a good-looking guy, that Andy Carter. Maybe next time for dinner if he asks me again. I need to get back to my hotel room and unwind.

*

Penny relaxed in her bathtub and sipped from a chilled Chardonnay she had poured herself. She reflected on how she, the daughter of an English aristocrat, had ended up working as a highly paid assassin for the US Government.

CHAPTER 2

Captain Fiona Irvine, British Army, waited to be asked to enter the Tactical Command Centre on the British base, just outside the Afghani city of Kandahar. She sat in the waiting area, noting the red light above the door was on, indicating a meeting was in progress. She sat upright in a foldable, unpadded, metal chair, with shoulders back and her hands in her lap. The base commander, Colonel Rupert Smythe-Jones, had summoned the captain.

It must be important if the Colonel wants to see me.

Fiona looked up as the light above the door changed to green, and the door opened. She stood to attention and looked into the windowless room, a hive of activity. Several operators were seated, headphones in place, eyes focused on the wall-lined computer screens. The screens surrounded senior officers in an eerie light as they grouped around a large rectangular, wooden trestle table.

The Colonel stood at the centre of the assembled officers with a pointer. In his strong, commanding voice, he was describing the locations of sightings of Taliban forces on a 3D model of the nearby rugged, mountainous terrain. As with the other officers, the Colonel wore the standard, multi-terrain pattern camouflage uniform the British Army wore. He was an imposing figure, a little over six feet tall, with greying hair and appeared to keep himself in good physical shape, unlike some of his fellow officers.

"Ah, Captain Irvine, come in," said the Colonel, indicating her to join him at the table with the other officers. She entered the room, stood to attention and saluted the Colonel as his eyes wandered down her body.

"Gentlemen, this is Captain Irvine. She is the sniper I have been telling you about. Stand easy, Captain."

I don't like the way he's looking me up and down. Fiona squirmed inside. *Makes me feel uncomfortable in front of the other officers.*

*

Fiona Irvine was the only child of Sir Peter and Lady Mary Irvine. Her Father had a distinguished career in the military, rising to the rank of Colonel in the Royal Fusiliers, before being wounded in the Gulf War, ending his service. Despite Lady Mary's protestations, Fiona had always wanted to follow in her father's footsteps and joined the 280-year-old Royal Fusiliers Infantry Regiment after completing a Science degree at Cambridge University.

Under her father's tutelage on the family estate in Hertfordshire, Fiona had shown an aptitude for target shooting, outshining all other recruits in the regiment. On active service in Afghanistan, she had quickly gained a reputation of being one of the top snipers in the entire British Army, rapidly rising to the rank of Captain.

*

"Captain Irvine, I would like to introduce you to Agent Andy Carter from the USA's Drug Enforcement Authority, the DEA," stated the Colonel as he turned towards the American, casually dressed in a white short-sleeved shirt, blue jeans and a pair of aviator sunglasses propped on his head.

Andy was around 6-1, 6-2 tall, with a slim muscular build, his bulging biceps evident in the short-sleeved shirt. Despite appearing in his early thirties, hints of grey hair were showing around the temple area of his close-cropped black hair. He stepped forward and extended his right hand towards Fiona.

"Howdy, Captain. You can call me Andy," he said in his Southern drawl. "I didn't expect...."

"Why I do declare," chuckled Fiona, mimicking Andy's accent. "Expect a woman!"

"Well, we better get down to business," said the Colonel sternly, seemingly annoyed at the friendly interaction between Fiona and Andy. "All of you gather around the model, and Agent Carter will explain why we are here today."

"Thank you, Colonel," began Andy as he picked up a pointer. "In the village of Nur Mohammed on the outskirts of Chaman, just over the border into Pakistan, our intel has advised us that a senior Taliban official, Ali Asgar, is holed up in the village. He is always on the move, his intel seeming to keep him one step ahead of us, so we don't know how long it will be before he's on the move again."

"What is the interest of the DEA in this operation?" Fiona asked.

"The sale of opium has been funding the Taliban's activities against our Allied forces, and we have been looking for him for a long time to stop his trade," detailed Andy. "Our informants have tracked him down to this village, and we need you guys to strike before we lose track of him again."

"Major Hazelman, would you please explain the details of the operation," said the Colonel, nodding towards his colleague.

"Thank you, Colonel," said Major Hazelman stepping towards the table with his pointer. "The plan, Captain Irvine, is to get you in a position in the hills above the village and eliminate Ali Asgar. Agent Carter will accompany you to ensure the target is correctly identified. We can't afford to miss given this rare opportunity."

"The terrain looks very rugged, so getting a position to take a shot won't be easy. I would also recommend we get dropped well away from the village. We can't risk the noise from a helicopter alerting them of a possible attack," stated Fiona.

"Good point, Captain," observed the Colonel as he moved his pointer on the model. "So as not to alert the target of our arrival, I propose we drop you on this plateau several kilometres from the village. You and Agent Carter can walk from the drop-off point to the high ground above the village. Ideally, you'll be in place ready to take the shot as the target heads to morning prayers around 0530 hours. Agent Carter will assist you in carrying your weapons and other supplies."

*

The unmarked, matte, black-painted Iroquois helicopter sat in the midnight darkness, ready for take-off. The pilot and payload officer dressed in civilian clothing awaited their cargo. The chopper was parked adjacent to an unlit aircraft hangar on the British Army base.

"Good morning, Agent Carter," said Fiona as Andy approached, dressed in non-identifying camouflage gear. She held a black balaclava in her right hand with a rifle bag draped over one shoulder and an automatic rifle over the other.

"All set?"

"Yes, all set, Captain," replied Andy. "We have about a 90-minute flight to the drop zone, then the hike to get into position to take the shot at sunrise."

"Given that we are going in without identification, I presume if we get caught, we are on our own?" Fiona observed.

"That is affirmative," replied Andy. "If that happens, I suggest a single shot to the temple would be the best option if capture was likely to occur. They won't treat you, a woman, very kindly at all."

With a thumbs up to the waiting pilot, the chopper's engine was fired up, and the blades began to whirr. The pair were helped to scramble aboard by the payload master, who strapped the duo into their seats and provided them with headsets for communication. "What have you got in the boxes?" Fiona asked Andy.

"Just a few things to provide some distraction to aid our escape," replied Andy. "There are some 40mm grenades and smoke bombs that I'll launch into the village with an M203 launcher after you take the shot. The launcher has a range of around 400m. Out of interest, what sniper rifle are you using?"

"Believe it or not, I use an American long-range semi-automatic rifle. It has an effective range of 1.8 kilometres," Fiona answered, tapping the rifle bag on her left shoulder. "It has a fantastic telescopic sight, and I also carry a suppressor and spare magazines," Fiona answered, tapping the rifle bag on her left shoulder. "It's not a lightweight at around 14Kg but comes with a fantastic telescopic sight. The other is a Nemesis Arms Vanquish 7.62, just in case, along with suppressors and spare magazines."

"Wow, that's some impressive weaponry, ma'am," noted Andy. "Wouldn't want to get on the wrong side of you."

The rest of the flight was in relative silence, with the nervous energy directed towards checking and re-checking the equipment. Andy loaded the diversionary explosive devices into a backpack and then studied the map under torchlight, going over the route to and from the village. A red light flashed above the cabin area, providing a 5-minute warning of the arrival at the drop zone. As the descent to the plateau commenced, infra-red goggles were activated, and the passengers scanned their surroundings for any sign of the Taliban lying in wait.

With the roaring rotors still whirring at full speed, the pair with goggles in place quickly unloaded their equipment and, with a final check, gave a thumbs up to the payload master. In seconds the chopper was gone under a powerful downdraft, whipping up a blinding dust storm. As the dust settled, the pair loaded up and began the difficult two-hour trek towards the village of Nur Mohammed, aiming to avoid any slips or falls with their dangerous load.

They arrived in the hills above the village just before 0500 hours, as the rays of early morning sunlight started to flicker on the snowcapped peaks of the Hindu Kush. From the recent drone surveillance, they identified the rocky knoll above the village as the best location from where Fiona was to take the shot at the target.

Peering down the steep slope into the valley below, they could see the village coming to life, with smoke starting to billow from the solid flat-roofed, mud-brick houses. Just before 0530 hours, the call to morning prayers could be heard crackling over the village imam's megaphone. Fiona did not have much time to set up and quickly unpacked the sniper rifle and accessories from the rifle bag. She rested the barrel on the bipod before setting the telescopic sight in place and zeroed in on the village mosque's prayer room entrance.

"I'll give you as much warning as possible as to which one is Ali Asgar. He's reasonably tall for an Afghani and tends to stand out amongst his men," said Andy.

He raised his binoculars to his eyes and began to scan the men beginning to gather in the village square.

"Got him. He's the tall guy with the black headgear and waistcoat over the white long-sleeve shirt."

Fiona adjusted her eyepiece and moved the rifle in her prone position in search of her prey.

"Contact," she confirmed and began to line up the high-ranking Taliban official in the crosshairs of her sniper's rifle.

It was an easy shot for her, with no wind at 400 meters. *Take a deep breath, slowly exhale, and gently squeeze the trigger.* With the suppressor connected, the rifle gave a gentle spit and a slight recoil into her right shoulder to send the bullet on its journey. In a fraction of a second, the target's head appeared to explode in the telescopic sight, creating an immediate frenzy of activity amongst those surrounding the now headless body, slithering slowly to the ground.

Heads began the scan the high ground in all directions above the village for the source of the attack, and indiscriminate firing of Kalashnikovs began to occur. This was the signal for Agent Carter to spring into action. He started launching grenades and smoke bombs down onto the village to aid their retreat.

"That was some shot, Captain. If you ever need a career change, I think I have the job for you in the DEA. Let's get out of here," yelled Andy above the noise of the explosions and rifle shots beginning to sound off from the Taliban members, who were continuing to pepper the surrounding hills, uncertain where the village's assailants lay.

They set off briskly, no longer burdened with the boxes of explosives and grenades.

"I'll confirm the pickup for 0700, and give me one of your rifles," said Andy as they moved to put distance between them and the enemy. "Without the extra load of the explosives, we should easily be able to return to the pickup point on time."

"Shit," said Fiona as a bullet ricocheted off a large boulder to their right. "They're onto us. Have you got any grenades left to give us a bit of cover while I return fire with Gertrude? Then I suggest we go hard, so put an urgent call in for a 0630 retrieval."

"OK, 0630. Let's go for it," replied Andy as he fired off his remaining two grenades. "Gertrude, you're kidding", he laughed.

Fiona set up her rifle, Gertrude, on top of a boulder and talked to herself as she prepared her telescopic sight.

"300-metres no wind." She fired off several rounds, easily taking out the advancing targets, their bodies flung backwards with the impact of the high-velocity bullets.

"That will slow them up for a while. Let's get moving out of here."

"Impressive shooting, Captain," noted Andy. *I could use her talents in the agency.*

The assassins made steady progress towards the pickup point, pausing periodically to ascertain whether they were still being pursued. They reached the landing zone and heard the welcome sound of the approaching chopper just as bullets again began to explode around them. Dust began to spit up from the ground edging closer towards them as the attackers began to find their range.

"Come on, you guys," yelled Andy as he looked expectantly towards the approaching roar of the helicopter.

"Fuck it," he shrieked as a bullet crashed into his left shoulder, causing him to drop his gun and stumble to the ground. He clutched the shoulder immediately, and blood oozed through his fingers.

"Stay low," called out Fiona as she returned fire. "Are you OK?"

"My left shoulder's stuffed, but I'll be ok," Andy replied. "Keep them busy. The chopper is nearly here?"

Dust swelled from the downdraft as the aircraft descended onto the plateau. Bullets began to bounce off its armour plating as the duo scrambled aboard.

"Go, go," yelled Fiona frantically as she waved towards the pilot and then turned her attention to Andy, who had collapsed on the floor, grasping his shoulder.

"That's a nasty hit," said the payload master, who had applied a dressing to the wound. "He's already lost a bit of blood and is probably just in shock. I'll get the pilot to expedite the return to base, as he'll need urgent attention. I'll radio ahead to have an ambulance on standby."

*

With the ambulance on its way to the base hospital with its patient, another vehicle pulled up in front of Fiona. The driver leapt out of the vehicle.

"Captain, Colonel Sir Rupert Smythe-Jones sends his compliments and would like a de-briefing with you at 1000 hours in his office after you have freshened up.

CHAPTER 3

After showering, Fiona put on a clean, pressed uniform and, with just a light touch of makeup, set off for the Colonel's office.

"Take a seat. The Colonel will be with you shortly," advised the soldier, seated at a desk, busily opening correspondence.

Fiona sat on a dark-brown leather sofa, her mind racing.

I hope Andy is ok. I'll see him as soon as I get this meeting out of the way. The Colonel is a bit of a political animal and is featured regularly in the British media claiming credit for successes in various missions in Afghanistan. It's rumoured he wants to join his younger brother, a current government minister when he retires.

The phone on the assistant's desk buzzed, "you can go in now," his voice brought Fiona back from her thoughts with a slight shake of her head.

Fiona strode into the office, stood rigidly to attention, and saluted the Colonel. "Captain Irvine reporting, sir."

"I hear congratulations are in order, Captain. Another successful mission. You certainly have built an enviable record as a crack shot. I am receiving ever-increasing demands for your services. Shame about that chap Carter getting wounded," observed the Colonel.

"Thank you, sir," answered Fiona. "I'll check on Agent Carter as soon as our de-briefing is completed. He took a hit to the shoulder just as we were boarding the chopper."

The Colonel stood up from behind his desk and guided Fiona to sit on one of the two dark-brown leather sofas on a large earthy-coloured Fukari rug.

"I understand he will be OK. Tea, Captain?" The Colonel asked as he sat in the matching leather chair opposite the side of the glass-topped, dark-timbered coffee table.

"Thank you, sir. I'll pour," said Fiona as she reached for the teapot. "How can I be of assistance concerning today's mission?"

"As you may know, my younger brother, Richard, is assistant to the Minister of Defence. Given your successes on the battlefield, the Government believes you would be a great asset in helping to meet the Government's agenda of recruiting more women into the forces. You are very photogenic, and the media will eat you up to coin a phrase," said the Colonel. "I can see the front-page headlines with you holding your rifle – Taliban leader taken out and such."

Fiona froze, and her mouth dropped open. Then she placed the teapot down on the table, her mind racing.

"Sir, my father, Sir Peter, is quite a public figure within the community, having had a distinguished military career," she said with a quiver in her voice. "If I was to be paraded in the media by the Government, I fear my family would become the target for every jihadist in the world. I would not feel comfortable appearing in such a promotion and put my family at risk."

"I do not see you have much say in the matter," replied the Colonel with pursed lips and a wrinkle on his brow. "I suggest you take your leave and consider the matter seriously. Otherwise, there will be consequences. I do not take insubordination lightly. I have promised the Minister of Defence we would help his drive to encourage more women to enlist and have volunteered your services. I look forward to your full cooperation in this matter."

I have always done what has been ordered of me, as is my duty without question, but endangering my family is another matter. What am I to do? Can I disobey such an order?

A sombre Captain Irvine was deep in thought as she made her way to the infirmary to visit Agent Carter.

*

"Agent Carter, I do declare," said Fiona as she walked into his hospital room, again trying a Southern accent to lift her mood. "How y'all doin'?"

Andy was sitting on his hospital bed, his left arm in a sling. "Will you give up on the accent," he mocked. "I've been better, lost a bit of blood, and I think the shoulder will take some rehabilitation after reconstructive surgery."

Wow, she's some woman. I can't get over those piercing blue eyes. I wonder if there's anyone in her life.

"Take a seat," he said, nodding towards a plain pinewood chair in the corner of the room.

"I have something to ask you," said Fiona as she lifted the chair and placed it beside Andy's bed.

"How can I help?" Andy asked. Sensing her mood, he looked at her with narrowed eyes.

"Were you joking when you said to contact you if I was looking for a career change, and if so, what did you have in mind?" Fiona asked.

"What has brought this on all of a sudden?" Andy probed.

Fiona stood and started pacing around Andy's bed, her right fist pounding into her left palm,

"The Colonel wants me to head up some crazy government-inspired campaign to get more women to join the forces. He must have been watching re-runs of Tom Cruise in *Top Gun* and wants to commit me to some promotional enlistment program for women. They probably want to feature me as some heroic female assassin with a gun in hand. I fear such a campaign will endanger all my family from jihadists. I'd never forgive myself if anyone in the family or a female recruit were killed due to any promotion that included me in some starring role. I have questioned my desire to stay in the army for the first time."

"Surely orders are orders as in any army?" Andy queried.

"Not when I have only two weeks to go on my enlistment," noted Fiona. "I doubt whether the Colonel would have been aware of that. Now, what did you have in mind concerning a career with the DEA?"

"I can't say too much till I get clearance, but I'm sure my organisation could employ you as an agent on a contract basis, as a non-US citizen, to undertake activities commensurate with your skills. I would think the pay as a gun for hire, plus bonuses, would be much higher than the earning capacity of a Captain in the British Army," smiled Andy. "How about we meet in DC at the DEA HQ after I'm out of here, and you confirm you'll not re-enlist?"

"You are on," said Fiona. "Given the circumstances, I do not see how I can re-enlist, and I look forward to seeing a fit Agent Carter in DC." She left the room with a casual salute.

*

Much to the chagrin of Colonel Smythe-Jones and his politically ambitious brother, Captain Fiona Irvine, now a civilian, stood on the footpath outside the DEA Headquarters in Arlington, Virginia, opposite the famous Pentagon building.

What will today bring? What has Andy got in mind for me? She turned and strode confidently towards the entrance.

Fiona presented her ID and signed in at reception, identifying the appointment with Agent Carter. With a Visitor's Badge lanyard around her neck, the receptionist directed her to sit on a huge light-grey fabric sofa in the spacious waiting area. She initially had felt strange dressing again as a civilian, but today she had dressed to impress Agent Carter and his colleagues.

*

Agent Carter smiled as he exited the elevator and saw Fiona seated on the sofa in the waiting lounge. He swiped his security pass on the exit turnstile and walked towards his guest.

Lookin' good in those dark grey woollen pants with matching jacket and those amazing blue eyes. She's growing her hair too. Andy thought when he saw Fiona.

Focus, Carter.

"How is that shoulder coming along?" Fiona asked as she stood to meet her host.

"Coming along OK, but the bullet shattered the clavicle, so I 'm not sure if it will ever be 100%," he replied as he swiped his pass to admit Fiona passed the security barrier and into the elevator. He pressed the button for the third floor.

"The agency Doc reckons I'll be on desk duties for some time."

Andy swiped his pass when exiting the elevator again to gain entry past a solid metal security door. Directly ahead, he escorted Fiona into a meeting room.

"Agent Denise Voss, meet Fiona Irvine."

Andy closed the door of the small meeting room and indicated to Fiona to take a seat at the round light-timbered table. He opened the Venetian blinds by twirling the long plastic control stick and, once seated, flicked a switch on a central panel to indicate the room was OCCUPIED.

Agent Denise Voss was similar in age to Andy, early thirties, around 5-9. She had a slightly olive complexion, short black hair and wore a dark-grey pants suit with low-heeled leather shoes.

"Agent Voss is the director of our South American field team," explained Andy. "She'll explain how we propose utilising your services for an important forthcoming operation."

"Thanks, Andy," said Denise, folding her hands over a closed manila folder labelled TOP SECRET. "We have already completed our background security checks on you. That side of things appears to be in order, backed by an exemplary service record with the British Army. Your reputation and skills are well-regarded, backed by Agent Carter's personal experience with you. On that basis, as a non-US citizen, we would be prepared to offer you a substantial fee to operate as a DEA contractor on an agreed fee per assignment basis."

"Before any contract is signed, you must complete our compulsory 12-week agency training program," Andy interjected. "The program includes training in various techniques including weaponry, self-defence, surveillance, communications and explosives."

"Sounds like a reasonable opportunity, and I don't have any problem participating in the training program," replied Fiona. "However, there is one thing I seek your assistance with. It's creating a completely new British identity. Once I complete the training program and sign up with the DEA, I will need a new name, passport, birth certificate and British National Health registration."

"Any particular reason for the change in identity?" Andy asked.

"My family is highly respected within the community, and I do not want them to be caught up in anything that may happen to me, especially if I was to be caught or killed while on assignment," stated Fiona.

"I see no problem for the DEA to work with our contacts within the British Government to create a new ID for you," answered Denise. "We can start some preliminary work immediately, so we can get you up and running as soon as you are certified."

"That is great," said Fiona. "Do you already have an assignment in mind for me?"

"That info will have to wait until your training is completed and you are officially contracted to the DEA," stated Andy. "The next intake for recruits starts next week."

"Fine by me. Nothing else is keeping me busy at the moment," responded Fiona. "The sooner I qualify, the better, and I can start my new life."

*

The 12-week training period had flown by, and Fiona was escorted into the same third-floor meeting room by Andy and was greeted by Agent Voss,

"I hear congratulations are in order. You passed top of your class, and as expected, you blitzed the target shooting."

"It was tougher than I expected," replied Fiona, shrugging. "You have a good bunch of recruits in this intake."

"Welcome to the DEA," added Andy with a smile.

"We better get down to business. Time is short for an assignment we need your skills for," said Denise. "In Columbia, there is a drug cartel run by the Manuel Munoz cocaine cartel. They operate freely based on providing regular funding to President Xavier Torres, who is very friendly with the communist regime in Cuba. A rival drug cartel headed by Hernando Gonzales supports an opposing candidate in the forthcoming elections, Fernando Casillas, a strong friend of the USA."

"Why take out this Manual Munoz?" Fiona asked.

"We want him taken out, so his funding to Torres is neutralised, and we can hopefully indirectly aid in the election of Fernando Casillas," Denise continued. "By using you to undertake the mission, we can claim to any subsequent Senate enquiry, hand on heart, that no American was involved in the killing of Munoz. We would claim the killing must have been orchestrated by a rival drug cartel."

"I have to get my head around this," said Fiona taking a deep breath. "You want me to take out one coke dealer to create a monopoly for another dealer who will continue to send coke to the States because he supports your preferred candidate? Wow! You guys work in mysterious ways. Suppose it helps the free world, so who am I to judge? What is the proposed fee?"

Ignoring Fiona's comment, Andy replied, "we would propose to pay two million in US dollars into your nominated Swiss bank. Half as a down payment and the balance on completion. However, remember that if you are caught or killed. You will be on your own."

Fiona took a deep breath. "Understood. Now about my new British identity. I've always wanted a fancy hyphenated name and decided to go with Penny Emmett-Jones. I couldn't find anyone with that name registered on the electoral roll."

I wonder whether Andy will ask me out for dinner. Fingers-crossed.

"That will be all. Thanks, Denise," said Andy. "I'll wrap up with Fiona while you start the name change paperwork."

After Denise left the meeting room, Andy said, "Fiona, or should I say, Penny, would you be free for dinner tonight?"

"I think I can fit you into my busy schedule," replied Fiona with a huge grin.

"I'll pick you up at seven," said Andy.

CHAPTER 4

Without access to the facilities of the British Army, Penny needed to establish a base from which she could continue to hone her skills. She wanted to remain in England, where she could reach most of the DEA's likely contract targets in one flight. Her parents were unaware of her new name and career, having been told she had taken a position with a security firm in New York City.

"I hope you come home to visit regularly, dear," said her mother, Lady Mary. "You know I don't like flying at the best of times, especially to America. You know what I think of those Americans and their abuse of the English language. They can't even spell properly."

"I will make sure I get back to visit you regularly," replied Penny. "I know you have told me you are not getting any younger and wondering when you will have grandchildren. And yes, I know Sir James's son Jonathan is single."

*

From Penny's research, she determined that the most strategic area to locate her base was in the English Midlands. The region of South Derbyshire in the East Midlands would provide access to Birmingham Airport for international flights, and the local East Midlands Airport would provide ready access to continental Europe. There was a regular train service available to London. Being based in the East Midlands also meant that Penny was unlikely to inadvertently bump into her parents, family members or friends, who were well ensconced in

Southern England. They rarely, if ever, travelled north of London.

Further analysis by Penny narrowed her focus to the village of Melbourne, located in the gently rolling hills between Derby and Nottingham. Melbourne featured Georgian-style architecture from the 18th Century. Buildings with flat exteriors built in brick or stone and featuring a white stucco finish. The village included around 50 shops, with cafes, bars and hotels, adjacent to the old mill pool, known as Melbourne Pool, picturesquely landscaped by Lord Melbourne, the British Prime Minister in the 1830s.

An online search had identified a property that was ideal for Penny's purposes and was shortly coming up for auction by White's Real Estate Agency, located in Melbourne village. She thought the property was ideal, an original three-storey Georgian farmhouse set on two acres, part of the recently sub-divided farm offering large lifestyle blocks close to the village. On a quiet Sunday morning, Penny cruised the M42 from her Birmingham Airbnb in her late model matt black V8 Range Rover to check out the property.

The farmhouse was set back around a hundred yards from the Melbourne - Ticknell Road and was a short walk across wheatfields to the National Trust's Calke Abbey. All the boundaries surrounding the property enclosed the farmhouse within a tall, dense hedgerow. At the rear of the house was a large barn with wooden walls, double sliding metal doors and a corrugated iron roof. The barn was big enough to have garaged the original farm's heavy machinery – tractors, harvesters, various tools and the like.

Penny pulled into the driveway and looked around. *This looks perfect. The three-story building had the classic symmetry around the central main entrance, with tall rectangular windows on the bottom two levels and small windows on the top, completed by a white stucco finish. Love it.*

With no one around, Penny surveyed the barn at the rear of the property. *I reckon that with the assistance of Andy Carter and the DEA team, I should be able to adapt the barn to my training and security requirements. The dense hedgerow would ensure privacy and added security.*

Penny was determined to acquire the place and decided to take the initiative and make a substantial offer direct to the property's listing agent, well above the indicated price range. She didn't want to risk exposing herself by bidding at a public auction. *You never know who could be in the crowd.*

On Monday morning, Penny called White's Agency.

"Good morning, White's Real Estate, Karen White speaking. How may I help you?"

"Good morning, Karen. My name is Penny Emmett-Jones. Over the weekend, I checked out the farmhouse property for sale on Melbourne-Ticknell Road. I would be very interested in discussing the property with you. How are you placed, say Wednesday around noon?"

Penny could hear pages being flicked over.

"That will be perfect. I look forward to meeting you then. We are on Derby Road, between the newsagent and the butcher shop. See you then."

*

On Wednesday morning, Penny drove slowly down Derby Road, the main street of Melbourne village, her eyes scanning the signboards of the shopfronts looking for White's Real Estate. Spotting the business, she turned left into Potter Street and parked the vehicle.

Penny had arrived earlier than the noon appointment, allowing herself time to explore the village on foot. She headed down Potter Street to Castle Street, which opened to a village square full of parked cars and surrounded by houses built up to the street front. Turning right, she headed past the White Swan Pub dating from the early 1600s and continued towards the famous Melbourne Pool.

After walking around the calm waters of the Pool and taking in Lord Melbourne's home and the spectacular Norman church, she looked at her watch. *Time for a coffee before meeting with Karen White.* Back onto Derby Road, she took a window seat in Forteys Coffee Shop and sipped on a café latte as she watched life in the village go by.

I like the feeling, the vibe of life in the village. I think I could be very happy here.

Just before noon, she noticed a professionally presented woman in her late thirties, dressed in a navy pants suit with blonde shoulder length check her watch, then entered White's Agency.

That must be Karen White.

Penny finished her coffee and, with her exit from Forteys accompanied by a tingle from the brass doorbell, made her way across the road.

*

Seated at a desk in the front of the office and having removed her jacket, Karen White looked up as she saw the elegant, well-presented woman enter her premises. She was around six feet tall, of slim build, well-tanned, with penetrating blue eyes and long, jet-black hair tightly pulled back into a ponytail. She wore black knee-high riding boots, beige jodhpurs, a white button-up blouse and a black oil-skinned shooting jacket. There seemed to be an aura of confidence about the woman.

"Good morning, I am Karen White. How may I help you?"

"Good morning, Karen. I am Penny Emmett-Jones, and please call me Penny. I have the noon appointment to discuss the property on Melbourne-Ticknell Road."

"Welcome, Penny. Yes, there has been much interest in the property. Good location and the house in excellent condition, with a price guide range of 700 to 800 hundred thousand pounds," noted Karen. "The auction is scheduled for Saturday week."

"That's what I want to discuss with you," Penny stated. "I have a very busy international travel schedule and would like to make an offer to acquire the property before the auction. I am prepared to offer nine hundred and fifty thousand today to take the property off the market."

Karen's jaw dropped, but she quickly gathered her composure, "I'll just go into my back office and give the vendor, Mister Lovett, a call."

Karen closed the door in the rear office and looked at Penny, sitting calmly in the front office while she called the vendor.

"Mister Lovett, it's Karen White. I have just received an offer before the auction of nine-hundred and fifty thousand pounds. Given there hasn't been much interest to date, I strongly suggest you don't go to auction and accept the offer."

Penny looked up as Karen returned to the front of the agency, "How did we go?"

"Congratulations Penny, you are the proud owner of a wonderful property and welcome to the village of Melbourne."

"I like the feel of the village," Penny nodded. "I think I will be very happy here. Will you take a cheque for the deposit?"

"That will be fine," answered Karen. "Welcome to the village, and I should also greet you as Director of the local Arts Festival."

"Thanks, Karen. Once I've settled in and completed some renovations, I might call you as I like to paint in watercolours. I see the potential to get my creative juices flowing with the lovely rolling landscapes surrounding the village," said Penny.

Penny and Karen's heads turned as the door of the agency opened. In stepped a woman in her late thirties. She was tall and slender, with dark brown hair pulled back into a ponytail. The woman was dressed in a navy-blue tracksuit emblazoned with the crest of a lion on the left breast.

"This is my friend Josephine Roberts," introduced Karen. "Josephine, meet Penny Emmett-Jones, soon to be the village's newest resident."

"Thanks, Karen and nice to meet you, Josephine," Penny said. "What about you, Josephine? What keeps you busy in the village?"

"I am just visiting, and please call me Jo," she replied. "Karen and I attended Oxford together, and she invited me to an exhibition of a local artist's work in the Melbourne Assembly Rooms this weekend. My claim to fame is my position as the English Women's Cricket team manager. We are arranging a training camp in the village for the forthcoming tour to Australia."

"I love cricket. How interesting. I thought I recognised the tracksuit you are wearing," said Penny. "I may be useful to the team someday with my paramedical background."

Little do they know that my skills were honed on the battlefields of Afghanistan.

*

The buzz of a mobile phone in her coat pocket distracted Penny as she extracted the phone from her coat pocket, glancing at the screen and moving away from the two women.

"Sorry Karen, Jo, I have to take this call. Speak soon."

Perfect timing, as usual, Mother.

"My dear, I've been trying to reach you," said her mother in an anxious voice. "Where are you? I can never seem to get you since you moved to America."

"For one thing, Mummy, there is a time difference between the UK and the USA," Penny replied, interrupting her mother. "Anyway, what can I do for you?"

"I was just checking in to find out when you will next be home for a visit," replied her mother. "I would like to arrange a party with the family for your father's birthday, and it would be great if you could attend."

"Promise, I will make it, Mummy," replied Penny. "Just text me the details when you have completed the arrangements."

I hope they never want to come to the USA on a visit. Thank goodness Mummy hates flying.

*

The money from the successful hit in Colombia provided sufficient funds for Penny to comfortably secure the title to the Derbyshire property. With the assistance of Andy Carter and his DEA resources, she completed works on the farmhouse and barn, turning the property into a secure operational centre for her future activities with the DEA.

Enhancements to the property included a satellite dish on the roof of the farmhouse that provided an upgrade in the communications capabilities. A sturdy electronic steel gate accompanied by security cameras was a deterrent for any uninvited motorists wanting to turn into the driveway off the main road.

The walls and roof of the barn were lined with sound-proofing materials, and a polished concrete floor was laid. An adjacent office area was outfitted with the latest computer equipment and CCTV screens. A windowless room with a solid steel door was added, home to a sturdy steel safe and racks housing a range of firearms – shotguns, handguns and rifles with telescopic sights and suppressors.

Armed with Gertrude, Penny was about to test out the shooting range for the first time when the red light above the office door began to flash, indicating she had a call coming through. Penny entered the office and picked up the phone's receiver on the office desk.

"What date is the Melbourne Festival this year?" a voice with a Southern US accent asked.

"I think it is October 8th," Penny replied.

"I had it in my diary for September 15th," the voice replied.

"I will check the date and call you back," Penny answered with a smile.

I wonder what Andy wants. Maybe he's coming for a visit.

Penny activated her VPN and hit the Andy Carter icon on her touch screen. After a short delay, he came online.

"Andy, good to hear from you, and the setup here is amazing. Thanks for all your help. You will have to come and check it out next time you are in the UK and see what your DEA dollars have created."

"Glad to be of assistance, and I will be coming to the UK. I have something important to discuss with you and will be in London Wednesday next week," Andy replied, immediately getting down to business.

"Meet you at the Mandeville Hotel, say 10 am, for coffee. I will book a meeting room under the name of Drew Collison."

*

The morning was chilly as Penny stepped out of the cab at London's Mandeville Hotel entrance. The doorman wore a crimson overcoat with gold braided epaulettes and buttons. He tapped his white, gloved right hand to the brim of his black top hat and, with a slight bow, opened one of the double glassed entry doors leading to the foyer. With a slight pause to gain her bearings, Penny stepped up to the concierge's desk.

"Meeting room for Mister Drew Collison."

"Certainly, Madam," acknowledged the concierge as he referred to his desk diary. "The Cambridge Room. Take the stairs through the door to the left of the elevators, down to the basement level."

Penny knocked on the door of the Cambridge Room.

"Come in," answered the expected Southern-accented voice of Andy Carter. "So good to see you," said Andy, completing a double cheek kiss while gently holding Penny's upper arms.

"It has been a while," replied Penny with a smile as her eyes adjusted to the low-level lighting in the windowless basement room.

Too long.

"Let me take off my coat. It's pretty warm in here." Penny draped the navy-blue woollen overcoat over the back of one of the heavy, red leather-bound chairs on either side of the long, glossy, black-painted timber board table.

"I'll get you a coffee. Café latte, I recollect," said Andy as Penny sat opposite Andy. He placed the mug of steaming coffee on the leather-lined blotter in front of Penny.

"The last time I saw you was at the de-briefing in the US Embassy in Bogota, Columbia, after the hit."

"Yes, that was when we said goodbye to Mister Munoz," Penny said with a smile.

"That was a master stroke," noted Andy with a large grin. "To take him out, sitting right next to the Cuban President and your getaway under the secret police's noses."

"I am grateful to Frederick Forsyth's book *The Day of the Jackal.* The book gave me the idea to use the disguise of an older woman hobbling along with the aid of a metal crutch that neatly housed Gertrude, my sniper rifle. However, it got a bit scary when they tracked me down after stupidly dropping that shell casing," said Penny as she reflected on the moment.

"Anyway, what brings you to London? You didn't come all that way to talk about old assignments with me."

"We have a problem in Australia that I need your help with," replied Andy.

CHAPTER 5

Electra tottered towards him in her towering red stiletto heels, tugging at her hip-hugging black leather skirt as she crossed the carpark. She knew Dominic liked her, but he seemed too hesitant to make any moves to ask her out.

"Was it a successful night?" Dominic asked with a quiver in his voice after lowering his passenger window.

Dominic had always liked Electra, with her long black hair and porn star looks. He had been waiting in his humble silver-grey Toyota sedan in the underground carpark of Kings Cross House of Pleasure for more than fifteen minutes, hoping to speak with her as she finished her overnight shift.

"It's been a bit quiet, but we've got the US Navy arriving in port in a couple of days, so that should keep us busy." Electra smiled at him, thrust her considerable chest a little further, and wriggled her hips, seeming to enjoy his evident discomfort.

Electra worked at the House of Pleasure, a high-class brothel owned by Gaetano Conti and his brother-in-law, Lorenzo Rossi, the patriarchs of the Western Sydney-based Conti family drug gang. From humble beginnings as migrants to Australia after WWII, the family had built their successful drug business from the demand coinciding with the end of the Vietnam War. The House of Pleasure, or the HOP as it was known around town, was established to launder the huge amounts of cash generated by the lucrative drug trade. Lorenzo's son Dominic had been appointed to manage the running of the HOP providing some level of separation from the risks inherent with having any direct involvement in the drug trade.

Electra glanced at her watch. "I am late. Gotta go," she said as she pressed the button on her BMW convertible's remote. "Catch you later."

Dominic watched as Electra stepped into the driver's seat, her skirt riding up, giving him a glimpse of her red underwear. He continued to stare and squeezed the front of his pants. *I'd love to get into that, but how could I impress her with what the fuckin' family pays me? I can only afford this shit heap of second-hand Toyota and have to live at home with my parents, for God's sake.*

The family's treated me like shit for long enough. I'm supposed to be the manager, and I don't even get a fuckin' reserved carpark. Doing all their donkey work, day in and day out and what thanks do I get? How could Electra ever look at me and respect me? I should be running the family business here in Aussie, not just this joint. Uncle Gaetano and Papa should've retired when my cousin Carlo turned rat on the family and is now safely hiding away in the Witness Protection Program (WPP). I reckon it's time to make a move.

As he watched Electra exit the carpark, Dominic hesitated, his hand paused above the glovebox before he reached to extract one of several burner phones. On his regular mobile, he checked Google for the number of the Australian Federal Police's (AFP's) hotline for crime reporting and chuckled when he saw the number 1-800-CROOKS.

This call will be the first step in me takin' over the whole fuckin' business, and Electra will be mine, and she won't have to work in the HOP anymore.

Dominic dialled the number.

"Crooks Hotline. How can I help you?"

Dominic placed his hand over his mouth and mumbled, "I'd like to report a drug delivery tomorrow mornin' at 8 am. The warehouse at 23C McDonald Lane, Kings Cross."

He immediately terminated the call and removed the SIM. He opened the car door and dropped the SIM on the ground, grinding it into the concrete with the heel of his shoe.

*

Detective Sergeant (DS) Tanya Layton of the Australian Federal Police (AFP) gently knocked on Detective Chief Inspector (DCI) Adam Charles's office door. As usual, his desk was piled with folders, representing the ever-increasing caseload for his Drug Enforcement Unit. He looked up and smiled as he indicated for Tanya to take a seat.

"What's up, Tanya?" Adam asked.

"We've just received a tip-off on the 1-800 hotline. An anonymous caller said a drug drop would be made at a Kings Cross warehouse tomorrow morning, 8 am," replied Tanya. "The caller quickly terminated the connection so that we couldn't trace the call, and from listening to the recording, the guy was trying to disguise his voice."

"Suspect he used a burner phone that now probably sits at the bottom of Sydney Harbour," noted Adam. "Better get the team together so we can plan the raid. Hopefully, it's not a false alarm to lead us away from a genuine delivery. That's happened to us before with one of these tip-offs."

Tanya quickly rounded up the Drug Enforcement squad and herded them into the large third-floor meeting room. Adam was already standing at the wall-mounted whiteboard, tapping a black marking pen. He waited while the team began scraping their chairs on the shiny, pine board floors to take their seats around the large rectangular, metal-framed, frosted glass-topped table.

"We've had a report of a drug delivery tomorrow morning at eight at a warehouse in McDonald's Lane, Kings Cross. DS Layton spoke to the real estate agent managing the property. They confirmed the warehouse is typically rented on a short-term basis, with payments usually paid upfront in cash," informed Adam. "The warehouse has been rented for a month by a company going by the name of Supa Trading, which doesn't have an official company registration. Interestingly, the warehouse is located only a few doors down from The House of Pleasure, owned by our friends, the Contis. I wonder if it is a coincidence?"

"I'll run you through the plan, then you better get home to rest up as we have an early start in the morning," advised Tanya. "I want you here at HQ by 6 am so we can get into position well before the advised delivery time."

*

A woman, her head down and dressed in a crumpled black trench coat and scruffy, laceless tennis shoes, slowly shuffled towards the El Alamein fountain dragging an old weather-beaten trolley behind her. Office workers avoided her as they hurried past, disappearing into the underground entrance to the busy King's Cross subway station.

Finally reaching the fountain, she sat on its knee-high parapet wall, settling the grimy trolley beside her. She pushed aside her tattered navy-blue straw bonnet with a limp artificial sunflower and looked around before spitting on the ground and muttering to herself.

Just across the road, a truck laden with a 20-foot Maersk shipping container was beeping a warning sound as it began to reverse into the driveway of a warehouse. The heavy steel roller door began to squeak and graunch as it slowly rose, revealing the loading dock and three men waiting to receive the delivery. No signage was on the front of the building to identify the commercial activities conducted within the anonymous dark, grey-painted building. Affixed to a frosty glass entry door to the side of the roller door was a faded sign advising that AJAX 24-hour Security Service monitored the building.

The old woman reached for her back as she stood and slowly hobbled over the road and headed towards the truck. The truck's nose protruded slightly into the street, so the woman had to step out into the roadway to get around the truck. "Careful, sweetheart. Don't trip," called out the driver.

"Fuck you," mumbled the woman, not looking up as she spat towards the driver.

"That's no way for a lady to behave," he grinned, reaching for his cigarettes in his shirt pocket.

Rounding the front of the truck, the woman stepped back onto the footpath and, unseen, suddenly accelerated into the recess of an adjacent doorway. She quickly removed her footwear, sunflower hat, blonde wig and trench coat, revealing an attractive woman around thirty with a bob of brunette hair, wearing a white, long-sleeve cotton blouse and blue jeans. Attached to her hip, on top of her jeans, was a black leather holster containing a Glock 19 handgun. She reached into the trolley, extracted a pair of black Skechers, and slipped them on. She then reached into her back pocket to retrieve a two-way radio.

"DS Layton in position," she whispered. "All set for go. The cargo has been delivered to the warehouse. Delivery door is fully open. Three suspects visible in the delivery dock, and the driver is standing in the street. Over."

Detective Tanya Layton edged along the wall towards the truck. She could smell the cigarette smoke from the relaxed driver as he stood on the footpath.

"Come on, you lazy fucks," he yelled. "Get the fuckin' container door open and the shipment unloaded. I haven't got all day. I must return the container to the shipping agent by this afternoon to avoid demurrage charges."

"You could give us a hand, you lazy prick, instead of standing out there puffing on a fag," snapped the retort from within the warehouse. "Have you lifted anything apart from your dick in your life?"

Using the truck and container as a shield, Tanya edged into the raised delivery dock area as the container doors swung open.

"It's a go, go, go," she yelled into the walkie-talkie, which caused a frenzy in the street.

Sirens started to wail, and red and blue lights flashed as cars emerged from adjacent streets.

"This is the police. Put up your hands. Lay on your belly. Hands behind your back." Police with raised guns rushed like bees towards the warehouse roller door.

The truck driver dropped his cigarette and stood rigidly with his hands raised. "What the fuck's goin' on," he quivered. "I'm just the delivery driver."

An officer pulled his hands down, turned his body around, and clasped black cable ties onto the compliant driver's wrists.

"Sit down and don't move came the firm instruction."

With her gun raised, Tanya scrambled up onto the delivery dock. She asked the two men inside the container to place their hands on the stack of cardboard cartons. As she reached for her handcuffs, she realised there was one missing.

"One suspect unaccounted for. We need to check the building."

Tanya cautiously made her way to the rear door to admit her colleague, who had been watching for anyone trying to escape the building.

"No sign of anyone coming out the back, boss."

Where the heck are you?

"You head up the stairs and check out the office, and I'll…" began Tanya as a hooter began to sound. "The bloody fire escape," she roared as she headed for the back door.

With her pistol poised, she reached the warehouse's heavy-steel rear door, tentatively pushed it open, stepped back, and waited. Receiving no reaction, she quickly dashed into the laneway and turned her body to check for anyone waiting for her behind the emergency exit.

A clatter from a rubbish bin being knocked over further down the street caused her to look down the laneway. A body dressed in black tracksuit pants with a matching hoodie turned left out of the laneway into the street to the sound of the squeal of brakes and the tooting of an irate motorist. He had a 100-metre start.

"Suspect heading east on Macleay Avenue," Tanya called on the two-way. "In pursuit. Over."

Tanya turned into the street and saw her quarry attempting to hail a taxi. A taxi pulled alongside the curb as she rapidly approached her target.

"Stop, police," she yelled, raising her handgun. The target had stopped and began to reach for the handle of the taxi's rear door. Tanya cautiously approached the solidly built man with her gun poised in her right hand.

"Police, put your hands on the roof where I can see them." She assumed a crouching position as her left hand groped for her handcuffs just as a patrol car screeched to a stop behind.

It's DCI Charles.

The brief distraction with Tanya briefly turning towards the patrol car gave the runaway a chance he needed. He turned his torso and swung with his right arm connecting with Tanya's hand holding the weapon. The gun was knocked from her grasp and crashed onto the footpath some distance away.

The assailant flicked back the top of his hoodie with his left hand, then with his right hand, reached to the small of his back from where he extracted a mean-looking knife. It was around ten inches long with a deeply serrated edge.

"What do you reckon bitch," sneered the man as he edged towards Tanya, thrusting the weapon threateningly backwards and forwards towards her face.

Tanya looked right and left, searching in vain for any backup. She slowly retreated from the deadly piece of steel glinting in the morning sun, her eyes fixed on her would-be attacker, looking for any hint of an attack in his eyes. The clunk of the taxi's passenger door caused the assailant to turn slightly towards the taxi. It was enough for Tanya to make a move. She slipped with the right side of her body to the ground and drove her right foot into the instep of the man's right foot. Simultaneously, her left foot hooked behind his right knee, pulling him forward. Off balance, he fell forward towards Tanya, who started to turn her body away to the left, away from the falling body.

The knife grazed her right arm, tearing the blouse, as the man fell forwards. Blood began to seep out onto the sleeve of her white cotton shirt. Ignoring the danger, she swiftly rolled onto the attacker's back and grabbed the knife, placing it against his throat.

"Don't move, you prick!" Tanya yelled; her heart pounded as she sucked in deep breaths.

"Nice work, DS Layton," called out DCI Adam Charles as he snapped on the cuffs and handed the captive over to an awaiting officer. "A very impressive manoeuvre. "Where did you learn that one?"

"I shouldn't have let him get to my gun," replied a crestfallen Tanya as she rose. "I was too slow. I'm out of practice. Luckily that self-defence training paid dividends. Otherwise, the situation could've been worse than a cut on the arm."

"What's that card fallen from his hoodie's pocket?" DCI Charles queried as he reached to pick the card off the footpath and read out the details. "The House of Pleasure, for all a gentleman's needs. Contact Dominic Rossi."

"I know that name. That's Carlo Conti's cousin," noted Tanya. "It may be a coincidence, or could The House of Pleasure be a front for that drug consignment we just nabbed?"

"Looks like you can't escape the Conti family," stated Adam. "I know you grew very fond of Carlo Conti while working undercover in Fiji and helping bust the Conti family drug packing setup."

"Yes, in the end, Carlo turned out to be a decent guy and providing evidence in the trial of his brother Guido caused the family to disown him," said a reflective Tanya. "What's the latest with his situation?"

"The Department of Justice agreed to admit him into the Witness Protection Program after he gave evidence in the trial in Fiji," said Adam. "Unfortunately, he was still not forthcoming about the Gonzales cartel's cocaine operations in Columbia. He seemed to be holding out and didn't reveal everything about his family's operations in Australia."

"Maybe he saw that as a way to protect himself and the family from retribution from Senor Gonzales for having given evidence?" Tanya posed. "Leave the family and me alone, and I'll keep quiet."

"Shit, you're bleeding," exclaimed Adam and he reached to grab Tanya as she started to slump towards the footpath.

*

Adam squatted down, scooped up Tanya in his arms, and carried her to the paramedics, rapidly rushing towards them, wheeling a gurney from the ambulance that had pulled up at the scene.

"Nasty cut on her right arm. No other identifiable injuries," Adam informed the ambulance crew, who quickly strapped Tanya onto the gurney and loaded her into the ambulance.

Tanya was soon underway to St Vincent's Hospital with the ambulance's siren blazing. Adam returned to his car and made his way to the hospital. Over the police radio, he advised his concerned colleagues involved in the raid that Tanya was en route to the hospital for minor treatment, probably just needing a few stitches.

Adam parked in the parking zone reserved for police vehicles and went to the Emergency Department. "DCI Charles," he said to the admissions clerk as he presented his police badge. "My colleague Detective Sergeant Layton was just brought in by ambulance."

"She's in casualty. Down the corridor, third cubicle on the left," the clerk advised with a cursory look at the police ID. "The doctor is with her."

The curtain was drawn on the cubicle, so Adam tentatively poked his head through the narrow gap. He saw Tanya lying on an examination table with her bloodied sleeve cut away, exposing the damaged tissue. A white-coated doctor leant over Tanya, poised with a hypodermic in his right hand. "Is she going to be ok?" Adam asked.

"It's a nasty cut, but she'll live," pronounced the doctor, who delivered the local anaesthetic into the wound area, preparing to suture the gash.

"Ow," cried Tanya, flinching as the needle entered the tissue. "I'll be fine," she said, reassuring Adam.

With the stitches in place and Tanya feeling much better, Adam removed his tracksuit top and handed it over to Tanya. "Here, take this and put it on, and I'll drop you home to rest up. You're not coming back into the office today. You can complete your report in the morning."

"Thanks, Adam. I'll write it up at home and get it back to you tomorrow," said Tanya as she cringed while slowly slipping her wounded arm into the sleeve proffered by Adam.

"No hurry," said Adam. "I'm just relieved you are OK. You've been a magnet for trouble recently," he grinned. "You've just got over the beating you received from Guido Conti in Fiji."

"Don't remind me," said Tanya as she exited the examination table. "I still get the occasional headache."

With Tanya gripping Adam's left arm, they headed out the sliding aluminium exit door of the emergency department. They were greeted by a barrage of flashes from cameras held by a wall of media personnel who began rapidly firing questions.

"Are you OK, Detective Layton? How big was the drug haul? Are all the crooks in custody?"

"How the hell did this pack of vultures know you were here," Adam told Tanya. "Some bastard's leaked this. They'll be in trouble if I find out who it is."

Adam raised his hand at the top of the stairs leading down to his vehicle, silencing the reporters.

"DS Layton must rest after being injured in today's Kings Cross drug seizure. A media conference will be held at 3 pm at police headquarters this afternoon to provide feedback on this morning's arrests and seizures. No more questions at this time, thank you."

"Thanks, boss," said Tanya as she slipped into the passenger seat while cameras flashed and reporters fired off questions. "I couldn't face those parasites at the minute. I got quite a grilling after giving evidence in the trial in Fiji about what the Contis got up to with their drug distribution network there. The bastards made me out to be some temptress who led a hardened criminal to betray his family. I was made to feel as though I was some sort of prostitute."

"They didn't make mention of all the heartache you saved by the destruction of the drugs that were destined for the streets of Sydney," said Adam as he pulled out into the traffic, with cameras continuing to flash on either side of his car.

"I wonder where Carlo will end up in the witness protection program and what is his new identity?" Tanya reflected. "What sort of life will he have with no family or friends? Starting from ground zero. I must admit I was starting to have feelings for him. He, in the end, was a nice guy who wanted a change from a life of crime."

Will I ever see him again?

"Come on, let's get you home to rest up after this morning's action," said Adam as he flicked on his indicator. Cameras flashed, and reporters spoke rapidly into handheld microphones as they slowly exited the carpark.

CHAPTER 6

Dominic watched as the raid on the warehouse unfolded. He peered through the cheap, red nylon curtains from the seclusion of his office in the front room of The House of Pleasure, just across the street at 18 McDonald Lane.

Despite the name, The House of the Pleasure projected a rather unassuming façade in the warehouse/ office section of Kings Cross. The two-storey building, including the upstairs windows, was painted dark grey. A single-panelled, frosted glass door sat at the top of the staircase leading up from the street, with a security camera monitoring any would-be entrant. A steep driveway with a boom gate, labelled STAFF ONLY, led underneath the building.

Madame Gypsy, a middle-aged woman, in a flowing floral kaftan, with flaming red hair and heavy pancaked makeup, entered the office.

"What's going on?" She asked. "Why have you got the lights off?"

"Looks like the cops are raidin' the warehouse up the road," replied Dominic as he stepped back from the curtain and turned to face Gyspsy. "Would you please excuse me, Gypsy? I need to make a confidential call."

Dominic waited until he heard Gypsy's footsteps retreat down the dark-timbered, polished hallway to the rear of the premises. He sat in the dark-blue fabric office chair and rolled over the plastic floor mat to access the PC perched on top of the black laminated IKEA corner desk. Leaning over, he reached down and fired up the PC while checking the local time in Columbia and noted it was early evening. With the PC primed for action, Dominic clicked on the screen's desktop icon HG.

After a brief delay, Hernando's long-serving assistant, Pedro, answered the call on the other side of the Pacific Ocean. Pedro was elderly, walking in his dark-brown, slip-on sandals with a shuffle. Wisps of straggly, grey hair fell onto the collar of his long-sleeved, white linen shirt that matched his long, white linen trousers.

"This is Pedro. How may I help you?"

"Pedro, this is Dominic Rossi calling from Sydney. I have an important message for Senor Gonzales. I need to speak with him."

"I am sorry, but that will not be possible. He's a busy man. I can relay the message for you," replied Pedro.

*

"Senor Gonzales, I have a message for you from a Senor Rossi in Sydney," said Pedro as he entered the study in the Gonzales' hacienda, located in the hills near the western Columbian city of Cali.

Senor Gonzales was seated at his desk, cleaning his revolver and nodded to Pedro, "what's up with our friends in Sydney?"

"Senor, it appears that the police have raided a recent delivery," responded Pedro. "He wants to speak with you urgently."

"Shit," exclaimed Gonzales. "I need Roberto. Get him for me as soon as he finishes the hit on the Munoz place in Pereira."

*

Roberto Rodriguez, the chief hitman for the Gonzales cartel, sat in the backseat of the SUV, cruising slowly down a quiet suburban street of the Western Columbian town of Pereira. He was undertaking surveillance of the headquarters and homestead of the now-deceased Manuel Munoz.

The killing of the head of the Munoz cartel by an unknown assassin had provided the opportunity for Hernando Gonzales and the Gonzales cartel to take over the whole of the cocaine business in the western half of Columbia.

Roberto's mission was to wipe out the remaining members of the Munoz organisation while the family was in mourning and before any new leader emerged.

Opposite the Munoz compound, in an upmarket area of the town, was a public parkland. The park, bordered by shady trees, included two soccer pitches and a large children's playground with roundabouts, swings, slides and a wall for aspiring tennis players to practice their shots.

Roberto took a vantage point on the far side of the parkland and, with binoculars in hand, began to monitor the comings and goings from the heavily walled compound. The compound was protected by tall, white stucco, thick stone walls topped with broken glass fragments. There was no property on either side of the compound, providing the numerous cameras with a clear 360 degree of the property.

Vehicle access to the property was via an electronic steel gate topped with coils of barbed wire. The only other access point into the compound was through a central, single, small steel door facing the street. Over the day, Roberto observed a regular movement of cars in and out of the compound – children to school, women to shops, and men to business.

The only time the small door seemed to come into use was when the children came home from school and made their way to the playground over the road accompanied by guards. The other occasion was when the hacienda staff went inside in the morning and headed home in the early evening.

The door could be the chink in the armour I'm looking for to gain access. I need to get a look inside the compound to see how the guards are placed and get information on the layout of the inside of the building.

The buzz from a drone flying over one of the soccer fields gave him an idea.

The following day, Roberto set up in the SUV with his laptop connected to a drone's camera operated by one of his men. The drone operator guided the buzzing drone to make ever-increasing circles until he got in a position to hover over the compound. The location of the drone over the property brought an immediate response. Two men came out of the compound's door and strode aggressively towards the soccer field.

It was quickly evident that the men were not happy with the drone's flight path and threatened the drone's destruction and physical violence on the operator if he continued to fly the drone in the neighbourhood. With apologies, the operator landed the drone and quickly departed the scene.

"Good job," said Roberto. "You got us a good look behind the wall. We have an armed guard at the vehicle entry, one at the central door and another in front of the main door to the hacienda."

Around 6 pm, the door again opened, and several humbly dressed men, likely to be labourers, exited the compound. Two men headed down the street towards the main road leading into the estate, and a solitary figure began to make his way across the parkland towards Roberto's vehicle.

Roberto and two of his men stepped out of his vehicle as the man approached.

"Got a light hombre?" Roberto asked as he pulled a pack of cigarettes from his shirt pocket.

"Get him," came the order, the man being grabbed and flung into the back seat of the SUV.

"Senor, what do you want? I am just a poor gardener. I have no money. Please let me get home to my family," begged the man as he was jammed between Roberto and one of his men, the vehicle screeching away.

"What is your name, my friend?" Roberto asked.

"Jose, sir. Please do not hurt me."

"No one will hurt you, Jose. I need your help with some information," informed Roberto as they continued towards the outskirts of town. "I want you to tell me about the inside of the compound where you work. How many men? Where do they work? Are they armed?"

"Sir, I cannot tell you that," replied Jose. "They are my bosses. They will not like me telling you such things. They will kill me."

With a grin, Roberto opened his tracksuit jacket and tapped on his shoulder holster. The gardener flinched at the look in Roberto's eyes.

"Head down that track," Roberto instructed the driver. The SUV left the main road and turned down a dirt road away from any housing.

"This looks like a nice place for a chat Jose. See my friend sitting next to you. He thinks if you are not prepared to use your tongue and tell us what we need to know, he might as well cut it out."

Roberto's man reached down his right leg, extracted a narrow stiletto blade from a sheath and began twirling it around in his hand. Without warning, he suddenly turned and slashed the blade across Jose's face. Jose shrieked in pain and brought his hand to his face. Blood began to ooze between his figures, and he started to sob.

"I will try and help you, sir. Please do not hurt me."

"That's very wise, Jose," said Roberto.

Over ten minutes, Roberto probed Jose's knowledge of the Munoz headquarters interior. Apart from the guards identified by the drone at the front of the property, an additional guard was next to the internal offices. There was a security room where another armed man monitored the security cameras.

To the left of the main entrance was a lounge area with a bar at the rear and two long couches on either side of a coffee table. On the right side was a large dining room with a huge dining table with matching high-backed chairs. The next door on the left down the hallway led to the kitchen-pantry area and the downstairs washrooms on the right. At the end of the hallway, a simple timber door divided the rest of the hacienda from the office area.

"What about the door to the offices?" Roberto probed. "Is it locked? Does it require a security code?"

"No, senor," replied Jose. "The guard who sits at the end of the hallway checks anyone coming into the office and security area. Next to the office door on the left is the upstairs staircase. The senior family members' bedrooms, bathrooms and living areas were upstairs. No staff apart from the maids are allowed in the family living areas. If I went upstairs, there would be big trouble for me."

"Thank you, Jose. You have been very generous with your time, and the information you provided has been very helpful," said Roberto as he opened the car door and indicated for Jose to get out. "I think you better get home to your family. It is starting to get dark."

Roberto pointed to the track and indicated for Jose to get going. With a bow, Jose turned and started to walk swiftly down the track back towards the main road. Roberto nodded to his stiletto-wielding associate, who removed a gun from his jacket pocket and began to affix a silencer to the weapon. Jose turned and, seeing the gun started to run. A spit of flame from the barrel saw Jose fall to the ground, the back of his skull torn from his head.

Roberto's men moved to the body and dowsed it in petrol from a jerrican. Then dragged it unceremoniously into the undergrowth. A flick of a cigarette lighter saw flames leap from the body.

"Back to the hotel, guys. We have a busy night ahead of us planning the meeting with our friends in the Munoz family," sneered Roberto.

*

The Munoz hacienda's main gate opened just after 3.15 pm when a large van arrived, having picked up the children from school. The children typically head out to the park at 4 pm after changing out of their school uniforms. At ten minutes to the hour of four, an SUV kangaroo-hopped to a stop right in front of the compound's central access door. The driver cursed as he pulled the lever to raise the hood and moved to the front of the vehicle while his three passengers headed to the rear and raised the hatch.

A vehicle pulled up on the other side of the road, and the driver called out. "Is that you, cuz? Are you OK?"

"Nice timing. Something has happened to the motor. It just died on me," the driver of the incapacitated vehicle replied.

"No problem, I'll get my tool kit," the other driver responded, heading to the rear of his vehicle accompanied by his two passengers.

A few moments later, the central door swung open, and a large, stern-looking man approached the vehicle and stopped in front of the gate.

"You fuckers can't stop here."

"We didn't plan the stop, my friend. My motor died. We'll be on our way as soon as possible. My cousin over there is a mechanic and is getting the tool kit from his car to take a look."

At that moment, the children's laughter could be heard as the door opened, distracting the hostile guard. As he turned and looked towards the door, the men from the two vehicles sprang into action. Bullet-proof vests were thrown on, machine guns grabbed from the rear of the two vehicles, and as the guard turned back to face the driver, a knife was driven into his chest. He clutched his chest, not comprehending what had just occurred. Blood gurgled in his mouth as he tried to yell a warning.

"Let's go," ordered Roberto as he stormed to the door and opened fire. The children's bodies and the two other outside guards were flung backwards from the impact of the bullets on their bodies.

"Come on, move, move."

With the element of surprise and all the outside guards taken out, the men stepped into the building. There was no one in the dining room. However, two women cowered on a sofa begging for mercy in the lounge area. Two men stood at the bar with wine glasses in their raised hands. Fear spread over their faces. Roberto smiled as he heard the cries of pain as the contents of a machinegun clip were emptied into the defenceless victims.

The group continued down the hallway with the smell of cordite in the air. Roberto signalled for two men to head upstairs while he checked the kitchen. Four women appeared to be busy preparing food. They didn't need to be told a second time to *vamos!* They quickly dropped everything and headed out of a side door.

A burst of gunfire could be heard from upstairs, followed by the call of "all clear." Roberto and the other men cautiously approached the homestead's rear and the closed door leading to the office area. He stretched with his right hand, pulled down on the door handle, and stepped back against the wall.

A burst of gunfire came from the rear, causing Roberto to reach into his backpack and extract two grenades. He removed the safety pins and hurled the explosives down the hallway. Screams followed the flash and boom of the explosions.

The cold-blooded killing rampage continued with no mercy as Roberto and his team stepped over the mutilated bodies of the remaining guards and proceeded to gun down the remaining occupants of the office area.

One of Roberto's men returned from his vehicle with a petrol container and began to spread the contents down the hallway. The fuel flowed easily over the tiled floor.

"Let's vamos. "The cops will be on their way," Roberto ordered as he sparked his cigarette lighter to life and bent down to place the flickering flame at the start of the trail of liquid destruction.

Roberto paused briefly as he looked back at the Munoz building and smiled as he saw flames engulf the property.

"I've got a hard-on just thinking about all those bodies being ripped apart. I'm going to have a good fuck tonight in celebration, but first, I must call Senor Hernando with an update. He is now king of all Western Columbia after obliterating the Munoz Cartel."

CHAPTER 7

"There are no Munoz family members alive, Senor Hernando," detailed Roberto from the Gonzales safehouse on the outskirts of Pereira. "We killed everyone on the property, then sent a clear message by setting fire to the place. I believe all the employees of the Munoz Cartel will be happy to work for us from now on."

"Good job Roberto. Congratulations to your team. Tell them tonight is on me, then I need you back home to Cali tomorrow," instructed Hernando. "We have a problem in Australia I need you to sort out as I've got to head to New York and meet with the Italians to discuss a deal."

"Wow, Australia. Always wanted to go there," responded Roberto. "I'll take the men down to Madame Maria's for a big night. They deserve it after this afternoon. Then I'll be back with you by tomorrow afternoon."

As he terminated the call, Roberto sat back in his chair. He unscrewed the cap from his bottle of tequila and took a long drink, then placed the bottle back on the table, leaned back and reflected on where he had come from over the past 20 years.

*

Young Roberto worked with his peasant farming parents in the basic cocaine manufacturing facility set up by Hernando Gonzales, a local gangster with connections in the city of Cali. The crude production took place high in the mountainous jungles outside the city. Roberto would help by collecting firewood to fuel the manufacturing process and be sent on errands into surrounding villages to buy food and other supplies.

The business was growing for Senor Hernando until early one morning, the tell-tale whoop-whoop-whoop sound of helicopters heralded a raid by the Columbian Federales on the site. Armed, uniformed men descended on ropes around the manufacturing site, yelling and firing indiscriminately, upending equipment and setting fire to the simple open-sided buildings.

Roberto's family slept under an open-air shelter away from the central manufacturing area, but the Federales were spreading out and rapidly closing in on the family. With all the commotion, his father grabbed the young Roberto by the arm and directed him to hide in the dense nearby bushes. Roberto was reluctant to leave his family, but a clip on the head got him moving into the hiding place.

With Roberto hidden away, his father and mother moved away from their shelter and Roberto's hiding place, their hands held high.

"No shoot. We surrender," Roberto heard his father cry, but to no avail as grinning Federales mercilessly gunned down him and his wife.

Several days later, Hernando, who'd been away on business to negotiate the sale of his latest batch, returned to the destroyed site. A hungry Roberto was the sole survivor. Hernando, with no family of his own, took Roberto under his wing and decided to care for him as if he was his son.

Times were now different for the successful Gonzales Drug Cartel, with even more potential following the destruction of the Munoz Cartel. There was now only a periodic raid to appease the Americanos. With the help of the local Policia chief, all the raids by the Federales were conducted well away from the main Gonzales manufacturing facilities. With the insatiable demand for the white powder to snort up their Americano noses, the wealth of Gonzales Cartel steadily grew.

Roberto stood, took another swig of tequila and, with a smile, gripped his crotch.

"Come on, guys. We're off to Madame Maria's. We've got an early start in the morning to get back to Cali, so don't misbehave too much."

*

Over the years, in the absence of a son of his own, Hernando saw Roberto as a likely successor to run the business. Under Hernando's guidance, Roberto was well-educated, including some time in the USA at a business college in LA. Hernando's only concern was with what he saw as an inherent cruel streak in Roberto that had the potential to cloud his judgement as a future leader of the growing organisation.

Hernando smiled and waved from his favourite rocking chair as Roberto pulled up his black Ford Explorer SUV and strode towards the steps leading up onto the verandah.

He's grown into a fine man. Tall, with broad shoulders, powerful arms and that short, jet-black hair. No wonder he's popular at Madame Carlotta's in downtown Cali.

The grey-haired Hernando Gonzales was fit for his advanced years. He was dressed casually in light blue denim jeans, with a white polo shirt from which draped a golden crucifix mounted on a thin gold chain.

Hernando was proud of what he had built from a humble camp in the tough Columbian jungles over the past twenty years. The opulent hacienda he had created was a testament to his success. With white stucco walls and an orange tiled roof, the centrally positioned hacienda was ringed by a thick whitewashed, broken glass-topped concrete wall three metres high. The only entrance to the compound was via heavily arm-guarded, double, thick, hard-timbered doors.

To the rear of the compound was the cocaine manufacturing laboratory hidden underground beneath a row of horse stables. Adjacent to the front gates sat two Raven helicopters with pilots on standby, ready to extricate Hernando from any threat posed by any unannounced raid by the Columbian Federales or a rival gang. Access to the compound was via a single road leading out through the dense jungle from the city of Cali. Various security devices and gang members provided regular feedback on the comings and goings on the access road to a security office at the gate.

The boundaries of the compound were well protected from unwanted incursions. A steep range of jungle hills rose from the property's rear. On one side, a large banana plantation, while on the other, a wide, fast-flowing, muddy river carried on down to the township.

"Coffee?" Hernando asked, swaying backwards and forwards in his rocking chair. He indicated for Roberto to take a seat.

"Gracias, Senor Hernando. Yes, please," replied Roberto, taking a seat. "How can I be of assistance to you today? You mentioned a problem in Australia."

"First, a coffee for Roberto, please, Pedro," ordered Hernando as Pedro stepped out onto the front verandah of the hacienda to greet Roberto.

"I presume your favourite, espresso with two sugars, with some Italian biscotti," said Pedro.

Pedro returned and served Roberto's coffee, with Senor Hernando declining another shot. Pedro retreated into the household and hovered inside the front door while Hernando spoke to Roberto.

"I have an important assignment for you to lead Roberto," said Hernando getting straight to business as Roberto took a sip of the thick, black, sweetened coffee. "Our business in the Australian Pacific region has taken a big hit. Yesterday, I received an inside tip from one of the family members in Sydney, Dominic Rossi. This latest shipment was supposed to help the Conti's make up for the loss in Fiji following the raid and closedown by the Fijian cops. They're now into us for around five million dollars."

"Holy shit," exclaimed Roberto. "No one had ever owed you that much before and lived to tell the tale."

"On top of that, Gaetano's son Carlo Conti has ratted us out to the cops in return for entering the Aussie witness protection program. His evidence in court caused his family to lose the business they set up in Fiji and left them owing us for the consignment we sent for packing in Fiji. In addition, it appears the DEA has started sniffing around."

"OK, what do you want me to do?" Roberto asked as he drained his espresso and focussed on Hernando.

"I need you to speak with Dominic and find out what's going on, then with my time required on other issues in New York, I want you to sort out the matter," stated Hernando.

"Luigi, this is Carlos calling. Please call me back on the VPN," said Roberto using pseudonyms on the open telephone line.

"Senor Roberto, thanks for calling," said Dominic.

"I hear things are going to shit with you, Contis, in Australia with the loss of another consignment," said Roberto getting straight to business. "What the fuck is going on?"

"Since the chaos following the raids on the business in Fiji, I believe running the organisation is getting too much for my Uncle Gaetano and my Papa Lorenzo. They're losing control, and I think it's about time they retired," said Dominic. "They don't even know about the raid. I'm heading out to speak with them to give them the bad news that the cops must have received a tip-off about the delivery. Leaks have never happened before in the business. Don't tell them I've told you about the raid when you speak with them. They'll be very unhappy and will stop me from keeping you informed of what's going on here."

"Well, the Conti family is now owing for two fuckin' shipments. The Fiji delivery where your cousin Carlo ratted us out to the cops, and now the second consignment," roared Roberto. "That's five million bucks plus interest that is now rapidly accruing. Nobody owes the Gonzales Cartel five million bucks and lives very long, no matter how long they have worked with us."

"I have been giving the matter much thought and have an idea," said Dominic as he cautiously interjected Roberto's tirade. "There's a Fijian gang starting up in Sydney called the K-gang. Their chief, Tiko Rokovou, wants to cooperate with us to distribute our dope here in Sydney. Tiko, based in Fiji, could re-establish the business my cousins Carlo and Guido tried to start up in Fiji, filling your Columbian Heaven (CH) into coffee pods, then shipping on to Sydney."

"I like that line of thinking," replied Roberto. "However, what about the money your family owes?"

"I plan to cover that as well," added Dominic. "The family business owns two properties, a distribution warehouse in western Sydney and The House of

Pleasure brothel in Kings Cross. The land value for both properties would be over five million. The titles could be transferred to you in return for cancelling the debt, and I could then take over the running of the business, working with Tiko. I'll talk to him about the Fiji business and see what can be arranged. Maybe you can help with any investment required to set things up in Fiji."

There was a brief silence before Roberto responded.

"You've given us plenty to think about. What about that snitch of a cousin of yours, Carlo?" Roberto asked. "He needs permanent silencing. Any clue where the bastard is hiding out?"

"The chicken shit has gone into the local Witness Protection Program, so no one knows his new name or where he now lives," answered Dominic. "He may not even be in the country. I no longer see him as a threat."

"You might not see him as a threat; however, I don't like the situation with Carlo alive and lurking in the background. He's still dangerous with what he knows about our respective businesses," mused Roberto. "That piece of dog turd needs to be drawn out of hiding and then dealt with before he decides to leverage anything more to the cops about the operation here in Columbia. Leave the matter with me, and I'll get back to you."

"Adios, Senor Roberto."

"Excuse me, Senor Hernando," Roberto said as he returned to the verandah. "Dominic has come up with what I believe is a good idea. We take over the Conti family's business properties in Sydney in return for settling the debt. Then we work with a group in the Fiji Islands called the K-gang to re-establish the CH packing business the Conti Family started to develop in Fiji. The K-gang is headed by a guy called Tiko Rokovou."

"What about the rat Carlo?" Hernando queried.

"He needs a knife straight up under the rib cage into the heart. I can already see the blood in his mouth," sneered Roberto. "I will develop a plan to lure the bastard out of hiding."

"Agreed," said Hernando. He paused before continuing. "I reckon if you take out his Papa, Uncle and maybe even this Dominic, that will surely bring him out from under the rock he is hiding. We take him out, and then we would control everything. We'd no longer rely on some other organisation to buy our CH. We'd work in with this K-gang and give them a cut, but we own everything."

"Yes, he would need to come out of hiding to console his poor grieving Mama. The family commitment would be too strong amongst those Italians for him to remain in hiding. One hundred per cent he would be compelled to see his Mama," mused Roberto.

"To get things moving, I'll suggest you speak with Dominic. Get him to speak with this Tiko, then see what he can arrange for you to meet with this Tiko in Fiji. Meantime you can start working on a trip to Sydney via Fiji. No doubt you'll need a visa for Australia," noted Hernando.

"I'll also check in with Dominic to see what weapons he can arrange for me in Australia," said Roberto. "Coming from Columbia at my age, I imagine I'll get a good working over by their Customs on arrival, and I won't be able to bribe anyone to bring in some decent firepower with me."

"I'm sure Dominic will be able to supply you with mobile burner phones, a gun with a silencer and anything else you need. You can arrange for him to meet you at Sydney Airport and organise accommodation for you," advised Hernando.

"What about these business properties the Conti's own?" Roberto asked. "Are they worth what Dominic indicated?"

"I know they have a warehouse in Western Sydney they planned to use to distribute the CH and the brothel called The House of Pleasure, close to the Sydney CBD," replied Hernando. "In a place like Sydney, I guess the land value alone would be worth the five million dollars owed to us."

"The House of Pleasure. I like the sound of that. I'm getting a hard-on just thinking about what delights await me. Maybe that's the place for me to stay," said Roberto as he stretched his arms and shoulders back and looked towards the hacienda's front door. "You OK, Pedro?"

"Sorry, sir. I was just looking to see if you had finished your coffee," Pedro replied as he turned and moved away from the doorway.

"What was that about?" Hernando asked.

"Pedro seemed to be listening to our conversation," Roberto answered. "I'm going to keep an eye on the old bastard."

"Forget it. He's been with me for years and fields all my calls," noted Hernando as he started to stand. "Go back to the office, call Dominic, and set up a meeting in Fiji on your way to Australia."

CHAPTER 8

Pedro returned to his room and locked the door behind him. The small room adjacent to the hacienda's kitchen was furnished with a single bed, a chest of drawers, a wardrobe and a writing desk, and an office-style chair and desktop lamp.

Pedro listened at the door and, hearing no activity, reached under his bed and lifted a floor tile, revealing a small cavity chipped in the flooring. The cavity housed a mobile phone and charger. He sat on his bed, turned on the device, and waited for it to connect to the network.

Why did my son not tell me he would smuggle drugs into the USA? He got himself arrested and then told the authorities about my situation. They offered him immunity from prosecution instead of life imprisonment, and here I am, forced to inform on my boss, who has been so good to me over many years.

With the mobile connected, Pedro hit the icon on his screen labelled Papa Bear. Within seconds the call was answered.

"This is Papa Bear, yes, Baby Bear?"

"Our friends are sending a key man to Australia very soon. His name is Roberto…."

Roberto began to pound on Pedro's door.

"Where the fuck are you? I've been calling for you."

"Sorry, sir. I'll be with you shortly," replied Pedro as he terminated the call and returned the mobile to its hiding place.

I'm going to have to be careful with Senor Roberto snooping around. He doesn't trust me.

He wiped away beads of sweat that had formed on his brow with a handkerchief and opened the door to be confronted by an angry Roberto.

"How can I help you sir?"

"Get me an espresso and make it quick. Bring it to the office," ordered Roberto, stepping aside as Pedro headed into the kitchen. Roberto peered into the room before following.

Something is going on with that old bastard. I don't trust him.

*

"You have a problem in Australia. Wow, that sounds intriguing. I have not been there for many years. It's a wonderful country but so far away, and it takes forever to get there. I did some backpacking there in my gap year before starting university," noted Penny. "What could there possibly be in Australia for the DEA that requires my skills?"

"Let me first give you a bit of background," said Andy as he leant forward in his chair. "We have an informant well-placed inside the Gonzales Cartel headquarters near Cali in Western Columbia."

"You mean the same Gonzales organisation related to the other drug lord Munoz. I made the hit on for you," interrupted Penny.

"That's the one," responded Andy. "Our informant advised that Gonzales is sending one of his senior men to Sydney to sort a mess created by the seizure of their last two consignments to a longtime customer, the Conti family. The family now owes the Gonzales Cartel over five million dollars."

"I imagine Senor Gonzales does not have too many people owing him money," observed Penny. "I hear on the grapevine those Columbian cartels are pretty ruthless."

"In addition to the money, there is a potential problem with Carlo Conti, the son of the Conti family, Gaetano Conti," informed Andy. "Carlo has much knowledge of the operation of the Conti and Gonzales organisations and is currently hiding in an Aussie witness protection program."

"Why is Carlo in a witness protection program?" Penny asked. "It is not common for the member of an Italian family to provide information to the police."

"I have a full report in my briefcase on the history of the matter for you to go through," stated Andy as he reached beside his chair and extracted a USB from his briefcase. "Look at this report at your leisure, but the bottom line for your assignment is to protect Carlo Conti. If they try to make a hit on him or any of the rest of his family, we hope that will be enough to entice him to reveal the detailed information he can reveal about the entire Gonzales operation so that we can close him down."

"Why, of all people, do you need to send me all the way to Australia? What about your local operatives in Australia?" Penny queried.

"From the info provided by our informant, Gonzales is sending one of his senior men. The call was cut short. However, the name mentioned was Roberto, so we believe our man is a ruthless bastard known as Roberto Rodriguez," said Andy. "I want someone with your skills to head up an operation to protect the Conti family and hopefully get Carlo to tell us what he knows about the Gonzales operation in Columbia."

"If this Rodriguez is planning to get to Sydney, I must get moving," noted Penny. "I want access to my equipment in Australia. Equipment I am familiar with and have tested, especially Gertrude. I know Australia is not the easiest place to get weaponry into. I will need your help with the authorities to get some baggage through their border checks. However, given the short time horizon, I may have a possible vehicle to get what I need to be carried into the country without going through complex diplomatic channels."

"OK, let me know what you need from our end, and I'll contact our operatives in Australia to get the necessary arrangements for your arrival," said Andy. "Knowledge of your presence in Australia will be restricted. Along with members from the DEA office in Sydney, there'll also be a couple of very senior members of the Australian Federal Police whom you can contact in an emergency only. I will provide you with their contact details before departure. Interestingly, in the report, you'll see our man Carlo Conti, had a relationship with an undercover cop in the Fiji Islands. By all counts, it appeared to be a mutual affair."

"Knowing the male of the species and given the romance you say this Carlo had with the undercover cop, she may well be another avenue that our friends at Gonzales HQ will aim to exploit to draw out Carlo," Penny posed. "She unknowingly may well be in significant danger."

"You could well be right," agreed Andy. "Keeping her safe will be an additional priority. Let's get something to eat, and we can discuss your exorbitant fee for service for this assignment. There's a nice little Spanish Tapas in a laneway just off Oxford Street, my treat before you catch your train back home. You will want to practice shooting on your new range."

"Any chance you will be in Australia for the operation?" Penny queried. "It would be great to work with you again?"

"Not likely at this stage," replied Andy.

She didn't seem happy that I wouldn't be directly involved.

*

There was a busy lunchtime crowd in the *Essential Tapas* restaurant. It was a chilly, overcast London day, so Andy declined an outdoor setting, and they were lucky to secure a quiet booth at the rear of the restaurant, adjacent to the warmth exuding from the kitchen. Over an array of dishes, including various slices of bread, hams, stuffed mussels, squid, olives and mushrooms, the pair enjoyed an exchange of small talk about their respective upbringings, where they went to school, what they studied, hobbies, interests and the like.

Sensing Penny was relaxed in his company, Andy looked around, then leant towards her and posed the question in almost a whisper.

"How did someone like you become the cool, calm person you present and in your chosen profession?"

Penny took a sip of her water, seeming to digest the question before answering,

"I will be honest with you. I was an only child born into a family with a long military history. I wasn't permitted to cry if I fell over and scraped my knee.

I was Daddy's girl and always had to be brave like him. At boarding school, I stood up to the bullies, and they soon knew it was wise to leave me alone. Joining the army became my only career choice after completing my degree at university. My Father personally drove me to sign up with his old regiment. The skill I developed with a rifle you know too well."

"Tough upbringing," added Andy as he signalled to the waiter to bring the bill for the meal. "I suppose you don't have time for anyone special in your life."

"You're right; I don't have time for that," Penny replied without hesitation as she checked her watch and stood up from the table. "Speaking of time. I need to head off if I'm going to make the 3 pm train."

Andy also stood and hugged Penny gently, "be careful in Australia. Especially with that Roberto. I look forward to getting your progress reports at HQ." He watched as Penny headed to the exit without turning back.

That is some beautiful woman. I wonder if I have half a chance to win her heart. She always seemed pleased to see me and wanted to know if I would be in Australia. Maybe I'm breaking through that tough exterior?

*

Penny paced up and down in her training facility office. She framed the conversation in her mind and then sat at her desk to call Jo Roberts at the English Women's Cricket team headquarters in London.

"Could I speak with Josephine Roberts, please? Tell her it is Penny Emmett-Jones calling."

"Hi, Penny. A nice surprise to hear from you," said Jo cheerfully. "What can I do for you?"

Penny stood and began walking around her office with her mobile on speaker.

"Maybe it's a case of what I can do for you," replied Penny. "Remember when we met in Karen's agency in Melbourne? I said I might be able to help you and the cricket team at some stage with my paramedical skills. Well, I understand you are heading off shortly on tour to Australia with the English women's cricket team, and the finances are pretty tight for the funding of support staff."

"Yes, you are correct. We head off Down Under in a couple of weeks," noted Jo, "and the travel budget is always tight, especially for support staff. How do you think you can help?"

"What if I paid for my travel and accommodation and provided the team with my medical skills? I could help the team by acting as a masseuse, a first-aider and the like," posed Penny. "All I would ask is for my equipment box to be shipped with the team's gear to save me the exorbitant excess baggage costs."

"Wow, that would be fantastic, Penny. The team would love to have someone with your skills on tour," said Jo. "I'll first need to square things off with the Cricket Council's management, but I'm sure they'll leap at the offer as we cannot get more funding. Including your training equipment with the team's gear should be no problem. I'll get back to you as soon as I get official confirmation."

"Cheers, Jo," said Penny. "I look forward to beating those Aussies on their home soil."

Problem solved. Gertrude, you are going to Australia.

*

"Andy, good news. I'm all set to get my gear to Australia in a couple of weeks as a trainer for the English women's cricket," advised Penny. "Now, over to you to arrange for my baggage to get cleared through customs at Sydney Airport. I'll give you all the flight information as soon as it arrives."

"That's great, Penny," replied Andy. "I'll get on to it immediately and let you know when I get the all-clear from the Australians."

"Gertrude will be very happy she can make the trip with me," noted Penny.

Shame you cannot make the trip, Andy Carter.

CHAPTER 9

Carlo Conti stepped off the flight from Sydney, his mind spinning with what lay ahead. So many unknowns.

Will a new identity and name provided by the witness protection program keep me safe from the Gonzales Cartel living in a new city? I've no friends and have left behind the woman and the family I love. I'm destined never to see them again for their safety.

Lost in thought, he went from the arrival gate to the baggage carousel to retrieve his suitcase.

"Mr Cerlik?" asked a gentleman holding a small whiteboard with the name Chris Cerlik written in black marking pen.

"Oh, sorry. Yes, I'm Chris Cerlik," he responded, his mind returning to the reality of his new identity.

"I am James Mahoney from the Department of Justice. I have all your documentation here. Driver's licence, birth certificate, passport, tax file number, the lease on a fully furnished apartment for six months and a mobile phone, all with your new identity. You'll need to use the documents to open a bank account. Once you have collected your luggage, I'll drop you off at your apartment, where you'll find a laptop computer all set to go."

"That's great, James," said Chris. "I wasn't sure what to expect under the WPP conditions, but you have made relocation easier than expected. I just have to get a job and keep myself busy."

"Here's my card should you need any assistance," said James extracting a business card from his wallet. "I am the only person in this city who knows about you and your new identity here in Melbourne. Please keep it that way and resist the temptation to call old friends and family for your and their safety."

"Here's my suitcase," noted Chris as he stepped forward to remove the large, hard, black plastic suitcase bearing a HEAVY tag from the baggage carousel. "Had to jam in as much as I could."

The drive to Chris's new residence was in relative silence. He peered out the passenger seat window taking in his new environment as dusk began to settle and the lights of this new world began to flicker into life. James provided some commentary to fill the silence.

"There's the Eureka Tower, Crown Casino, Melbourne Cricket Ground and Rod Laver Tennis Centre," he highlighted as the journey unfolded.

"Bigger than I expected," was all Chris could manage in response as he stared out the passenger side window.

"Here's your new home," said James as he pulled his car into the visitor's carpark in front of the 12-storey Junction Tower. "You're on the 7th floor with a nice city view. You are in Camberwell Junction, with easy access to trams, trains and shops. In this location, you'll be able to easily get around the city until you buy yourself a car."

James removed a plastic card from his shirt pocket and used the item to gain access to the building. Entering the building, James led Chris across the glossy, cream-tiled floor to the bank of two elevators on the far side of the foyer. He pressed the UP arrow, and the left-hand elevator door immediately opened. James scanned the card again inside the confined, mirrored elevator and pressed "7". The elevator silently made its way to the seventh floor, and Chris still lost in thought, seemed startled as the elevator pinged on its arrival. James wheeled Chris's suitcase exiting the elevator, heading down the quiet, brightly lit corridor to the apartment door and scanned the electronic entry key.

"It's a one-bedroom apartment, fully finished and as agreed, the WPP picks up the rent for the first six months to get you on your feet," informed James. "There's a laptop for you on the kitchen bench; the password is 1-2-3-4. Other than that, call me anytime if there are any problems. Here is an envelope with $500 cash as a starter for food and transport while you look for some work."

With a firm handshake, James turned and was gone, leaving Chris staring at the closed apartment door, his mind spinning with information overload. He turned and began to scrutinise his new abode.

James has provided me with a few essentials to get me started. I can't fault how the program has looked after me.

The open plan lounge/dining had a two-seater dark-brown fabric lounge chair facing a low, dark-brown wooden coffee table. The furniture was completed with a square wooden dining table with two metal-framed chairs and a wooden sideboard matching the coffee table with a small wall-mounted TV above.

To the right was a kitchenette – double basin sink, stove, refrigerator and bench providing a barrier to the lounge dining area. A quick look in the refrigerator revealed some milk and a few basics such as bacon, eggs, orange juice and bottled water.

Chris stepped across the room and opened the double glass sliding doors leading onto a narrow balcony. He peered over the chest-high railing down into the street below. He chuckled at the sound of the ding-ding of the tram rumbling through the intersection.

It's going to take some gettin' used to. Hope I can sleep OK.

Chris returned to the kitchen bench, flipped open the laptop's lid, and booted it up. As prompted, he entered the code and accessed the online employment agency SEEK through Google. He pulled up one of the four light-coloured timber-topped, chrome-legged stools wedged under the kitchen bench and hunched himself over the screen.

*

Vera Mueller, the owner of the Powerhouse gymnasium in Melbourne's eastern suburb Camberwell, smiled as she heard the busy chatter of the group arriving for the 9 am HIIT (High-Intensity Interval Training) Class.

The door opened, and the many women attending the HIIT class burst into the gym's lobby. With their fobs poised, they scanned through the turnstile laden with gym bags, towels, and drink bottles, ready for a vigorous 1-hour session with Chris.

"Good morning, Adrienne, Anne, Alison, Vicki, Sandy, Robyn, Jo and Pam," greeted Vera as she enjoyed reeling off the names of the regular members of the HIIT class. "Hope you are ready for a tough workout this morning. He looks in a mean mood today, even though he's wearing his RELAXED T-shirt."

"For sure. Bring it on," the women answered in chorus as they went in anticipation to the centre of the gym floor, having placed their personal effects around the perimeter.

"Good morning, ladies," boomed Chris as he greeted the class in his deep baritone voice. "Ready to get those bodies moving? Let's get warmed up with some stretches before you start swinging those kettlebells."

*

With the women preparing for their program, Vera reflected on the day Chris Cerlik entered the gym to apply for the trainer's position she had advertised on the SEEK website. Since the Covid outbreak and the resultant lockdowns, it has been difficult to recruit trainers, with a lot of competition from other gyms in the area eager to find staff with many trainers exiting the industry.

Vera could immediately see that he would be popular with her clientele. Chris was powerfully built with a huge chest and bulging biceps, enhancing his stocky build. He had a full head of close-cropped jet-black hair and was around 30 years of age, and as a trainer, he had kept himself in good shape.

Chris presented Vera with a range of documentation – A Victorian driver's licence, a Working With Children Card, Trainer's Certificate. Vera only gave the documents a cursory look. She didn't want this man going anywhere else.

"All your paperwork is very professionally prepared, and you are well qualified," stated Vera, "When can you start?"

"Well, I recently moved to Melbourne and am keen to get to work as soon as possible," Chris said. "How about straightaway?"

Vera extended her hand. "You're hired. I'll get the paperwork together. You can take the employment contract home to review and bring back a signed copy tomorrow morning. In the meantime, I will update the website announcing your appointment and offering your services as a personal trainer. Are there any classes you prefer to conduct?"

"As per your advertisement, my favourite is HIIT," Chris replied.

*

"Great workout, ladies," yelled Chris as he turned off the Village People's YMCA beat, which had been pulsing through the sound system. "I look forward to seeing you all back for the next class. Give yourselves a big clap."

"Hey Chris, are you going to join us girls for a coffee this morning," asked Adrienne.

Chris was just about to reply when something clicked in his mind, and he turned towards the wall-mounted TV as the newsreader fired out the lead story on the mid-morning bulletin.

What's that? Is that my Tanya?

Hero cop of Fiji fame, DS Tanya Layton, was injured in yesterday morning's raid on a Kings Cross drug warehouse. Her arm was badly cut by a dangerous serrated-edged dagger while arresting the notorious crime figure, Deon Hodgkison, the alleged leader of the Renegades Motorcycle Gang. Detective Layton had been instrumental in closing the infamous Conti family's drug operation in Fiji and arresting the Conti twins, Guido and Carlo. She had been badly beaten while operating undercover by the now-deceased Guido Conti. Carlo Conti famously co-operated as a star witness for the prosecution in the case and is now in the witness protection program. His whereabouts…

"Sorry, Adrienne, I've got to attend to an important matter that's just come up. " Next time," said Chris, quickly turning and heading for the staff room. He opened his locker and retrieved his mobile phone, accessing the ABC TV App. Chris replayed the news bulletin.

WPP or no WPP, I've got to see her and make sure she is ok.

With the gym quiet after the HIIT class and the ladies headed for coffee, Chris approached Vera, "I may need to head up to Sydney at short notice.

There's a family member taken ill, and I may get a call if things worsen. I'll inform you if we need to cancel any classes or PT sessions."

"Thanks for letting me know," replied Vera. "Give me as much notice as you can. Hope everything is ok."

CHAPTER 10

Dominic pulled up in front of the Mount Willsmore warehouse in Sydney's outer western suburbs, screeching to a stop. He had called his Uncle that morning and told him he had bad news and would be there in the hour to update the family.

The family-owned warehouse was solidly built of red bricks and starting to show its age, with hints of rust appearing on the corrugated iron roof. The facility had served the family well in facilitating their role in the booming Sydney drug trade.

Honking the car horn, Dominic waited for the steel roller door to open. He sat impatiently, his fingers drumming on the steering wheel as the door made the slow, ear-piercing, screeching journey to the top, then drove into the warehouse. He was greeted by his Uncle Gaetano Conti and Papa Lorenzo Rossi, who hustled towards him as he stepped out of his car.

"I see you guys have been busy," noted Dominic as he looked around the warehouse. "Tidiest it's looked in a long time."

"Take a look around," said Gaetano pointing out to Dominic the work that had been done. "With the latest shipment due to be delivered today, we're ready to have the cash rolling in again to compensate for what we lost in Fiji. I've had the walls painted and cleaned up the racking, and we have a forklift on order. No expense spared."

"What's so important that you had to call us out to the warehouse and not tell us over the phone?" Papa Lorenzo asked as he steered Gaetano and Dominic towards the office.

The office was located at the far right-hand end of the building. It was open at the top but encased in scratched, chipped, dark wooden panelling in the bottom half and glass at the top. A central door opened onto a bank of four, four-drawer light grey metal filing cabinets. To the right of the filing cabinets was a large, solid dark wooden desk strewn with paper and to the left, a round, dark, dusty, timbered meeting table surrounded by four collapsible metal chairs with plastic seats and backs.

"Have you had the place scanned? Is it safe to talk in here? With what I have to tell you, I don't want the fuckin' cops listening in," said Dominic as he stopped in his stride and looked around the office.

"Had the place scanned this morning by Frank. The office is safe for us to meet," replied Lorenzo as the men took their seats around the meeting table.

"I've got fuckin' bad news," said a glum-sounding Dominic, his eyes fixed on the tabletop. The fuckin' coppers raided the Kings Cross warehouse this morning and got the lot. They must've got a tip-off."

"Holy fuck. How in God's name," yelled Gaetano as he pounded his fist into the tabletop, causing it to wobble on its uneven legs. "We're now into Gonzales for two consignments making the debt at least five mill, and he won't be happy. Where am I goin' to get that sort of money in cash? He has the reputation of being an unforgiving, ruthless bastard."

"There's also the matter of the Fiji Islander K-gang," added Dominic. "As you know, I had arranged for them to start distributing for us here in Sydney. Now that Guido and Carlo are no longer with us to direct operations at a street level, I met with their chief, Tiko Rokovou, here in Sydney to finalise the deal."

"Before we worry about the Fijians, I need to give the bad news to Hernando," said Gaetano. "I'll call him to discuss what we can do to rectify matters, and you, Dominic, can smooth over matters with the Fijians. See if you can buy us some time. I don't want them bringin' in their own shit into the market and starting up against us. Bad enough with competition from the Middle Eastern gangs."

*

After checking his watch and mentally calculating the time in Columbia, Gaetano texted Hernando.

Need to speak. Urgent.

He paced up and down with his stomach churning, waiting for confirmation that Hernando would be prepared to speak with him. His heart began to race when his mobile pinged a few minutes later.

Gaetano checked the message, *VPN thirty minutes.*

He sat in the warehouse office a lone figure, strumming his fingers on the top of the desk, having dismissed Dominic and Lorenzo. He booted up the PC, ready to utilize the VPN for the call. He checked his watch and clicked on Hernando's icon on his computer screen.

After a short delay, a voice with a strong Latino accent answered.

"Buenos dias, Senor Conti. To what do I owe the pleasure?"

"Buenos dias, Senor Gonzales. I am afraid it's bad news," answered Gaetano. "Your latest consignment was seized in a police raid this morning in Sydney."

After a long pause, Hernando replied harshly, "Failure is becoming a regular theme with your family. You now owe for two shipments - the shipment to your sons' failed venture in Fiji and this consignment to Sydney. You have over five million US Dollars outstanding. When can I expect payment?"

"Hernando, I don't have that sort of cash lying around the place," said Gaetano, his voice quivering. "I'll immediately speak with my family in Sicily to get the money I owe you, but I'll need time to get the money together and transferred to Australia, then on to you. You know you can trust me. We've worked together for many years, and I've never let you down."

"You've been a good customer for years, so I will give you a little time to pay the debt, but not too long. Business is business, you understand! I can't set a precedent with other customers," said Hernando in a firm voice. "In addition to what you owe me, there's also the matter of your son Carlo."

"He's dead to me," Gaetano quickly interjected.

"That may be so, but I'm concerned he may have provided much useful information to the DEA in the US. Carlo's evidence in the trial of Guido resulted in our key distribution centre in Acapulco being raided and closed down," said Hernando angrily. "Carlo also knows a lot about our operation here in Columbia, and that information would be very dangerous in the wrong hands. I can't risk him divulging that information to the Americanos."

"You would've known by now if that information had been shared with the DEA," noted Gaetano. "As far as I'm aware, he hasn't given any more information."

"I fear he's using what he knows as a bargaining chip to extract more money from the Americanos who want to shut me down. I need to take him out quickly to make sure he's permanently silenced," said Hernando.

"As I said, he's dead to me," said Gaetano. "You have my ok to go ahead and take the snitch out if you can find the rat."

"I can't risk any more problems in Australia, so I'm sending my right-hand man Roberto Rodriguez to take charge of sorting out the problems we have with your organisation," stated Hernando. "He has my full authority to discuss with you an idea I am considering to take our business forward. Once I've confirmed the arrangements, I'll get back to you, and I expect your full cooperation in helping him flush out your son and agreeing to my new business plan."

"That's assured," replied Gaetano, nodding. "Let me have the details when they are available."

I wonder what this new business plan is. It doesn't sound as though it will be negotiable. What will it mean for the family going forward?

"Thanks, Gaetano. Adios for now, and I do not want to hear from you again on this matter. Everything is to go through Roberto from now on. I am too busy with other matters."

Hernando stood up from behind his desk and opened the office door to see Pedro standing there. His clenched fist raised, ready to knock. "Sorry, sir. I was coming to check to see if you needed anything."

"No, I'm fine, thanks," replied Hernando.

Roberto is right. Something is going on with Pedro. He always seems to be around when I'm on a call.

*

Dominic returned to the HOP and went straight to the office to contact Tiko via the security of the VPN. An excited Dominic made the call, "hey, bula man."

"Bula bro," replied Tiko. "What's the news?"

"I've spoken to the man I'm dealing with in Columbia, and he says you're on. You can go ahead to secure the property. He'll finance the deal in return for a percentage of the action," informed Dominic. "Given what the family went through to buy the property in the first place, I suggest we use your name to avoid going through the same lengthy approval process required for non-Fiji citizens."

"My cousin has confirmed we can get it for under a mill. The Government wants to end the bad press created by the saga," Tiko said. "I'll let you know when I need the money to make the payment."

"As part of the process, one of the top guys will pass through Fiji on his way to meet with me in Sydney," added Dominic. "He wants to meet you, check the setup, and finalise a deal. His name is Roberto Rodriguez, and he'll be in contact."

*

"Sorry to disturb you, Senor Hernando," said Pedro. "I know it's late, but I have just received a message from Dominic Rossi in Sydney, who would like to speak with you."

"I'm busy with the problem in New York. Roberto's now in charge of sorting Australia. Get him to take the call if he's free," said Hernando.

"Certainly, senor," responded Pedro.

"Yes, Pedro?" Roberto snapped as he reached for the remote and paused the program he was watching on the big screen in the lounge room.

"Senor Roberto, so sorry to disturb you so late, but I have had a message from Dominic Rossi, who said the matter was important. Senor Hernando has instructed all the Australian matters are now to be directed to you," informed Pedro.

"Set up the VPN and let Dominic know I will call in ten minutes," ordered Roberto.

*

"What is so important you must call me at this hour?" Roberto asked.

"Sorry to have disturbed but I thought it was important information to help you plan your travel," said Dominic. "I've spoken with Tiko in Fiji; through his contacts, he should be able to secure the Fiji property with all the packing equipment for under a mill. I was bold enough to tell him to go ahead before anyone else became interested."

"Good work," replied Roberto.

"I also informed him that you are a key man with the Gonzales Cartel and will visit him on the way to Sydney to inspect the facilities and formalise working arrangements with him," informed Dominic. "It's all starting to come together. I look forward to taking charge and working with you when we retire the old guys."

"Bueno," replied Roberto. "I'll start working on my travel plans, including getting a visa for Australia. In the meantime, I will also start planning a shipment of CH to send to Fiji so we get the cash flowing. I look forward to seeing that piece of dog shit Carlo at the bottom of your famous Sydney Harbour when I'm in Sydney. Bye for now."

Roberto stood from the desk and went to the partially closed office door. *What's that noise?* He stepped into the hallway and noticed Pedro retreating towards the kitchen.

What is it about that Pedro recently? He always seems to be hovering around. I have to say something to Hernando about him in the morning.

CHAPTER 11

With the assistance of her taxi driver, Penny could load her suitcase and large, heavy, fibreglass equipment chest onto a trolley discarded by an earlier traveller, lying next to the taxi rank. On entering Heathrow's Terminal 4, Penny headed towards the QANTAS check-in counter, where other members of the touring cricket team were assembled at the group check-in counter.

It looks like it is going to be economy class.

Penny smiled and waved at Jo Roberts, who, as Team Manager, was checking the documentation of the team members to make sure no one had left their passport at home.

"Good evening, Penny," greeted Jo. "With your height, I hope you don't mind flying in economy. I'm afraid travel had a limited budget. At least we'll get a short stop-over in Singapore to stretch the legs."

"That will be fine," replied Penny as she presented Jo with her documentation for checking and wheeled her baggage up to the check-in counter. "My team tracksuit is comfortable, and if you could get me an aisle seat, I'll be able to get up and stretch my legs during the flight."

"I'm sure we can arrange that for you," said Jo. "After all, you are kindly paying your airfare."

With everyone checking in, the team approached the airport security entrance.

OMG, that's a squad of Royal Fusiliers entering the building and Sergeant Taylor and Corporal Robinson heading right towards me.

Penny reached into her bag and grabbed her sunglasses, quickly placing them on as the squad strode past.

"That looks like Captain Irvine. I heard she resigned her commission," said Sergeant Taylor as he slowed and directed Corporal Robinson's attention to the group of passing women.

Penny began to quicken her stride as a voice came from behind, "Captain Irvine."

"I think that soldier was calling out to you," noted Jo, who increased her pace to keep up with Penny. "Said Captain something."

"Must be a case of mistaken identity," said Penny as she continued to head swiftly to the security entrance without looking back towards the men.

*

Given take-off in the late evening, most passengers reclined their seats and aimed to try and get some sleep straight after the meal service. Penny tried to relax and stretched her long right leg into the aisle. However, she found it difficult to relax and continually tried to find a comfortable position.

Her mind was racing after what she had read in Andy's report about her mission in Australia. It was going to be a complex operating environment. There were several possible scenarios with the Conti family, the likely presence of a Gonzales hitman and DS Tanya Layton used as potential bait to lure Carlo out of hiding. Then there was the lunch with Andy in London.

I like Andy. He's good-looking, brave and has a good sense of humour. Could he be someone in my life?

The cabin lights coming to life caused Penny to snap forward in her seat and rub her eyes.

Come on, Penny. Get yourself together. You can't allow yourself to have the luxury of having a man in your life with your chosen career.

"You were deeply asleep," said Jo, seated across the aisle from Penny. "They'll be serving breakfast shortly, as we're a couple of hours out of Singapore."

"Must have been tired. Had a busy time before the flight. At least it helped the time pass," replied Penny. "I'm looking forward to walking around the terminal in Singapore before the final leg to Sydney."

*

The stopover allowed Penny to get her body moving amongst the endless corridors of glittering shopfronts in the Singapore Airport Terminal. Back onboard, after downing a couple of 500ml bottles of water, she felt more relaxed and began to engage with other cricket team members.

"Ladies, for those of you who have not met her as yet, this is Penny Emmett-Jones, our team trainer and masseuse," said Jo as she stood up from her seat and pointed Penny out to the team members clustered together in the surrounding seats.

Penny rose out of her seat, rotated her body, and waved, acknowledging the smiles and cheers from the team members.

"I look forward to getting my hands into you lot," she grinned, sitting back down.

The passengers began to quieten again as darkness descended on the cabin as the aircraft crossed the coast of Australia, just near the port city of Darwin. In another few hours, Penny would be arriving in Sydney. With her team members grabbing some sleep, she re-opened the envelope containing the information provided by Andy. Penny reviewed the names of officials in the DEA's Sydney Office and the key officials within the Australian Federal Police who were aware of her mission and could be contacted in an emergency.

Andy proposed that Penny should prioritise contact with the Conti family and warn them of the likely threat they would face from the Gonzales cartel. News of the threat might entice Gaetano Conti to provide evidence in return for protection. She planned to discuss her plans with her DEA team. Backup would be essential for such a meeting.

Penny also planned to make informal contact with Detective Sergeant (DS) Tanya Layton. The aim would be to get the opportunity to put a system in place to monitor her safety, given the prospect that Gonzales could use her as bait to draw Carlo out from the safety of the witness protection program.

Penny's mind whirled while the rest of the team attempted to gain more sleep before the touchdown.

Will I be able to find Carlo Conti and convince him to provide evidence against the cartel? Will I be able to save his father? What has Gonzales got in store to entice Carlo out of hiding, and who will he send from amongst his accomplices to undertake the task?

*

It was a tiring flight, especially having to cram her six-foot frame into an economy seat along with the other members of the cricket squad.

Maybe I should have been a snob, travelled business class, and not be stuck in economy. However, they are great, and it was good to get to know some of them, she reflected as she extracted her carry-on baggage from the overhead locker.

Finally stepping off the aircraft, Penny raised her arms and stretched. With a shake of the legs, she was off to complete the arrival formalities for entry into Australia.

"What brings you to Australia, Miss Emmett-Jones?" The Border Force Officer asked as he checked the photograph and Australian visa in Penny's UK Passport and examined her arrival form for any declarations of contraband.

"I am part of the English Women's Cricket Team support crew," Penny replied. "Come to thrash you Aussies on your home ground."

The officer paused and waved to a colleague who presented with several stripes on his shirt epaulettes. They looked at the computer screen, and with a nod from his superior, the officer stamped her passport and annotated her arrival form.

"I don't know whether I can let you into Australia, and I certainly can't wish you good luck," he joked. "Welcome to Australia."

Penny collected her suitcase and equipment chest as it dropped down from the delivery chute, loaded her trolley, and headed towards the Customs Hall exit. She handed her declaration card to the Border Force officer, who maintained a stern façade and directed her to the exit door after discreetly placing the card in his trouser pocket.

Penny waited for an exhausted Jo to emerge from the Customs Hall. "You were lucky. They didn't inspect your luggage. They wanted to open all our cricket bags and inspect every item for soil remnants. Luckily, we got the tip before departure to clean everything thoroughly to avoid any hassles with the Aussie agricultural inspectors."

"As agreed, I have made accommodation arrangements here in Sydney," said Penny. "I will call you in the morning about the timing of the first practice session for the team and make my way out to the ground. The team will look forward to a massage to recover from the flight."

"Sounds like a plan. Catch you later," replied Jo as she gathered the rest of the squad for the bus trip to their team hotel in the city centre.

Penny scanned the faces behind a metal barrier as Jo headed away. Her eyes moved left and right, finally identifying a sign with her name. The sign was held by a slightly built woman of Asian appearance. She appeared to be in her late 20s or early 30s and around five feet four inches tall, wearing a dark-grey pants suit over a white button-up blouse.

"Hi, I'm Agent Wong," said the woman with an American accent as she extended her right hand. "Agent Carter has asked me to assist you in Australia. I have a car waiting outside for you."

"Seems unusual to have a DEA operation here in Australia, Agent Wong," observed Penny. "You are a long way from home."

"Please call me Sandra. Let me give you a hand with all that luggage. You certainly don't travel light," said Sandra with a grin. "The crime gangs get big prices here in Australia for illicit drugs, especially cocaine. The selling prices make Australia a major hub for the re-distribution of drugs around the globe, including the US. We work closely with the AFP and share intelligence between our respective organisations."

"What are the plans for the day?" Penny asked. "I have plenty to discuss with the team about my operation here."

"Well, depending on how you feel after the flight, I propose you come into HQ. We can brief you on what we know about the Contis and the famous Detective Layton from the AFP's Drug Enforcement Division (DED)."

"Sounds good to me," replied Penny. "After you drop me off at the hotel, I can unpack. I will then go for a run to clear my head. I want to avoid laying down immediately to get into the local time zone. It was hard to get adequate sleep in an economy seat over the past 24 hours while in transit."

"Tell me about it. With our recent budget cuts, we have to travel economy back to the States," said Sandra, who smiled as she clutched her back. "Say I pick you up from the front of your hotel at 3 pm? That will give you a few hours for your run and something to eat. And, per your instructions, your room is allocated next to the fire exit, no higher than level 3."

*

Penny scanned her security key and entered her hotel room. Light beamed in through the open curtains. *Ah, a hint of lemon-scented air freshener.* The room was spacious enough for a dark-grey linen two-seater couch, with two single chairs around a dark mahogany coffee table adjacent to the window.

Penny continued to explore the room, and to the right of the entrance was a modern bathroom dripping with chrome fittings and an array of the usual accessories such as shampoo and conditioner. The cupboards on the left of the entry in matching mahogany included a good-sized safe suitable for her handguns and ammunition. Penny sat on the end of her bed, and her eyes felt heavy. Her body screamed for her to drop back onto the pillows when a knock at the door, followed by the word "concierge," got her moving.

She slowly stood, stretched her arms over her head and opened the door. She seemed amused as she watched the concierge struggle to lift her heavy equipment chest off the trolley.

"Over next to the coffee table will be fine, thank you." Penny reached into the pocket of her jeans and extracted a British five-pound note. "Hope this is ok," she said. "It is all I have."

In seconds the money was whisked out of her hand, and with a nod and a smile, the concierge about turned and was gone.

Eyeing her equipment chest lying on the floor, Penny turned and opened the hotel room door and swiftly affixed the DO NOT DISTURB sign on the exterior door handle. Kneeling next to the chest, Penny entered the PIN on the combination lock. A scan of the contents indicated nothing had been tampered with during the transit from London Heathrow.

Included in her deadly cargo were several aluminium tubes of various lengths and diameters that shielded the contents from the prying eyes of any x-ray machine operatives. The tubes were tagged with labels such as cricket bats, uniforms, medical kits and the like. Penny unscrewed the end cap of the longest tube and extracted Gertrude, holding the gun with a look of admiration as she gently placed the weapon on her bed.

Other tubes were similarly opened, and the contents were placed on her bed. The contents included her backup rifle, several handguns, ammunition, a medical kit, infrared night glasses and an array of electronic equipment, such as listening devices. Penny checked the listening devices to ensure they were operational and fully charged before placing them in the room's safe, along with her handguns and knives.

As Penny started to pack away her equipment, her mobile phone pinged. It was Agent Wong with a message confirming pick up at 3 pm in front of the hotel.

Penny looked out of her window, which presented an uninspiring view of the building on the opposite side of Martin Place.

I did not notice any parklands to run in, so maybe a 5BX workout, a hot shower and a light room service meal will freshen me up. Maybe grilled fish with a Greek salad will do nicely.

CHAPTER 12

Agent Sandra Wong was waiting in her car in the hotel driveway when Penny stepped out at precisely 3 pm. "Did you get a rest?" Sandra asked.

"Hi, Sandra. I was very tempted to nap, but I unpacked my bags, pressed some clothes and did a 5BX routine I use for hotel rooms. After a hot shower and a bite to eat, I am feeling reasonably ok," said Penny as she gently patted her stomach. "I fought the temptation to grab some sleep but figured I would not be able to get up if I did so."

"Our office is nearby in a building overlooking Sydney Harbour," explained Sandra. "Only a few minutes away, so hopefully, you won't get the urge to nod off in the car."

"It will be nice to see the famous Sydney Harbour Bridge and the Opera House again after so many years," Penny said. "Better than the view of the building opposite my hotel room."

Sandra drove into the underground carpark of the Credit-Suisse building adjacent to Circular Quay. After parking the car, Sandra guided Penny to the elevators and scanned her security pass. In the elevator, she again scanned her security pass and pressed the button for the 42nd floor. The elevator opened onto an unoccupied desk and a solid wall with a handleless central doorway. There was no signage indicating the occupants of the office. Sandra scanned her security pass, and the door opened inwardly.

Behind the door, Penny entered a world akin to a beehive. People rushed everywhere, others busy on phones, eyes affixed to computer screens. Doors adorned with *Meeting In Progress* signs filled a nearby corridor.

"Sorry, but with my rank, my office doesn't rate a harbour view," said Sandra. "However, the main meeting room is free, so come in and take a look."

"Wow," exclaimed Penny as she beheld the panoramic vista of the Bridge, the Opera House and the magnificence of the Harbour perfectly framed on the floor-to-ceiling windows.

"It is as beautiful as I remember from all those years ago when I last visited Australia as a student. But I suppose we better get down to business."

Sandra guided Penny to her small office and closed the door. "As I said, I don't rate a view," said Sandra with a laugh. "I get the blinding reflected light from the building next door. As you stated, we better get to business before your jetlag kicks in."

"From studying Agent Carter's briefing notes, we have a very complex situation," said Penny.

"Agreed," responded Sandra, "especially adding the likelihood of a Gonzales hitman arriving on Australian soil into the mix."

"The whole situation would make a great book or movie," smiled Penny.

"I understand that after your discussions with Agent Carter, you are proposing a two-step plan," noted Sandra.

"Correct. Firstly, I will need your help to obtain a contact number for Gaetano Conti. I want to shock him with the news of a possible hit on the family by the Gonzales cartel. The information may entice him to cooperate with us if we offer the family protection," informed Penny.

"Secondly, I want to closely watch the AFPs, Detective Layton. She'll likely be a focus of attention for our hitman, intending to use her as bait to draw Carlo Conti out of his unknown whereabouts in the WPP."

"As you know, the AFP cannot share the details of Carlo's whereabouts and identity within the WPP," noted Sandra. "You should also be aware that we have received an update about developments in Fiji. Agent Carter has confirmed that the Fijian Government has sold the Contis coffee packing business in Savusavu under their Proceeds of Crime Act."

"Do we know who purchased the business?" Penny asked.

"Our intel tells us that the business was bought by a low-level local drug criminal, Tiko Rokovou, who reportedly heads a growing entity called the K-gang, with emerging interests in Sydney," said Sandra. "According to our informant, the money required to buy the business was provided by none other than the Gonzales Cartel."

"That certainly does not bode well for the Conti organisation's longevity, I fear, with Gonzales already making moves on this side of the Pacific," noted Penny. "I better contact Gaetano Conti as soon as possible and see if I can gain his support, given what we know about the Gonzales' plans."

"I'll email you the Gaetano Conti's contact details and information on Detective Layton. Now from the look of you, I better get you back to your hotel so you can get some rest," said Sandra as she stood up, picked up her handbag, and retrieved her car keys. "You have done well but are starting to nod off."

*

"Come in, Tanya. Take a seat," said DCI Adam Charles as he pointed to the chair on the opposite side of his permanently file-cluttered desk. "We need to go over the raid on the Kings Cross warehouse and fill in the paperwork generated by you ending up in the hospital for stitches."

"It's nothing serious," mumbled Tanya looking at the floor and instinctively reaching for her injured arm. "I'm fine. It was only a few stitches and a tetanus shot."

"Nothing serious. You could have been killed with the knife that bastard Hodgkison drew on you," stammered Adam. "Not to mention you losing control of your weapon, something the internal affairs guys don't like. I'll do my best to bury the paperwork."

"Thanks, boss. That should be easy from the look of your desk," Tanya smiled. "I fixed Hodgkison up with a jiu-jitsu move I'd been practising in the dojo with my instructor."

"Yes, I was very impressed watching you perform that very slick move," said Adam with a grin as he relaxed in Tanya's presence. "Back to business. The anonymous tip-off we received on that consignment no doubt cost someone a lot money."

"We've taken many drugs off the street," noted Tanya. "That someone will undoubtedly still have to pay a very unhappy supplier. I see you picked up a business card that slipped from that slime-ball Hodgkison's pocket."

"Yes, it was for The House of Pleasure in Kings Cross, located only a short distance from the raided warehouse. The card featured none other than the name of Dominic Rossi as the Manager," replied Adam. "He's a nephew of the infamous Gaetano Conti and son of Lorenzo Rossi. The location near the warehouse can't be a coincidence. With a bit of digging around, I found that the sole director of the House of Pleasure is Maria Conti," stated Adam as he referred to a document in the open folder on his desk. "She's Carlo's mother. I bet the woman has no idea about her appointment as a director and has probably never heard of the House of Pleasure and the services it provides."

"For sure, there'll be a link with the shipment and the Contis," said an agitated Tanya, her voice rising in anger. "With another shipment, old man Conti must be trying to make up for what they lost in Fiji."

"With this latest consignment being seized, I bet old man Conti must be into his suppliers in South America for a large whack of cash. They'll not be very happy," said Adam. "I think we need to keep an eye on the Contis. They'll have to get up to something big time to raise the cash to pay for the lost consignments."

"I wonder whether Carlo, or whatever his name is now, has any idea what is going on with his family," pondered Tanya.

"With their statement about disowning him and him in the WPP, I doubt he's looped in," said Adam. "He could even have been relocated overseas and is unaware of what is happening with the family."

"I hope he's doing okay. In the end, he turned out to be a great guy," said Tanya as she turned away from Adam and blinked away a tear from her eye.

*

Penny sat up in bed after a refreshing night's sleep, the jetlag becoming but a memory. She stretched, leapt out of bed, headed to the bathroom to wash her face, and scrubbed her teeth. Penny then commenced a vigorous 5BX routine with a selection of exercise music from Spotify on her mobile phone. As she began to perform some cat stretches after the routine, there was a knock on her door announcing the arrival of her breakfast tray.

The waiter placed the tray containing a plunger of black coffee, granola muesli with oat milk, and freshly squeezed orange juice onto her coffee table. The waiter presented Penny with the bill she signed and added a tip that brought a smile.

"Just leave the tray outside your door when you've finished, ma'am."

After thirstily draining the glass of orange juice and hungrily devouring the bowl of muesli, Penny poured a mug of coffee and opened her PC on her lap. She noted Sandra's email containing the requested contact information on Gaetano Conti and DS Tanya Layton's home address and usual routine.

After she finished her coffee, Penny began to pace up and down in her room. Her mind was racing as she began to plan the day.

First up, I will call Jo to see how the team is going and save her from trying to track me down. I will need to terminate the arrangement with the team if things heat up with the Contis. Next, I need to head into the office and meet with Sandra to record the call to Gaetano and work on a plan to monitor Tanya Layton.

"Hi, Jo, Penny here. How has the team settled in? Getting over the jetlag?"

"Everyone seems to be recovering OK. Only a few of them have been hit a little more than the others. How about you?"

"I am doing ok. Thought I would pop out and see you and the team this morning as I may have something on this afternoon with some old friends."

"That would be great, Penny. I know I would welcome a massage. You can come to the Sydney Cricket ground near the CBD. Entry is via the Service Gate Number 9, and we will set up our headquarters in the Visitors Room in the Members Stand."

"See you around 10," confirmed Penny as she searched for Agent Sandra Wong's number.

"Good morning, Sandra," said Penny.

"How did you sleep?" Sandra asked.

"Nice and refreshed, ready for action," replied Penny.

"What's the plan for today, Penny?"

"I have a commitment with the English cricket team I need to honour. Then, I will head into your office to call Gaetano Conti," Penny replied.

"Yes, I'll set up a recording device," said Sandra. "See you later this morning."

*

"Sorry for the late start this morning Sandra, but as mentioned, I committed to a session with the cricket team," Penny said. "To save complications arising from further involvement, I will tell them I must return to England on an urgent family matter."

"Yes, you can't take the risk once things start to heat up with the Contis," responded Sandra. "I am all set to record the call to Gaetano Conti."

Penny dialled the number and indicated to Sandra to hit the record button.

"Mr Gaetano Conti, my name is Andrea Pinkston."

"I don't know you. How did you get this number?" Gaetano asked. "It's a private number."

Unfazed, Penny stated. "It is not important how I have your number. What is vital is that I must inform you that your family is in imminent danger from a long-time associate of yours, Mister Hernando Gonzales."

"I don't know whom you're talking about, Miss Pinkston," stammered Gaetano. "I don't know anyone by that name." An agitated Gaetano fired out questions to his unknown caller. "Who are you? Where are you from?"

"Mr Conti, I can assure you this line is safe, but again I repeat, your family is in danger, and we must talk. I suggest I give you ten minutes to think about what I have said and expect your call back on my number within the next ten minutes. The choice is yours. You have nothing to lose by speaking with me."

*

Gaetano looked at his phone screen as the call terminated. His mind was racing with unanswered questions.

Who the fuck was that? What and how does she know what Gonzales is up to? She's right. I've got nothing to lose by speaking with her. Hernando is certainly not happy with what I owe him. I better give Dominic a call.

*

"Dominic, it's Uncle Gaetano. I've just had a strange call from a woman who spoke with one of those fancy English accents straight out of the movies," said Gaetano. "She said she had information regarding danger to the family from Senor Gonzales and wanted to urgently speak with me. Somehow she had my private number. I need to speak with her to find out what she knows."

"Uncle. I'm sure there's nothin' to worry about," Dominic said. "Roberto's coming out to Australia to sort everything out with us. Must be the cops trying to scare you into saying something."

Shit. I'll have to tell Roberto about this.

"Call me after you've spoken with the bitch, Uncle," Dominic said before hanging up.

*

"Miss Pinkston," stated a curt Gaetano. "

"Thank you for agreeing to speak with me, Mr Conti." Trusting a stranger in your line of work is difficult, but you need to hear what I say."

"My line of work. Interesting, go on," said Gaetano.

"Life is dangerous in your line of work." Penny paused for effect. "Fortunes are won and lost, friends and enemies created. It is also on the public record about your sons, their activities in the Fiji Islands, and their involvement with the Columbian Gonzales drug cartel."

"I'd like you to get to the point," Gaetano irritatedly said as he shuffled in his seat. "The Fiji Islands had nothin' to do with me."

"From my well-informed resources, I know your family likely owes Mr Gonzales and his cohort a considerable sum. He has a reputation for being very ruthless, showing no mercy to those indebted to him," explained Penny.

"Ah…" Gaetano was about to interject and thought better of it, "sorry, please continue."

"I have been made aware that a hitman is en route to Australia on the orders of Mr Gonzales, and you have reason to fear for your life," said Penny. "I advise you to be very cautious, and it may pay to put your trust in the authorities to get you out of harm's way."

"So, you are a stinkin' copper," yelled Gaetano as he stood and started to pace up and down.

"Do I sound like a local police officer to you?" Penny asked, remaining calm. "I cannot make you do anything. It is up to you, but I wanted to give you this information. Only you can decide what you want to do. I am just trying to help you by passing on what I know from reliable sources."

"As I said, I don't have a fuckin' clue what your talkin' about," Gaetano snapped.

"You have my number," said an unruffled Penny as she stood. "Call me any time. I will help you if you decide to cooperate with the authorities."

*

Gaetano immediately called Dominic, who quickly answered the call.

"What did the bitch say, Uncle?"

"She must have inside info," Gaetano replied. "She knew about Fiji and the family's involvement with the Gonzales cartel. And get this, she knew about the money owed to Gonzales and stated that Hernando was sending a hitman to Australia, and we needed to be aware of the danger."

"As I said, Uncle, the cops are just trying to make you spill the beans. I'm sure there's nothin' to worry about."

Gaetano started to sound more relaxed. "Your probably right. There's nothin' to worry about. Just those fuckin' cops makin' trouble. Anyway, I've got her number, just in case."

*

Dominic was sitting in the office at the HOP when the call came from Gaetano. A quick check of the CCTV showed the girls were all busy.

At least some cash is coming in courtesy of the US Navy with that destroyer in port. However, I need to get the fuckin' drug business up and goin' again. Hopefully, Roberto will come good for me once we meet, and I can finally take over the business now that all those cousins of mine are out of the fuckin' way.

With his office door closed, Dominic fired up his PC again to connect with Roberto. It would be early morning in the jungles of Columbia, and Roberto would be unhappy about being disturbed so early. However, the information about Andrea Pinkston was too important to hold back.

After following protocol and contacting Pedro, a sleepy-sounding Roberto answered gruffly.

"This better be fuckin' urgent, Dominic."

Dominic was straight to the point, "An English bird called and talked to Gaetano about a threat from the Gonzales organisation to take him out with a hitman and suggested he seek refuge from the cops."

"Fuck me," roared Roberto, fully aroused from his sleep. "Who is this bitch, and how did she know about a hitman? I'm goin' to have to sweep the phones and check for bugs. There must be a leak. Where's Pedro?"

"She reckons she's not a fuckin' copper but claims her information came from informed sources," continued Dominic.

"What about your uncle?" Roberto asked. "What did he say?"

"Told her to piss off, he wasn't interested, but he does have her number," added Dominic. "I'll watch him if he tries to contact her."

"I'll also have a look from my end to see what I can learn about this, Miss Pinkston. Keep me informed of any developments, and I'll confirm my travel arrangements with you shortly," stated Roberto as he terminated the call.

Maybe I might be in charge of the organisation sooner than I thought possible. I deserve a nice glass of Scotch and finish with a relaxing blowjob from Randy Mandy. Let's see if she's finished with that Yankee naval officer.

CHAPTER 13

"Sandra, as expected, he thought I was a police officer trying to coerce him into providing information on Gonzales," said Penny. "However, he did seem shaken when I mentioned the possibility of a hitman and suggested he should seek protection from the authorities. However, he does have my number."

"You have sewn the seed with him to cooperate," acknowledged Sandra. "I'll let Andy know how you went with Gaetano, and now we should put the second part of the plan into action by aiming to establish a close connection with Detective Layton. If the hitman takes out either his Dad or Tanya Layton, I believe it is 100 per cent certain that such action will draw Carlo from wherever he now resides within the WPP."

"I will start operation Tanya tomorrow," said Penny. "I am due for a good workout, and Larry's Gym, you highlighted as part of her routine, sounds just the place. She's had an interesting career working undercover in Fiji. I look forward to meeting her."

*

From the information provided by Agent Sandra Wong, Penny knew DS Tanya Layton spent regular lunchtime breaks working out at Larry's Gym. The gym was in a laneway running off George Street in Sydney's CBD, near AFP's Headquarters. Ten minutes before noon, Penny checked her FitBit and sat in a window seat of Giovan's Coffee Shop opposite the police building's entrance. The sign above the doorway proclaimed the best coffee in Sydney. Penny ordered a double hit espresso coffee, some biscotti and a small bottle of San Pellegrino sparkling water. She maintained an eye on the entrance while feigning to read a previous customer's newspaper left on her table.

Penny had just finished her coffee and opened her water when she saw a woman with a gym bag over her shoulder.

That's her. It looks like it is a workout day. Penny finished her water in one swallow and, after checking the bill, left cash on her table and was out the door in pursuit of Tanya.

Tanya made a left turn down a shadowy laneway a couple of hundred metres down George Street from the entrance to AFP's offices. According to Sandra's datasheet, Tanya entered the premises, identified as Larry's 24/7 gymnasium, by a small white timber sign with faded black lettering above the glass entry doors.

Penny peered through the double glass doors and saw Detective Layton. She was chatting to a tall, blond, youthful-looking, muscular man in a tight white singlet emblazoned with *Larry's Gym* by the reception desk.

Entering the gymnasium, Penny paused while her eyes adjusted to the fluorescent lighting and strolled up to the desk.

"Can I help you?" the young man asked Penny.

"I am not sure if it is possible," commenced Penny. "My name is Penny Emmett-Jones, and I am touring Australia with the English Women's cricket team. We have just arrived in Sydney to commence our tour of Australia. I would like to know whether it be possible for me and any fellow team members to use the gymnasium while we are in Sydney on a casual basis?"

"That's fantastic," interjected Tanya. "I've started playing cricket a bit myself. You've got to help them, Tony. You could get the newspaper to take photos of the team working out and get good publicity for the gym."

"I'll check with the boss, but with what Tanya here has suggested, I reckon we could do something for you, Penny and the rest of the team. By the way, I am Tony Whittaker, and this is the internationally famous Sydney detective Tanya Layton."

"Stop it, Tony," said Tanya as she punched his arm.

"Ow. That hurt, detective," grinned Tony.

"Let me show you around Penny while Tony speaks to the boss."

"Thank you, Detective Layton," said Penny. "I better make sure I behave while I'm here in Australia."

"Please call me Tanya, and I love your posh accent. Just like the royal family," Tanya said with a laugh. "It's pretty basic here, but Larry and his trainers do a great job. I come most lunch times, casework permitting, of course, but I'm taking it a little easier at the moment after a bit of an injury while on the job," she added as she instinctively reached for the spot on her wounded arm.

Tanya proceeded to provide a tour of the facilities to Penny. The gym was created from a converted warehouse, with the original brickwork painted glossy cream. Without access to direct sunlight, several fluorescent light fittings dropped from long chains from the high ceiling. Directly behind the reception area was a boxing ring encircled by punching bags, speedballs and racks of boxing gloves of various sizes and colours. Centrally located at the rear were doorways indicating OFFICE to the right and CHANGE ROOMS to the left. The left-hand side of the gym housed the usual equipment - cross-trainers, treadmills, mounted cycles and racks of various pieces of equipment designed to build every muscle of the body.

"This will be fine. The gym has all the equipment the rest of the girls in the team would need," said Penny. "Hopefully, Tony can get the owner to do a deal for them."

"How about you come around to my place for dinner tomorrow night?" Tanya asked. "Nothing flash. Just steaks and salad with a nice bottle of Aussie red."

"Sounds perfect. You Aussies are certainly hospitable. I do not believe you would be invited back to someone's abode in London, having just met them in a gym," Penny smiled. "I will give you my mobile number, and you can send me your contact details."

Wow. It could not have been a more successful introduction. Invited to her place for dinner. Better get those bugs ready to install.

"Penny, Larry says he would be very happy to host you and the team as honorary members of Larry's Gym, as long as we can get a few photos for the media and maybe even a television crew to film the team working out," said Tony with a beaming smile. "Hopefully, you can introduce me to a few of the girls. They may be able to give me a few tips to improve my batting in return for me providing them with some personal training."

"Oh, Tony. Please, improve my batting," said Tanya with a groan.

*

Penny was feeling quite pleased with how the afternoon had turned out, especially with being invited to her target's place for dinner.

Penny thought these Aussies were far too friendly as she retrieved her equipment box from her bedroom cupboard and dragged the heavy, bulky container towards the coffee table. She swiftly affixed the DO NOT DISTURB sign on the door's exterior and moved the security chain into position.

Kneeling next to the equipment box, Penny entered the PIN on the combination lock and flipped open the box lid. A quick scan confirmed that all the contents were in order. Her mobile phone pinged. The message was from Tanya confirming dinner at her place for 7 pm the next evening, along with the address in the suburb of Randwick. Checking the address on Google Maps, Penny noticed Tanya lived nearby the Sydney Cricket Ground.

I can meet Jo and the team at their practice session tomorrow afternoon. Then as discussed with Sandra, I will speak to Jo and tell her I need to return to England on a family matter and regrettably cannot continue on tour with the team. I need to focus 100% on the mission. I can head off to Tanya's from the cricket ground for dinner.

Penny checked the listening devices to ensure they were operational and fully charged. She placed a few units in her black leather shoulder bag and returned her equipment box to the bedroom cupboard, ensuring the box was locked.

*

The following morning Penny headed to Larry's gym for a workout.

"I am seeing the team this afternoon at the cricket ground during their training session and will let them know about your offer of using the gym," said Penny. "The team manager Josephine Roberts, I am sure, will contact you so you can arrange the promotional photos. The girls will love the exposure."

"Look forward to meeting them," smiled Tony.

"Anyone available I can spar with in the boxing ring?" Penny asked.

"The boxing crowd usually workout in the afternoon and evening," replied Tony. "However, I can put the gloves on if you like."

"Thanks, Tony, that would be great," Penny said, heading towards the boxing gloves rack.

*

"Good afternoon, Jo," said Penny as she walked into the changing room at the Sydney Cricket Ground.

"You look like you have come straight from a gym session," noted Jo.

"We are very observant," replied Penny. "Yes, and that relates to some good news for the team. I worked out at Larry's gym in the city, and they offered free membership for the team while they were in the Sydney part of the tour."

"Excellent news Penny. How did you manage that?" Jo asked.

"I was looking for somewhere to work out near my hotel yesterday afternoon and wandered into Larry's. They are a very friendly crowd," noted Penny. "Here is the business card for the manager Tony Whittaker. Give him a call, and in return for a complimentary membership, you will need to arrange a time for some publicity shots to be taken."

"Fantastic news. I will call him, as it has proven difficult to use the facilities here at the cricket ground with all the Aussie men and women players about the place," said Jo.

"With the good news, I am afraid there is some bad news," Penny said, adopting a serious tone.

"Oh dear, what's happened? Nothing serious, I hope."

"I received a call early this morning from my Father saying my Mother has taken very ill," said Penny. "My Father wants me to return home as soon as possible."

"The timing could not have been worse. We've just started the tour," exclaimed Jo shaking her head. "Are you sure you've got to go back?"

"Yes, I am afraid so," Penny said, nodding.

"I guess family comes first," said Jo reluctantly, "I hope she is going to be ok."

"Thanks for your understanding, Jo," replied Penny. "I wouldn't forgive myself if something terrible happened to her."

"I understand," said Jo. "I will let the team know, and thanks for arranging the gym and the associated media coverage will be an added and unexpected bonus to promote the tour."

*

Penny sat in the Uber en route to Tanya's residence.

It helped to get rid of that obligation with the cricket team. I can now focus on Gaetano and Tanya.

Penny checked the devices in her bag just before pulling up in front of Tanya's apartment block. She stepped out of the Uber and noted it was a small block of apartments with six apartments over three levels.

There was no elevator, and Penny climbed the two flights to the top level. She poised outside the screen door and was about to press the illuminated doorbell mounted to the right of the doorway when she heard two voices inside. Along with Tanya's laughter, she could hear a man's voice.

That is a nuisance. A guest. Placing the listening devices with a fellow guest or a partner watching my movements may be difficult.

With a press of the doorbell, a smiling Tanya greeted her with a glass of white wine. "Hey Penny, come meet my boss DCI Adam Charles."

"Hi, Penny, pleased to meet you," said Adam extending his right hand towards Penny. "How are you doin'?"

"Very well, thank you," Penny said, noting Adam's firm grip. "I am slowly getting over the jetlag."

Penny mentally scanned the apartment. Immediately on the right was a small, functional kitchen with a bench providing a barrier to the compact lounge dining area. On the left, a closed door led to what Penny presumed to be the bathroom. A small square dining table was set with three placings. Bamboo placemats were adorned with two glasses, one already filled with chilled water with condensation dribbling down the side. On either side of the mat were a fork and a serrated steak knife, with a dessert spoon and fork at the top of the mat.

It looks like two courses with the promised steak. I guess Aussies love their steak.

"Take a seat, and I'll get you a wine," said Tanya indicating the fawn-coloured two-seater couch. "What will you have?"

"That white you have looks fine, thank you," replied Penny as she noted Adam making himself readily comfortable in one of the two single lounge chairs.

They obviously have a comfortable working relationship.

"Cheers," toasted Tanya as she took her seat. "Welcome to Sydney, and good luck with the tour." They clinked their glasses.

Penny looked around. "I have just had some bad news. My Mother has become ill, and I must return home as soon as possible. It means I will have to miss the tour with the team."

"Oh, that is terrible news. You've only arrived," said Tanya. "I hope she'll be ok."

"She has not been well for some time," answered Penny, "but enough of that. I don't want to spoil the mood. Tell me all about you being a famous international detective, which Tony mentioned at the gym yesterday."

"There's not much to tell," responded Tanya. "Bottom line is that I worked undercover in the Fiji Islands and helped bring down the manufacturing centre set up by an Aussie crime gang."

"Tanya is very modest," interrupted Adam. "She…."

"Enough of that chitter-chat. I'm starved, let's eat," said Tanya as she stood and guided her guests to the table. "As promised, porterhouse steaks, greek salad, fries and a bold South Australian Shiraz. I hope you don't mind, but I've done them medium."

"Medium is fine, and I love your Australian Reds from my last trip here as a student." Penny raised her glass to her nose. "Wonderful bouquet."

*

"Thanks for a wonderful dinner Tanya and it was great to meet you, Adam. I am sorry I have to return to the UK, but I hope our paths cross again in the not-too-distant future," Penny said as she hugged Tanya and then descended the stairs to the waiting Uber.

"All the best," chorused Tanya and Adam. "Hope your Mother is OK."

It was a nuisance. Adam was there as well tonight. I must return to Tanya's apartment to put the listening devices into place. The locks for a police officer's abode looked very basic, and there was no security system, so there would be no trouble getting in and out relatively quickly.

CHAPTER 14

"How are your travel plans coming along for Fiji and Australia?" Hernando asked Roberto.

"My Australian visa came through ok, but one thing that has caused me serious concern is the feedback I received late last night from Dominic about the mysterious English woman who spoke to his Uncle Gaetano on the phone," stated Roberto.

"What did she say to Gaetano?" Hernando asked.

"Dominic said she contacted Gaetano unannounced and introduced herself as Andrea Pinkston. From all my investigations through our network, I can't find anyone who has heard of this Andrea Pinkston. I presume she used a false name," responded Roberto. "According to Dominic, Gaetano told this woman to fuck off, though she did leave her contact number."

"So, we definitely have a leak, which brings us back to Pedro and his recent behaviour," stated Hernando. "Leave him to me. I can assure you he'll be sorry."

"Given the situation with this Andrea Pinkston, I will travel as Enrico Sanchez of Bogota Travel International, meeting with Mr Conti of Willsmore International Travel. Gaetano has been advised of the details in case he gets a call from Immigration on my arrival in Australia," informed Roberto. "I've also packed a couple of spare passports under different names just in case. Our friend at the Columbian Passport Office was most helpful once I told him where his children went to school."

"What about our Fijian friend Tiko?" Hernando asked.

"All good. I spoke with him, and he will pick me up at Savusavu Airport. He'll provide accommodation at his residence located at the coffee packing business. Evidently, there are plenty of spare beds on the estate's grand hacienda," replied Roberto. "While in Fiji, Tiko will show me around the business, and we can discuss plans for him and his K-gang to take over the distribution for the Contis operation in Sydney."

"The sooner you get to Sydney and finish off the Contis and get the K-gang in place running the business, the better. Give me a call from Fiji after you meet with Tiko, and let me have feedback confirming their capabilities," requested Hernando.

I'll also arrange for Tiko to come to Sydney immediately to get the operations in place. Getting Gaetano to sign over the businesses will make the job a lot easier to set up the new infrastructure without him and Lorenzo Rossi in the picture," advised Roberto.

*

After the long transit from Bogota to Fiji, an exhausted Roberto, using the false identity of Enrico Sanchez, cleared customs and immigration formalities at Nadi International Airport. Exiting the customs hall, he smiled as his body felt the tropical heat and humidity, sweat droplets starting to dribble down his back. It was just like being home in the jungles of Columbia. With help from the Fiji Tourism ground staff official, he was directed to the domestic terminal for the domestic flight to Savusavu after he exited the Customs Hall.

Roberto entered the building and noted the row of check-in counters at the rear. The domestic terminal was not air-conditioned. A string of overhead fans circulated the hot tropical air above several long rows of joined, black metal framed chairs padded in dark-red plastic material. He stepped up to the check-in counter and was surprised when invited to step up on the weigh-in scales.

"80 kilos, plus 22 kilos for the luggage," called the airline official to his assistant, who recorded the data on his clipboard with a short stubby pencil. "Gate 3, and we'll call boarding in about 20 minutes."

Roberto sat under a whirring overhead fan and felt sleepy when the boarding call came through. Roberto slapped himself gently on his prickly, unshaven face and went to the gate. He noted his fellow passengers start to clamber up the rear stairs of the small twin-engine Twin Otter aircraft.

Holy shit! What am I flying in?

Roberto bumped his head as he had to stoop and shuffle his way to his seat in row 2, just behind the cockpit. With seat belts fastened, the co-pilot delivered the safety instructions above the plane's engines' roar as it rumbled onto the runway and headed to the take-off point.

Roberto gave his seatbelt an extra tug, and then with a sudden lurch, the engines roared into life. With the co-pilot's hand pressing down on the captain's hand on the throttle, the aircraft began to tear down the runway. In a gut-wrenching moment, the Twin Otter leapt into the sky.

Whoa, I didn't fuckin' expect this. Hernando, what have you got me into? Holy Mary!

Relieved at successfully becoming airborne, Roberto leant into the aisleway and peered into the cockpit. He identified the altimeter and could see the craft had settled down at just under 8-thousand feet. Finally feeling relaxed and with the throb of the engines, Roberto quietly nodded off to sleep, until he was aroused about 40 minutes later by a voice - *make sure your seat belt is securely fastened, and please review the safety card.*

The plane gradually decreased altitude as it descended a long tranquil bay surrounded by rugged hills covered in dense foliage. Roberto's heart raced as the pilot made a sudden sharp turn to the right, flying over the top of the Savusavu town centre. He clutched the armrests of his seat as the plane appeared to be only a few metres above a myriad of rooftops and could see people in the street below looking upwards at the descending aircraft. Then, passing over the top of the hill backing the township, the captain abruptly dipped the nose. Roberto saw a narrow, short runway dead ahead through the open cockpit curtain.

Roberto made the sign of the cross and then resumed his tight, knuckle-whitening grip on his armrests. The Twin Otter hit the ground with a screech from the tyres and hurtled towards the ocean at the far end of the runway. To his relief, the pilot pulled up the aircraft well short of the waves crashing onto the large boulders marking the end of the landing strip.

As soon as the aircraft came to a stop, Roberto quickly unbuckled his seatbelt and stood, stooped in the aisleway, keen to get off the aircraft. He made his way down the wobbly rear stairs and quickly made his way to a couple of wooden huts, which constituted the Savusavu Terminal. The small buildings acted as check-in counters, with scales on either side of a central arrivals/ departure zone. The luggage was manually extracted from the plane, loaded onto a hand-drawn cart, and hauled to the arrivals area for retrieval by the passengers.

With his luggage removed from the cart, Roberto began to scan the waiting crowd. He noted a tall, powerfully built, youthful-looking Fijian man approaching him with his right hand extended.

"Bula, and welcome to Savusavu. I'm Tiko. You must be Roberto."

"I am so pleased to meet you, Tiko," Roberto replied. "I wasn't expecting the small plane that brought me to Savusavu and that approach to the runway."

"Local airports can be a bit of a surprise to visitors." Tomasi grinned.

He wore faded blue jeans and a dark-green Hawaiian shirt depicting tropical scenes of palm tree-lined beaches. Black trainers and rimless sunglasses pushed back onto his close-cropped, wiry Fijian hair completed his attire.

"I am sorry, but I probably smell a bit," said Roberto as Tiko retrieved his suitcase and guided him towards a waiting Land Rover. "I've been in transit for over 24 hours and need a shower, shave and something decent to eat."

"We'll get you sorted at my place. The property, Tradewinds Coffee is only a short drive from here," said Tiko. "Once you freshen up and have something to eat, I'll show you around. Then we can head into the local yacht club for a relaxing drink and dinner tonight."

After about a ten-minute journey, the vehicle crossed a narrow bridge with a well-worn sign affixed to the bridge with faded lettering, *Slow Down Wailailai Village.*

"Tradewinds Coffee is just on the village's other side," said Tiko. "Several of the coffee company's employees reside in the village. Typically, the business has the ladies on the packing line and the men responsible for the bean roasting, warehousing and shipping functions. On the left, you can see a number of the huts, called bures in Fiji, located right on the waterfront. They're typically backed by small jetties where the villagers keep fishing punts."

Tiko turned left off the main road, rumbled across a thick metal grate sitting over a deep stormwater drain, and pulled up in front of a gate. To the right of the entrance was a one-metre by one-metre recently painted sign, with bright red capital letters identifying the premises as the *Tradewinds Coffee Company, General Manager – Tiko Rokovou.*

Tiko got out of the driver's seat and opened the gate. After driving through, he stopped, closed the gate and headed towards an array of buildings occupying the foreshore.

"On the right, you can see the homestead where I live. You'll note it has a nice wide verandah for enjoying a cool drink in the evening to watch the setting sun. The house is very comfortable and comes fully furnished with three bedrooms, an office and is fully air-conditioned you'll be pleased to know. Dead ahead down the left fork in the driveway is the office and packing shed where the crushed coffee granules are filled into their pods and boxed for shipment. The green bean storage bin, roasting shed, and coffee grinding equipment are down that right fork."

"The property looks as though it was very well-planned," observed Roberto.

"Yes, the original developer, Mister Phillips, did a great job. Through the gap in the sheds, you can see the jetty and the company boat, the *Coffee Queen,* is moored on the waterfront. Unfortunately, the boat was damaged when Guido Conti, one of the previous owners, tried to make his escape. It should be repaired shortly and used to deliver the packed cartons direct to the wharf area. Having our own transport will save the company significant overhead costs and ensure we control the shipping process until the consignments are loaded directly onto the inter-island ferry services to Suva. From Suva, the goods will be shipped directly to Sydney. I understand the K-gang may become of greater service to your organisation."

"We can talk more about that this evening," replied Roberto. "It is a very impressive facility; I can see why the Conti's were attracted to the property.

Getting our product into Australia, disguised as legitimate coffee pods, was a brilliant idea."

"From what I heard in the local media, Guido Conti fucked everything up for the Contis. They could have established something really special here," stated Tiko. "However, the Contis stuff up has allowed our respective organisations to get this place humming. Let's get you freshened up, and we can chat more. I'll brew some of the local coffee for you to sample."

*

After his relaxing shower, Roberto opened the front screen door and joined Tiko on the verandah. Roberto was invited to join Tiko on one of the outdoor teak seats surrounding a matching teak side table. On the table was a tray laden with a coffee pot, two mugs and a tray of biscuits. "Try the coffee," invited Tiko. "All Fijian produce."

Roberto picked up his mug containing the black brew and took a tentative sip.

"Wow, that coffee was magnificent, even for us Columbians who love our coffee," said Roberto as he saluted Tiko. "I like the bitterness of the high-intensity blend. Anyway, we better get down to a bit of business. Tell me about your organisation and how you will manage the business. You can then give me a tour of the place."

"It may surprise you, but I studied economics at Auckland University but unfortunately discovered the joys of smoking pot," said Tiko, easing back in his chair, extending his legs and placing his arms on the armrests. "Getting arrested in New Zealand meant I was deported back to Fiji and lost my scholarship from the Fiji Government. The contacts I made in Auckland set me up to bring weed into Fiji, where I targeted the tourist market around Nadi."

"I don't meet too many university-educated crims in my work," smiled Roberto. "What did you do next?"

"With guys from my home village, who I explicitly trust here in Fiji, along with family and friends who migrated to Australia, we set up what we called the K Gang, only dealing with weed, no hard stuff. The K is short for the Fijian word meaning strong, spelt k-a-u-k-a-u-w-a," explained Tiko.

"How did the link come with the Contis?" Roberto probed.

"With the arrest of the Contis here in Fiji, the family's business was heavily compromised, with the cops in Australia keeping a close eye on them. Mr Conti, via his nephew Dominic made contact with my people in Sydney to help move product for them," explained Tiko. "I flew to Sydney and met up with Dominic, who offered us the opportunity to trade in the more profitable hard stuff, including your Columbian Heaven. He also told me about what happened here in Fiji, which got my mind spinning; the rest is history. Through Dominic, our organisations were introduced, and here we are today. With your financial backing, we secured the property."

"We will agree for you to receive a fair percentage of the profits," stated Roberto.

"Sounds good to me, given Senor Gonzales has put the money up," said Tiko, heading inside. "Wait here, and I'll get us a couple of cold beers."

While sipping on their beers, Tiko detailed how he found out details about the auction of the Tradewinds Coffee property. He had spoken with the local Savusavu property agent, Gary Tyler, whom the Government had commissioned to conduct the sale. Tiko learned of the other parties interested in buying the property and business. Unexpectedly, Tiko was the only person to attend the onsite auction on the day and could purchase the property at a bargain price.

"I like it. You are a good operator Tiko," said Roberto as he drained his beer.

"I'll get us another one," said Tiko as he readied himself to stand.

"Hold off on the beer. Another beer in this heat, and I'll be asleep," said Roberto with a grin. "Save it for tonight. You better finish your tale, then we should look around the facilities."

"OK," said Tiko as he relaxed back into his chair. "As indicated, I began to talk with Dominic, given the move to set up the K-gang in Sydney. With the loss of Gaetano's sons Carlo and Guido from the Conti business, Dominic agreed to work with me, with my K-gang, to sell Columbian Heaven in Sydney for a slice of the action. However, given the recent seizure of a large consignment, I hear things are not going well with the Conti empire. I suspect that is why you secured the business here in Savusavu. Maybe to run the business yourselves?"

"Very astute, Mr Rokovou," stated Roberto, his eyes focussed on Tiko's. "We will do much business out of the Tradewinds Coffee packing sheds. I'll need to work on getting the pipeline of CH into Fiji back up and running. Do you mind if I use your VPN to speak with Mr Gonzales?"

"Certainly," replied Tiko. "Come with me. Get the call out of the way, and we'll tour the property and then head into town to get something to eat."

*

"You made it to Fiji," greeted Hernando as the call went through on the VPN. "What do you think of our man Tiko Rokovou."

"In a word, impressive," said Roberto with conviction. "He is getting ready to re-open the Conti facility and will be set up to get production humming once we re-establish supply lines of CH. With the packing line operating in Fiji, Tiko's people on the ground in Sydney, and us taking over the Contis warehouse and other properties in Sydney, we have the potential to build a very substantial business. Tiko is happy to work on taking a fair share of the profits."

"That does it," said Hernando. "You know what you have to do in Sydney."

"Yes, confirming that I'll take out Gaetano, Lorenzo and Dominic once they have signed over the various properties. That will surely bring Carlo out of hiding for the funeral and to see his Mother, and then I'll kill the fuckin' rat. The other concern is to see if I can find out who was the English woman who visited Gaetano. Who is Andrea Pinkston, and how did she know what is happening?"

"As an aside, I want nothin' to happen to Mrs Conti. She retains the family home, ok?" Hernando stated.

"No problem," assured Roberto. "Get back to you from Sydney when the job's done with Gaetano, Lorenzo and Dominic, and we have Tiko ready to get up and running."

"I'll also start work on getting some shipments of CH to Fiji," indicated Hernando.

Roberto terminated the call and returned to the verandah to join the waiting Tiko.

"Spoke to the big boss, and we are all set for my assignment in Sydney. I suggest you join me in Sydney to set up operations with you and the K-gang. You can follow on a few days behind me, so there is no link between us arriving on the same flight into Sydney."

"Excellent. Let's get this factory tour underway, then into town," said Tiko. "We may be able to find a bit of action at the Coconut Palms Nite Club. I understand the club was a bit of a favourite place of Guido Conti's."

*

Hernando stood up from his desk after finishing his call with Roberto on the VPN and opened the office door to find Pedro outside with a tray of coffee and biscuits.

"Sorry, sir. I was checking to see if you would like some coffee," said Pedro.

"No thanks," responded Hernando as he withdrew a pistol from his desk drawer and placed it on his desktop. "We need to talk, Pedro. Take a seat."

CHAPTER 15

Tiko pulled up in front of the Copra Shed building, home of the Savusavu Yacht Club. It sat atop the water in a secluded bay adjacent to the township. The club offered a pleasant watering hole for members and visitors to enjoy a Fiji Bitter, surrounded by craft from around the world and to watch the setting sun.

After signing in his guest as Enrico Sanchez, Tiko directed him to sit on a high-rise barstool under a shady beach umbrella that offered protection from the late afternoon sun.

"I'll get the beers," said Tiko.

As Tiko and Roberto clinked their stubbies of beer, a man approached with a broad smile. He was dressed in faded blue jeans with a dark-green bula shirt depicting tropical scenes of palm tree-lined beaches. Black trainers and rimless sunglasses pushed back onto his broad forehead, completing his attire.

"Hi Tiko, you are already taking advantage of your club membership and bringing in a guest. I'm Gary Tyler, Commodore of the club," he said, extending his hand towards Enrico.

"I should say, bula," replied Roberto.

"That sounds like a Latino accent to me," probed Gary. "Don't get too many Latinos in Savusavu. What brings you here?"

Before Roberto could reply, Tiko interjected.

"My friend Enrico is from South America, and we are considering importing more coffee beans as we can't get enough supply here in Fiji...." Tiko flinched and stopped talking mid-sentence. "Sorry, Gary, we've got business to discuss."

"OK, catch you later. Nice to meet you, Enrico," said Gary as he headed towards other visitors seated at another table.

"Tiko, you said too much. I didn't like the way he was asking questions. Sorry to have pinched you under the table," said Roberto. "I will probably have to change the way I enter Australia. One can't be too cautious in my line of work."

"Sorry, I wasn't thinking. I was trying to keep Gary happy," responded Tiko. "Finish off your beer, and I'll grab a couple of pizzas to take back home."

*

Back at Tradewinds Coffee and after eating his meat-lovers pizza, washed down with a glass of red wine, Roberto entered the study to access the VPN. After a few seconds, the call was answered by Dominic,

"Hi, Tiko."

"Dominic, it's Roberto Rodriguez. I'm calling you from Fiji."

"Hi Roberto," replied Dominic. "Have you got your flight details so I can arrange to pick you up at the airport?"

"That's why I've called," said Roberto. "I am using a false passport to enter Australia as Enrico Sanchez, so I don't want you at the airport just in case there are problems and they try to track my movements. I'll make my way to your business, the House of Pleasure, tomorrow evening your time."

"Are you sure?" Dominic asked.

"Yes, that's what I want to do," answered Roberto. "See you tomorrow night."

Roberto shut down the computer and joined Tiko on the front verandah for another beer.

"I spoke with Dominic in Sydney and didn't mention what we discussed. It is best that he doesn't know much about our plans and becomes suspicious. As a precaution, given your friend Gary Tyler's questioning, I've made alternative arrangements for my arrival in Sydney."

"Again, I'm so sorry. I wasn't thinking," said Tiko. "Gary is that friendly sort of guy, easy to talk to, and that's how life is in a small community."

"DS (Detective Sergeant) Chand, this is Gary Tyler from the Savusavu Yacht Club."

"Hi Gary, I remember you from all that business with the Conti Brothers. I bet you are happy Savusavu has quietened down again, and the drug trade is no longer operating out of Savusavu," replied DS Chand.

"That's the reason for my call," said Gary. He paused and took a breath before he continued. "The local gossip is that the guy who bought the Tradewinds Coffee business, Tiko Rokovou, has links with the drug trade. He has joined the yacht club, and last night he came into the yacht club with a man he introduced as Enrico. Enrico had this very heavy Latino accent, and there was something about him. He was solidly built, with very mean eyes and seemed sleazy. It's hard to explain, but I had this gut feeling as he appeared evasive and didn't want to make polite conversation. Tiko said he was a coffee supplier from South America."

"That's interesting. I wouldn't imagine Tiko Rokovou having too many South American contacts," stated DS Chand. "Thanks for the heads up. I'll look into it."

DS Chand terminated the call and immediately dialled the direct line of SS (Senior Sergeant) Viliame Naqima at Fiji Police Headquarters in Suva. "SS Naqima."

"Sir, it's DS Chand from Labasa Police."

"Ah, the media personality DS Chand of Labasa and Conti Brothers fame," joked SS Naqima. "What can I do for you today?"

"Some interesting information from Gary Tyler at the Savusavu Yacht Club has just come through, " DS Chand replied. "Ever since those American yachties were involved with the Conti Brothers, Gary has maintained vigilance on the comings and goings of people at the yacht club. He called me this morning and mentioned our friend Tiko Rokovou. We've been watching Tiko since he bought Tradewinds Coffee, and he was at the club last night. Gary said he was with a man who spoke with a heavy Latino accent and was visiting from South America. He went by the name Enrico, but Gary didn't get any family name before this Enrico seemed to shut down the conversation."

"That does sound strange. I can't imagine Mister Rokovou would know too many people from South America. I'll mention it to our friends in Sydney, just in case there is a link. I know they have been getting reports of increased activity of a Fijian gang in Sydney, reportedly linked to Rokovou."

"Did you get a description?" Viliame asked.

"Yes, Gary described him as well-presented, with close-cropped jet-black hair, olive complexion, muscular body and aged in the early thirties," replied DS Chand.

The chain of calls continued with SS Viliame Naqima now calling his colleague DCI (Detective Chief Inspector) Adam Charles of the Australian Federal Police. Viliame dialled the direct line number he had in his contact list. The phone rang, and he was about to hang up when an unfamiliar voice answered.

"DCI Charles' phone."

"Good morning, SS Naqima from the Fiji Police in Suva. May I speak with DCI Charles? It is important."

"I'm so sorry. DCI Charles is appearing in court today, giving evidence and will not be available until late this afternoon or early evening. I'll leave a message on his desk," replied the voice.

"Thank you for your help. He has my number," said Viliame.

*

Roberto knew from previous experience in the USA that his appearance, young age, and Columbian passport would likely ensure scrutiny by the Australian Border Force officials on his arrival at Sydney Airport.

As soon as he presented his passport to the female immigration officer, she was joined by an older male officer with tell-tale stripes on his epaulettes, indicating someone more senior in rank.

"Come this way, Mister Sanchez."

Roberto was directed towards a raised bench and indicated to place his suitcase on the raised, stainless steel inspection bench and open it. The officer began busily flicking through the pages of the passport.

"Do you speak English?"

"Yes sir," replied Roberto with an American lilt, maintaining rigid eye contact with the official. "I was educated in the USA."

"What brings you to Australia, sir?" the officer asked, raising his eyes from the passport.

"Business," was the quick, confident reply. "My company Bogota International Tours, arranges for ecotours through the Columbian and Peruvian parts of the Amazon jungle. I am here to meet with Mister Gaetano Conti of Willsmore International Travel to discuss potential package tour arrangements for his clients. Here is my meeting schedule and Mr Conti's contact details."

The officer examined the document.

"I'll be back with you shortly."

He went into a sparsely furnished office, two chairs, one on either side of a simple pinewood desk with a telephone, closing the door behind him. He closed the office's venetian blinds before sitting at the desk and punching the telephone number from Roberto's document.

"Willsmore International Travel, how may I help you?" answered Gaetano on the burner phone he had set up for this situation.

"Mr Conti, this is Officer Sam Rogers from Border Force at Sydney International Airport. Are you expecting any overseas visitors today?"

"Yes. We expect Mr Enrico Sanchez from Bogota International Tours in Columbia. He has an appointment to meet me at my Mount Willsmore office tomorrow morning. I checked, and his flight from Fiji was said to be on time. Is there a problem?"

"Thanks, Mr Conti, that's all I needed to know. There is no problem, just a formality," replied Officer Rogers. He disconnected the call and headed back into the arrivals hall.

"All appears in order Mr Sanchez. I spoke with Mr Conti, who confirmed your business connection. We'll check your luggage quickly, and you can be on your way."

The officer took swabs from the interior of Roberto's suitcase and carry-on bag, then disappeared into a room that appeared to be equipped with a range of drug detection equipment into which he placed the swabs.

Roberto stood calmly and began to slowly repack his luggage.

"All is in order, Mister Sanchez. Thank you for your patience and co-operation. Welcome to Australia," said Officer Rogers.

*

It was late afternoon when Adam Charles stormed back into his office and slumped into his chair.

"That bloody defence lawyer," he raged to Tanya, sitting at a desk outside his office door. "Thinks he is so clever. I thought he was auditioning for a TV show the way he strutted around like a peacock before the jury. I need a coffee."

"Sit there. I'll get one for you, black and two sugars," yelled Tanya through the door. "You'll need some sweetening up from the sound of things."

While Tanya was making his mug of coffee, Adam began to trawl through the usual pile of yellow Post-it messages that had accumulated on his desktop. His eyes riveted onto the message from Viliame Naqima as Tanya entered the office and carefully placed the mug of hot coffee on his desk.

"What's up?" Tanya asked, noticing a sense of urgency on Adam's face.

"There's a message from Viliame in Fiji. He wouldn't have called me unless it was important," Adam replied as he picked up his mobile and selected Viliame's number from his contact list.

"Adam, bula," came the response from Viliame. "I was just about to head home."

"Sorry, it's late. I forgot about the two-hour time difference. I have been tied up all day in the witness box with a smart-arse defence lawyer," sneered Adam. "What can I do for you?"

"It may be more of a case for what I can do for you," replied Viliame. "From Guido Conti's court case, you may remember DS Chand from Labasa Police."

"Certainly, he's an excellent detective," noted Adam. "He did a great job in tracking down and arresting Guido."

"Well, he received a call from Gary Tyler, the Commodore at the Savusavu Yacht Club. Gary reported that Tiko Rokovou brought a South American friend he introduced as Enrico to the yacht club," explained Viliame. "Gary went on to say that he had a feeling about the guy, whom he described as pretty sleazy. Enrico cut off Tiko when describing his actions in Fiji. "So Gary didn't get a family name?"

"With the intelligence, we received from our American friends, this Tiko definitely appears on their radar. Now with a South American involved, I would have to suspect our friends in the Gonzales cartel could well be involved in re-establishing what the Conti's were originally planning for Fiji and Australia," noted Adam. "I'll get our Border Force people to watch out for any South American named Enrico entering Australia. Thanks for the heads up."

"Glad to be of help. Keep me informed so we can move on Tiko once we have enough evidence," said Viliame. "We need to remove that scourge from both our countries. Catch you later."

"Tanya, what's the name of the senior guy at Sydney Airport Border Force?" Adam asked. "I'll call him and ask him to keep an eye out if our friend turns up in Sydney."

"Sam Rogers, he's a nice guy, always been very helpful," said Tanya. "I'll text you his number so you can add it to your contacts."

"Officer Rogers, this is DCI Adam Charles of the AFP. DS Layton gave me your name."

"Yes, Tanya Layton. She's a good operator. How can I help?" Sam Rogers asked.

"We received intel from sources in Fiji that we should keep an eye out for a man of South American origin with only a first name available of Enrico. He's described as well-presented, with close-cropped jet-black hair, olive complexion, muscular body and aged in the early thirties."

"Holy shit," came Sam's immediate response roaring down the phone line. "I saw him myself. He fitted the profile of being a high-risk entrant for carrying drugs. He had documentation about him being a travel agent to arrange tours with a company called Willsmore International Travel. I called the number and spoke with a Mister Gaetano Conti, who established the bona fides of Mister Enrico Sanchez."

"I need to see your CCTV footage urgently," requested Adam. "We need to note who picked him up at the airport and where he went. We want to have him under close surveillance."

"We'll do all we can to help," Sam said. "See you shortly. You know where to come."

CHAPTER 16

As soon as he exited the Sydney Airport Customs Hall, Roberto followed the signage to the taxi rank. He opened the rear door of the silver-coloured Mercedes sedan with 13CABS in black lettering emblazoned down the length of the vehicle and scrambled in with his luggage into the back seat, and closed the door.

"Hilton Hotel, thanks," stated Roberto, who retrieved his mobile phone from his jacket pocket and accessed his international roaming login.

Despite attempts by the driver to engage in polite conversation, Roberto continued to be occupied with the phone, with his fingers busily tapping at the screen. After around 30 minutes in the relatively light afternoon traffic, the driver pulled up in front of the Pitt Street Mall entrance to the hotel, where a staff member promptly opened the car door for Roberto.

"Can I help you with your luggage, sir?"

"No thanks. I'm OK," said Roberto as he waited for the driver to process the credit card payment on his hand-held terminal.

"Reception is immediately on your left after you enter, sir."

Roberto strode into the building and, without looking towards the reception desk, walked past the concierge, who was coming towards him with his hands extended to assist with Roberto's luggage. The surprised concierge watched as Roberto headed directly towards the escalators that took him down a level to the hotel's George Street exit. He placed his suitcase on the footpath and hailed a passing yellow-coloured taxi.

"House of Pleasure Kings Cross," directed Roberto, bringing an immediate smile to the driver's face.

*

"Fortunately, we have good timelines on Sanchez's arrival," said Officer Sam Rogers as he started to scroll through the CCTV footage of the Customs area.

"Look, there he is, talking with me while I'm inspecting his documentation. After I made the call to Mister Conti, he was cleared, and you can see him make his way to the taxi stand. He got into a 13CABS, vehicle registration – XAA 001."

Adam called the administration office of 13CABS. While initially hesitant in providing driver and customer information, the company soon obliged with the polite threats made by DCI Charles and the words Australian Federal Police. The company indicated that the driver, Mohammed Rafiq, was in the process of dropping off a fare and would call back as soon as he completed the transaction.

Adam sat in Sam Rogers' office, fingers thrumming on the desk, causing Sam to look at his visitor. Adam stopped, stood and began to pace when his mobile rang,

"DCI Charles," he quickly answered.

"Sir, this is Mohamed Rafiq, the taxi driver you wish to speak to. Have I done something wrong?" Mohammed asked. "My student visa permits me to work."

"No. You are fine. I want to ask you about a passenger you picked up at the airport late this afternoon," explained Adam. "It's important that we locate him. His name was Enrico Sanchez."

"I remember the name from his credit card. He was not very friendly and was totally occupied with his mobile for the entire journey," said Mohammed. "I dropped him at the Pitt Street Mall entrance of the Sydney Hilton Hotel."

"Thank you very much, Mohammed. You have been most helpful. Sorry to have disturbed you."

"A pleasure, sir," said Mohammed with relief evident in his voice.

Adam immediately called the hotel, "Hilton Hotel, reception. How can I help you?"

"This is DCI Charles of the Australian Federal Police, Security, please. The matter is urgent."

Adam spoke to the head of security and indicated he would be on his way to the hotel and wished to view CCTV footage for the reception area for the period, mid to late afternoon. He also asked to check for any registration under Enrico Sanchez, travelling under a Columbian passport.

*

On viewing Adam's police ID, the concierge directed him to the security office on the first floor.

"DCI Charles," Sean Hewettson, head of security, greeted Adam as he stepped out of the elevator. "Follow me to the control room, and you can check the CCTV footage. I have the period you requested primed on one of the monitors."

"Thanks, Sean. Much appreciated."

After some instruction from Sean, Adam sat at the desk and began to scroll through the footage.

"Got him," came the cry from Adam as he eagerly sat forward in his seat. "Can you zoom in for me, please, Sean?"

"There you go," said Sean as he leaned forward and manipulated the zoom control on the computer's screen.

"Shit," exclaimed Adam. "I see him. Look, he's ignored the concierge and walked past the reception desk towards the downward escalator leading to the rear exit."

Sean switched cameras, and they followed their man to the point of his exit via the revolving door leading into George Street.

"The clever bastard," said Adam as his clenched fist pounded on the desk.

"He must be a pro. He's figured we may be on to him and has taken precautions to remain undetected. Can you switch to a street camera?" Adam asked.

"Sorry, privacy crap and all that. The council wouldn't allow us to mount a street camera above the George Street entrance," explained Sean.

"Thanks for your help Sean," said a disconsolate Adam as he stood and returned to his car.

On reaching his car parked at the hotel entrance, Adam called DS Layton.

"Tanya, get the team together. We need to get some plans together around tracking this Mister Enrico Sanchez, especially given his use of Gaetano Conti as a referee to get into the country. We need to know what he and the Contis are getting up to. It can't be good news."

*

On his return to HQ, Adam went straight to the main meeting room where Tanya had assembled the two key operatives in the drug detection unit – James Aidney and Rod Gregson.

"I know you're all busy, so thanks for meeting at short notice," said Adam. "I want to update you on recent developments associated with our friends, the Contis. Sources have informed us that Tiko Rokovou has acquired the Tradewinds Coffee business in Fiji. Tiko began his career in the drug trade as a small-time operator in New Zealand. He was caught selling weed, arrested and deported back to Fiji. He has come onto our radar with the emergence of a group called the K-gang. The K-gang's presence coincided with the Contis empire's decline."

"Further intel from our American and Fijian friends indicates that the Gonzales cartel has contacted the K-gang in Fiji. They see the K-gang has the potential to re-ignite what the Contis were trying to set up in Fiji," said Adam as he began to annotate key points on the whiteboard with a black marker pen.

"To that end, a suspected Gonzales' cartel member, likely travelling under a false identity as Enrico Sanchez, arrived at Sydney Airport this afternoon. We tracked him to the Hilton Hotel, where he, unfortunately, disappeared out the rear entrance of the hotel, where we lost him with the lack of CCTV coverage."

"It sounds as though he anticipated some surveillance, so he must be a professional operative in the way he knew the layout of the hotel," added James. "He knew what he was doing and was well prepared."

"That's for sure," agreed Adam. "The other interesting snippet of info is that he used our friend Gaetano Conti as a referee to enter Australia. Gaetano used the guise of being the head of a company called Willsmore International Travel. It is a registered company but doesn't appear to trade to any great extent. It will be a miracle if they have booked a single airfare."

"What's the plan from here, boss?" Tanya asked.

"Tanya, I want you and Rod to maintain surveillance outside the Conti's place in Mount Willsmore in case our friend Enrico turns up there to meet with Gaetano. I will circulate photos we got of him from Border Force at the airport," detailed Adam. "James, I want you and your team to see what you can pick up on CCTV locations around the city. Let's see if you can track this Sanchez down. Also, we must watch for Tiko Rokovou in case he enters Australia. So, Tanya, you'll need to maintain a close liaison with your friend Senior Officer Sam Rogers, in Border Force. I know it's getting late, but let's get on with it," said Adam, clapping his hands together.

"I'll need to go home and pick up some gear for the stakeout tonight," said Tanya. "Back within the hour, and I'll hit the road with Rod."

*

Penny left the Uber in front of Tanya's apartment block and checked up and down the street.

Good, no sign of her red Mini Clubman sedan.

Late afternoon there appeared to be little activity emanating from the other apartments. With a final check of her black leather shoulder bag, Penny made her way to Tanya's top-floor landing.

As a precaution, Penny pressed the illuminated doorbell and waited. Penny opened the screen door without hearing any response and extracted a set of lock picks from her bag. Given the basic nature of the door's lock, Penny was inside the apartment quickly. She surveyed the bathroom and bedroom before placing her bag on the kitchen bench and extracting the listening devices she planned to put in place.

The minute size of the devices would make them difficult to see. One was placed inside the cover of the sub-woofer sitting underneath the wall-mounted TV. Next, Penny grabbed a stool from the kitchen bench and, kneeling on the stool, placed a second device within the centrally located light fitting. A final device was planned for Tanya's bedroom when Penny suddenly stopped.

That was a car door and shit. I can hear Tanya's voice. Penny moved over to the partially opened sliding door leading onto the balcony. *She's on her way to the stairs. Think.*

"I'll make us some sandwiches and a Thermos® of coffee, Rod," called out Tanya as she headed to the stairwell. "I'll be ten minutes."

Penny placed the stool back into position and quickly looked around to see if she had left anything out of place. She removed one of her golden hooped earrings and placed it between cushions on the two-seater couch before exiting the apartment and locking the door behind her.

Hearing Tanya climbing the final stairs to the top level, Penny pushed the doorbell and looked expectantly at the front door. She turned in response to a greeting from Tanya.

"Penny, what are you doing here? Thought you'd be long gone headed back home by now."

"Yes, flying out tomorrow morning," responded Penny. "I was taking a chance you might be home this afternoon as I have lost an earring. The earrings were given to me by my Mother for my 21st birthday and had some sentimental value. Do you mind if I take a look inside? I may have lost the earring while sitting on the couch."

"Sure, no problem. Come and take a look while I get a few things together," invited Tanya as she opened the front door. "I've got a colleague down below, and we are on a stakeout tonight, so I was getting some gear together, along with something to eat."

Penny made a pretext of looking under the couches before removing the cushions on the sofa.

"Here it is. I am lucky. Mother would never have forgiven me if I had lost the earring," she beamed, holding the trophy aloft.

"That's great. I bet you're relieved," said Tanya. "Can I give you a ride back into the city? It'll be no trouble."

"No, I am fine. I have already booked an Uber," said Penny. "Sorry to have bothered you. I will get going and leave you in peace. It certainly has been great meeting you."

"Likewise, Penny and all the best to your Mum," said Tanya as she began removing bread, butter, mayonnaise and filling from the refrigerator.

Penny closed the door behind her and rapidly entered the street as an Uber pulled up.

That was too close for comfort.

*

Roberto paid the driver and stood in the street looking up a flight of concrete stairs to the rather unassuming entrance to a place with such an exotic name. *It doesn't look like any House of Pleasure from what I can see from here in the street.* Roberto pressed the glowing buzzer on the wall beside the chrome-plated door handle.

A voice crackled out of the intercom, "Yes, how can I help you?"

"Mister Sanchez to see Mister Rossi."

The door buzzed, followed by an audible click, and Roberto entered the foyer and closed the door behind him. As Roberto's eyes adjusted to the dim, red-lit corridor, he noted a long narrow passageway with a series of numbered doors leading off to the left and right.

A door on his immediate right labelled OFFICE opened, and a woman stepped out.

"Hi, Mister Sanchez. I'm Gypsy, the manageress. Take a seat on the couch, and I'll call Dominic. He's been expecting you. He's out back in the storeroom."

Gypsy walked to her desk behind which were a series of security monitors. The screens constantly switched between various cameras located in and around the building.

"Dominic, your visitor has arrived," Gypsy announced on the intercom.

"Hi, Enrico," greeted Dominic a few moments later as he entered the office. "Please excuse us, Gypsy. I need to speak with our guest."

Dominic waited for Gypsy to leave before he closed the office door. "Everything ok at the airport?"

"No problem. Once Immigration called your uncle, I went through the clearance process very quickly," replied Roberto. "But to more important matters, we need to meet with Gaetano and Lorenzo as soon as possible. Mr Gonzales wants to clear up the large debt and has demanded that this business, The House of Pleasure and Lorenzo's warehouse be signed over to him to clear the debt as you suggested."

"While I proposed the idea, I can't see they'd readily agree to the deal, despite the debt," answered Dominic. "The properties have been in the family for your years."

"Hernando sees your support as important in this matter, especially with your potential to take over the operation in Australia. He appreciated your help in letting him know about the raid that caused the loss of the last consignment," explained Roberto.

"What we need you to do now is get the deeds of sale drawn up tomorrow with your lawyers and arrange for us to meet with Gaetano and Lorenzo in the evening to complete the signing of the documents. You need to stress that Senor Gonzales has intimated that there will be severe consequences if they don't comply with the opportunity to clear the debt. I can assure them that the business they established will continue to operate as long as the rent is paid on time. Apart from paying rent, it should be business as usual as far as they are concerned. We can inform them about your situation once the paperwork has been completed."

"Wow, that's going to be a busy day tomorrow. I will get onto Gaetano and Lorenzo tonight," said Dominic. "Now, we better get you organised. You can have room 14, the last door on the left. As a treat, I have arranged for our best hostess, the lovely Electra, to keep you company tonight."

With a wide grin, Roberto picked up his suitcase and laptop bag and followed Dominic down the corridor. Dominic stopped in front of Door 14 and gently knocked before entering.

"Ah, Electra. This is a very good and important friend Enrico. I would like you to look after him this evening."

Wish it was me. All in good time, Electra.

"My pleasure", said Electra licking her lips, fluttering her eyes and thrusting her ample breasts forward.

Electra stood at the foot of a queen-sized bed adorned with a red satin bedspread and a wall of pink-coloured cushions at the head of the bed. Dim, pink-shaded lamps sat atop the bedside cabinets and provided the only lighting in the room. Roberto examined Electra from head to toe, and the smile on his face indicated he liked what he saw in the petite woman. She stood in what appeared to be diamond-encrusted towering stilettos with sheer stockings clipped onto a pink bodice.

Roberto placed his suitcase and laptop bag at the foot of the bed and pulled Electra towards him.

"Electra will do just fine," Roberto said as he turned to Dominic. "See you in the morning, and get on to Gaetano and Lorenzo. I want no delays."

Dominic left the room and closed the door behind him. He paused outside the door and heard Electra exclaim.

"Oooh, Mister Enrico, you are a very naughty boy. We are going to have some fun tonight."

*

Dominic returned to the office. He sat at the desk and reflected on what he had just heard from Roberto.

Take over the running of the organisation. Fantastic. I can show those old fools what I can do to build this business and return it to its former glory. Their days are over, and they can retire to a life of playing bocce at the Italian Club.

They won't like the business about signing over the properties to Gonzales but too fuckin' bad. What choice do they have? They owe Hernando Gonzales a fortune. Signing them over is a good deal and better than the likely alternative of a body bag at the morgue.

Before heading home for the evening, Dominic sent text messages to Lorenzo and Gaetano – 'I met with Roberto Rodriguez, Hernando's man. I must speak with you both first thing in the morning. Please arrange a teleconference for 8 am for me to update you.'

CHAPTER 17

"Thanks for getting together for this important call," began Dominic. "As mentioned in my text message, I met with Hernando's key man Roberto Rodriguez last night. He brought with him some serious news of demands from Hernando to settle our debt."

"What's this fuckin' serious news and demands," stammered Gaetano. "I told him I'd get his fuckin' money from the family in Sicily."

"Well," Dominic paused before continuing. "In return for forgiveness of the five million debt owed to Hernando by us, he wants the family business properties signed over to him."

"Bullshit, we've worked all our lives for those buildings," yelled Lorenzo. "Who does he think he is, making demands on the Conti and Rossi families? Think of all the money we've made for him over the years. The ungrateful bastard."

"That's well and good, Papa, but I fear the consequences of not signing will be severe, the way Roberto put it," said Dominic trying to retain a calm voice. "It is a good deal for such a huge debt that will otherwise prove difficult to repay. On the positive side, Roberto stated we could continue to operate out of the properties by paying rent, so not a complete loss. It will enable us to rebuild without the burden of a huge debt. With the profits, we can soon buy other properties."

There was a long silence before Gaetano uttered.

"You're right. We don't have much fuckin' choice with that ruthless bastard

Hernando. Five million bucks of debt forgiven for a couple of old buildings, and we can rent the buildings you say to keep the business running, and we get to keep our homes?"

"Yes, there was no mention of the family homes," confirmed Dominic. "I can get the deeds of sale drawn up by our lawyer Alberto Russo this morning, and I'll bring Roberto to the warehouse tonight to sign the documents. How about I get there with our visitor around nine?"

"OK, thanks for organising everything, Dominic. But we still need to be cautious with this, Roberto. Hernando is ruthless, and we should be prepared for the unexpected with him," said Gaetano. "I suggest you come armed and prepared if there's any funny business."

"Roberto appears to be nice and relaxed after we extended to him the company of Electra last night, so he should be in a good mood," responded Dominic. "However, I'll be prepared just in case the situation gets out of hand."

"Electra, you say. The lucky bastard," chuckled Gaetano. "If I was only ten years younger."

After finishing the call with Gaetano and Lorenzo, Dominic called Alberto Russo and explained what was required and that he would pick up the paperwork late afternoon.

"Gaetano agreed to the transfer?" Alberto asked, expressing doubt about the instruction. "I'll give him a call to verify, ok."

"No problem Mister Russo," replied Dominic. "My Uncle will confirm everything, and I'll drop into your office at four to collect the documentation for signing."

Next on Dominic's list was Roberto. He left the HOP's office, reached room 14 and gently tapped.

"Enrico, are you ok?" Dominic asked, using Roberto's cover name in case Electra was still in the room.

"Couldn't be better. That Electra is fuckin' amazing. I think I'm in love. I'll take her back to Columbia with me," Roberto said as he opened the door. "I'm starvin'. Let's get some breakfast. I need a coffee."

Dominic peered over Roberto's shoulder, noting Electra had gone.

How I wished I was with her and not you, one day when I'm runnin' the show.

"Come on, let's get something to eat and a strong coffee. There's a café just around the corner."

*

"There's a car parked up the street," said Mama Conti. "A man and a woman have been parked there all afternoon."

"Must be the bloody cops keepin' an eye on us since that raid on the Kings Cross warehouse and that Andrea woman who called us. Told you she was a cop," noted Gaetano. "I'm heading out with Lorenzo to the Mount Willsmore warehouse tonight. I'll go into the basement, use the concealed door, and head out into the laneway. I'll meet Lorenzo down the road and keep well away from the prying eyes of those dumb cops."

Gaetano headed out the front door and down the front stairs. He used the pretext of checking the mailbox to look up and down the street, noticing the white sedan sitting about 100 metres down the street. The light from the street lighting revealed two heads in the front seat of the darkened vehicle.

"Those idiots get paid for that," Gaetano muttered as he returned inside and called Lorenzo. "Lorenzo, I've got a couple of cops sitting in the street, so I'll head out via the laneway and meet you around the corner, well away from those prying eyes. See you in 15."

*

"Gaetano is heading out to the letterbox," observed Tanya. "I guess he won't be going anywhere tonight. Let's call it a day. You can return to duty at seven tomorrow morning, and I'll relieve you early afternoon. No need to continue to tie the both of us up with so little happening."

"Sounds like a plan," said Rod. He needed no inducement to turn the ignition key and head homeward.

*

Lorenzo and Gaetano sat quietly in their car in the side street and watched as the two occupants of the white sedan completed a three-point turn and exited the cul-de-sac leading to the Conti's home. With the police observation vehicle gone, Lorenzo fired up his car and headed off to the family warehouse located on the Mount Willsmore industrial estate, a ten-minute drive away.

There was little activity this time of night in the darkened industrial estate. Lorenzo pulled up in front of the warehouse's roller door and pressed the remote he retrieved from the central console. With a screech, the heavy steel door began the slow climb to the top of its track. Lorenzo drove inside and left the warehouse door open for the arrival of Dominic and their VIP guest from South America.

They made their way to the office at the rear of the building, guided by a security light and turned on the lights. They placed four office chairs around the central wooden table, ready for the signing of the documentation. With the chairs in place, Gaetano entered the adjacent kitchenette and brought back two cans of beer. They made themselves comfortable and waited.

"I wonder what this Roberto's like?" Gaetano pondered.

"If he's Hernando's man, he'll be a tough bastard," noted Lorenzo. "I bet he's killed a few people in his day."

As they were taking the last swig from their stubbies of beer, vehicle headlights were seen approaching the warehouse. Gaetano and Lorenzo drained their beers, stood and made their way to the entrance, ready to greet the overseas visitor. Dominic drove into the building and waved to Gaetano and Lorenzo.

"Roberto, my Uncle Gaetano and my Papa Lorenzo," introduced Dominic.

"Come into the office. I'll grab us some beers," said Gaetano as he headed to the refrigerator. "Close the door, Lorenzo."

The men sat around the table as the door began its screeching, metal-on-metal journey. Dominic opened his briefcase and extracted several documents that he had spread out on the table.

"These are the title deeds for the Mount Willsmore warehouse and the House of Pleasure properties," stated Dominic. "Mister Russo personally prepared the documents, so everything should be in order and ready for signing."

"Can you excuse me for a minute?" Roberto asked. "I'm busting for a piss. Should have had one before we left the HOP."

"No problem, it will give me time to quickly look at the documents", replied Gaetano. "You'll see the light switch is on the wall as you open the door."

Inside the privacy of the toilet, Roberto knelt and lifted the right leg of his jeans. He removed his handgun and checked the weapon turning off the safety. The left leg was home to a razor-sharp stiletto blade which he also removed and admired the glint of light reflected from the stainless-steel blade. With the weapons provided by Dominic back in place, Roberto made a final check that the pistol's silencer was in place in the right hip pocket of the sports jacket and turned out the light as he returned to the office.

Roberto re-entered the office as Dominic continued his explanation of the documentation.

"You'll note that for tax purposes, Alberto has put values in the sale deeds well below the debt owed to Hernando Gonzales. The aim is to minimise the capital gains tax you must pay. You both need to sign at the bottom of the page above where your names are printed, and I will witness your signatures," explained Dominic.

With the signing in progress, Roberto asked, "I hear you had a visit from a mysterious English woman warning you about a possible hit on you from Hernando. Tell me more. Hernando is most curious to learn more about this mysterious woman."

"Nothin' to it, really," replied Gaetano. "I told her to fuck off. I wasn't interested. Haven't heard from the bitch since."

Gaetano reached into his trouser back pocket and removed his wallet, extracting a piece of paper and placing it on the table.

"She gave me this number and said to call her anytime. Her name was Andrea Pinkston, and as you said, she claimed I was in danger from my good friend Hernando."

With the documents signed, everyone smiled until Roberto got to his feet, extracted a pistol and placed the weapon on the tabletop. With concerned looks towards each other, Gaetano and Lorenzo pushed back their chairs and started to stand.

"Sit down," said Roberto in a firm voice as he picked up the pistol and waved the gun at Gaetano and Lorenzo. "Thank you for signing, gentlemen, for which Hernando thanks you very much. Now there is another point of business of great importance to Senor Hernando. He wants you to tell me where that scumbag Carlo is hiding."

"He's in the witness protection program," stammered Gaetano. "We've no idea where the cops have stashed the snitch. He could be living overseas for all we know."

"You'd have us believe that he doesn't contact you from time to time to speak to his precious Mama," sneered Roberto as he threatened Gaetano by waving his pistol in his face. "Things will not go well for you if you don't tell me what I need to know."

"I told you, Dominic, that we couldn't trust Hernando, so you know what to do," said Gaetano as he looked towards Dominic. Dominic remained motionless in his seat. "Dominic," repeated Gaetano with concern on his face. "What the fuck? Do something."

Gaetano and Lorenzo relaxed as Dominic stood and placed his hand inside the open briefcase on the table. "Sorry," Dominic said as he looked away from Gaetano, extracted a packet of black cable ties from inside his bag and tossed the pack towards Roberto.

"You fuckin' dog Dominic. You're betraying your own family? You Judas," yelled Gaetano.

"Shut the fuck up," ordered Roberto as he smashed the butt of his pistol into the side of Gaetano's head. "I'll ask one more time. Where is Carlo hiding out?"

Gaetano began to weep, "I've told you the cops have stashed him away. I've wanted nothin' to do with him since he ratted on his brother."

With his gun pointed at Gaetano, Roberto indicated for Dominic to open the pack of cable ties. "Tie the bastards down," he ordered Dominic.

Dominic hesitated, but a nudge from Roberto's hand holding the gun got him moving. The cable ties restrained Lorenzo's and Gaetano's arms to the arms of the wooden chairs and their legs to the legs of the chair. Unable to make eye contact with Gaetano or Lorenzo, he stepped back from the table.

Roberto began to walk slowly around the table, a smug look on his face. He began to hum quietly, then suddenly swivelled with the pistol barrel held in his right hand, driving the pistol butt into Lorenzo's fingers strapped to the arm of his chair. Lorenzo shrieked in pain. Roberto continued to pound away, turning Lorenzo's fingers into a bloody, pulpy mass.

"You're next, Gaetano," threatened Roberto as Lorenzo slumped unconscious into the back of his chair. "Tell me what I want to know. We don't need to make this hard for you."

"What, and then you'll kill us anyway," shouted Gaetano. "I can't fuckin' tell you what I don't know. He's in the fuckin' witness protection program."

"This is your final warning Gaetano," said Roberto as he pressed the pistol's barrel firmly into Gaetano's nose, causing blood to trickle from Gaetano's right nostril.

With no response from Gaetano, Roberto roared, "I've had enough of this shit." He reached inside his jacket pocket and extracted the silencer he expertly twisted into position onto the weapon's barrel.

Without warning, his silenced pistol spat out two shots. Red marks appeared on Gaetano's and Lorenzo's foreheads, and brain matter splatted onto the office wall. Tears trickled down Dominic's cheeks as he rushed to the bathroom.

The sound of Dominic vomiting brought a laugh from Roberto, followed by, "you're weak as piss Dominic. Come on. We have to clean up the scene. No fingerprints, and wipe everything down with disinfectant to remove any DNA remnants."

"Why did you have to kill them? They told you the cops hid away Carlo," said Dominic as he wiped away some drips that had started forming on the nose's tip.

"They were going to get it anyway," said Roberto as he paused and added, "and then there was one. One more Conti to go," said Roberto as he replaced the pistol inside his ankle holster and picked up the piece of paper. He dialled the number and waited for an answer.

"Andrea Pinkston," came a cautious answer to the call. "How can I help you?"

"Ah, our English friend," said Roberto. "This is to inform you that your *sapo (snitch)* is no longer with us, compliments of the *Padrino* (Godfather)."

Roberto abruptly terminated the call and tossed the paper onto Gaetano's lifeless body.

"Hey, Dominic, what's the major TV news channel here in Sydney."

"Channel 12 is very popular," replied a sombre Dominic as he reached automatically for a wad of tissues in his jeans pocket and began to dab at the tears forming in his eyes.

I didn't expect this. I just wanted to take over the business. I have to be careful. Otherwise, I'll be his next victim.

Next, Roberto checked the newsroom for Channel 12 on Google and called the number on his mobile.

"I'd like to report a shooting at a warehouse in the Mount Willsmore Industrial Estate. Building 6. I can see a bright light shining from the open doorway, and I can see what I think are at least two bodies in the office of the building."

"Sir, can I have your name…."

"Come on, Dominic, let's return to the HOP and step on it. I like a good fuck after killing someone. Electra better get ready for a long night; this bull has a raging hard-on and is ready to fuck her brains out."

CHAPTER 18

Penny stood frozen, looking at her mobile phone screen.

That was a Latino accent, and he used the words sapo and padrino, typically used in Columbia. Gonzales's man must have taken out Gaetano. I better get onto Sandra and prepare for the likelihood of Carlo Conti coming out of hiding. He'll want to be with his Mother, irrespective of the witness protection regulations.

"Sandra, Penny here. Bad news. Our Columbian friend called me from the crime scene to gloat that he had taken out Gaetano Conti. I'm not sure about Lorenzo or Dominic, but as we discussed, Gonzales is undoubtedly working to bring Carlo out of hiding to ensure the hitman takes him out."

"That's terrible news and comes straight after you warned him. I'll come by your hotel and pick you up in 30 minutes, and we'll head into the office to discuss plans," said Sandra.

"Thanks, Sandra. I'll activate the devices I placed at Tanya's apartment just in case our man Carlo turns up there," Penny said.

*

This is Vanessa Jeffries from Channel 12 News. I am reporting from outside Building 6 in the Mount Willsmore Industrial Estate. We have just had a report of a shooting in the building and, on arrival, found that no police are in attendance. There appears to be no movement from inside, and we have advised the police of the situation. They have confirmed that they are on their way to the scene. Wait, I can hear the police sirens and red and blue lights flashing as I see one, two, no three police vehicles roar into the estate.

*

"What happened, Tanya? You and Rod were outside his bloody house tonight," said an exasperated Adam as he stood outside the police incident tape and started to dress into the protective crime scene attire.

"How did Gaetano give you the slip?"

"I'm so sorry," replied Tanya. "He looked as if he was retiring for the night, and we decided to call it a night and planned to be back in position first thing in the morning."

"I'll check out the situation with the crime scene team, then we better head off to speak with Mrs Conti and deliver her the bad news," said Adam as he ducked underneath the blue and white chequered tape. "You better make your way here asap."

There was a hive of activity outside the entrance to the warehouse, where a spotlight had been set up adjacent to a Crime Scene Investigation Unit trailer. Police scientific officers clad head to foot in white coveralls were engaged in various evidence-gathering activities - taking photographs, swabbing for DNA, checking for fingerprints, and ascertaining the trajectory of bullets. One of the officers signalled for Adam to come over to the office table in the centre of the room.

"What have you got, Peter?" Adam asked.

"Two aged males with single gunshots to the forehead. It would appear the place has been wiped down as no fingerprints are evident, and it smells of bleach. It appears to be most likely a planned hit as there is no evidence of a struggle," detailed Peter. "As you can see, the victims were tied into their chairs using cable ties. On the floor next to one of the bodies, we found this piece of paper with a name and a mobile phone number."

"Thanks, Peter. Tell me if you come up with anything else of interest," Adam said. He took a photo of the paper on his mobile before placing it in an evidence bag and then headed back to the waiting Tanya at the entrance to the warehouse.

"Find anything useful?" Tanya asked.

"On the floor next to Gaetano's body was this piece of paper with the name Andrea Pinkston. Does the name ring a bell?" Adam queried.

"Nothing that comes to mind," replied Tanya. "I'll get someone to track down that number. In the meantime, I suppose we better go and check on Mrs Conti and break the news to her. Hopefully, nothing has happened to her."

As the detectives headed towards their vehicle, they were illuminated by the bright, blinding light emanating from the top of a mobile TV camera.

"Vanessa Jeffries, Channel 12 news. We were the ones who called in the hit. Can you give us an update? Can you confirm if the bodies were members of the Conti family?"

"Sorry, Vanessa, we cannot provide any details at this time," said Adam as he focused on the camera lens. "We will need to formally identify the bodies and advise family members before confirming any details of the deceased with you."

Undeterred, Vanessa tried again to extract information from DCI Charles.

"Well, I have some information about the person who called us with the tip on the hit. It may be helpful to your investigation. How about you give me an exclusive interview when you can?"

Adam paused before replying, "I think something can be arranged, Vanessa. What have you got for us?"

"The person who called in the crime spoke with a heavy Latino accent. He sounded almost gleeful about what had occurred, almost as if he enjoyed what had happened."

"Thanks, Vanessa. We'll arrange a press conference in our headquarters meeting room in the morning. I'm sure someone forgot to notify the other networks of the time of the conference," responded Adam with a smile.

Adam brushed off attempts by the reporter to ask any further questions and rapidly made his way to his vehicle along with Tanya. "From Vanessa's info, we are looking for Gonzales's hitman. We better transmit a nationwide release to all police jurisdictions and Border Force to be on the lookout for our man who calls himself Enrico Sanchez."

Adam and Tanya pulled up in front of Conti's house and noticed a dull light coming from the front room. They momentarily gathered their thoughts before Adam nodded to Tanya, and they made their way up the front steps and pressed the doorbell, hands poised above their gun holsters. After a slight delay, the light for the front verandah came on, and a tentative, soft Italian accented voice came through the door.

"Who is it?"

"Mrs Conti, it's DCI Charles and DS Layton from the Australian Federal Police," replied Adam as he spoke into the intercom and held his ID up towards the camera above the door.

The door was slowly opened, just wide enough for Mrs Conti to view Adam's police ID that he held up to the locked screen door.

"Can we come in?" Adam asked. "We need to speak with you urgently. It's about your husband and your brother Lorenzo."

Mrs Conti reached to unlock the screen door, then stepped aside as she fully opened the front door, indicating for the detectives to head into the lounge room. She picked up the TV remote, turned off the device, and invited the detectives to sit on the sofa.

"What is so important? Why do you need to come to my home at this late hour? Do you want to speak with my husband? If so, he is not at home."

Adam paused and then coughed before drawing a breath and then continued,

"Mrs Conti, I have terrible news. This evening we attended a crime scene at a warehouse in the Mount Willsmore industrial estate where we found what we believe are the bodies of your husband and brother Lorenzo."

Mrs Conti drew her hands to her face and began sobbing, rocking backwards and forwards in her chair.

Before Adam could continue, Tanya moved over to Mrs Conti's chair and squatted beside her as tears began streaming down her face. She placed a hand on Mrs Conti's arm.

"Can I get you some water, Mrs Conti?"

"My Gaetano. My Lorenzo."

"I don't think we can speak with her tonight, Adam. She's too upset. I'll see if she has a local parish priest or family member we can contact," said Tanya.

"Mrs Conti, do you have a parish priest or family member we can call?"

Mrs Conti looked up, wiped away her tears, and deeply breathed. "Please call Father Alessandro. He is the parish priest. His number is next to the telephone in the kitchen."

Adam stood and headed to the kitchen to get the number while Tanya continued to console Mrs Conti. Adam dialled the number.

"Father Alessandro, this is Adam Charles from the Australian Federal Police. We are at the Conti residence in Mount Willsmore."

"What's happened? Are the Contis OK?" Father Alessandro asked.

"I'm sorry to inform you that her husband and brother have been shot and killed, and Mrs Conti has asked for you," Adam explained.

"I'm on my way. I'll be there in five minutes."

"Mrs Conti, Father Alessandro is on his way. I need to return to the office, and Detective Layton will stay with you until Father arrives. I'll be back in the morning as we must speak with you to see if you can help us with any information that may help us identify the killer."

*

Roberto leapt out of Dominic's car as soon as he parked underneath the House of Pleasure. He appeared to be in an aggressive mood as he bounded up the stairs leading to the rear entrance and purposedly strode to the HOP office.

"Gypsy, I need to make a call, so find yourself something else to do to keep busy. Then I want to see Electra," Roberto said loudly. "In room 14 as soon as I've finished my call."

"Your command is my wish," Gypsy replied with a sneer as she got up from behind her desk and started to leave the office just as Dominic arrived. Gypsy took Dominic by the arm and led him back into the corridor.

"He wants me to get Electra for him. She's one of our biggest money earners, and he's in an aggressive mood. I'm concerned about what he may do to her and how he carries on."

"Do what he says. Keep him happy," snapped Dominic and entered the office, closing the door behind him. "Take a seat, Roberto. I'll set up the VPN for you to call Hernando."

"When we're finished, I'm going to fuck Electra's brains out. I love a good screw after taking someone out. All that blood has given me a raging hard-on," said Roberto, unable to keep still, his legs shaking and body rocking. "Did you see the brain splatter on the wall? A beautiful sight to behold."

"Here you go," said Dominic, moving the computer mouse towards Roberto. "Just click on the HG icon."

That's my dad he's talking about. He's shown no emotion about the murders. I'll need to be careful.

Roberto asked Dominic to leave the office and clicked on the indicated icon. After a short delay, a cheery voice answered the call.

"I hope all went to plan?"

Yes, Hernando, those *sapos* Gaetano and Lorenzo are dead," said Roberto. "They didn't expect a fuckin' thing, and everything is signed over to us. You can now work on getting CH to Tiko in Fiji to pack and for his boys in Sydney to start selling the shit."

"Good work. What about Dominic?" Hernando asked. "The weak bastard chucked his guts up when I put the bullet through Gaetano and Lorenzo's heads."

"I suggest we keep him around a little bit longer. We will need him to watch over his aunt, Mrs Conti, just in case Carlo shows up to see his mother once the news about the hit gets out. I ensured the local TV news station got the scoop on the hit. Carlo will no doubt soon learn about what happened to his Papa, and I'll need to be ready to take him out," detailed Roberto.

"Agreed, let's keep Dominic on the scene until you get set up with Tiko and the K-gang," said Hernando.

"Tiko is coming to Sydney in the next couple of days, and once we have everything in place, Dominic can join his family members in the cop's body bags," added Roberto

"I also need to track down Detective Layton, whom Carlo had a hard-on for. Given the death of his Papa, he may seek her out, and we can use that to our advantage."

With the call terminated, Roberto opened the door and called for Dominic.

"Tell that old woman Gypsy to get me, Electra, now," Roberto ordered and strode to room 14. He sat on the bed and began to undress immediately.

"Please look after Electra," pleaded Dominic. She is one of our most popular assets."

"Get her here and quick. I've got a raging hard-on," snapped Roberto.

Dominic waited outside the room for Electra to arrive.

"Enrico is in a strange mood Electra. Just look after him and try to make him happy so he cools down."

"Yes, Dominic," replied Electra. "He was very kind and gentle the other evening. I'm sure everything will be OK."

Dominic hesitated outside the door and listened. He heard a slap followed by a shriek and Electra's quivering voice.

"Please don't hurt me, Enrico."

Dominic cringed after another slap. "Shut up bitch. Get on the bed. This doggy is coming for a hard ride."

Dominic poised his hand above the door knob but turned and began to walk away as more cries could be heard from room 14.

What have I done to my family? What have I done to let him hurt Electra? Will I be next on their list? What should I do?

*

The following morning, Father Alessandro greeted Adam and Tanya at the front door of the Conti home.

"Detectives, Mrs Conti has taken the news very badly, and last night we needed to call her doctor to provide some sedation to help her sleep. I suggest you don't question her for too long," Father Alessandro advised as he led the detectives to Mrs Conti waiting in the lounge room.

"I know it is not a good time, Mrs Conti and I appreciate you agreeing to speak with us. I want to ask you a few questions to help us catch whoever did this terrible thing to your husband and brother as quickly as possible."

"I'll try. I want you to catch whoever did this to my family," Mrs Conti answered, her hands clasped in her lap as she looked at the floor.

"Was there anything unusual about your husband going to the warehouse last night?" Adam asked. "It appears to be quite late to have gone to the warehouse."

"Not especially. My Gaetano said he met with my brother Lorenzo and mentioned needing to speak with an overseas visitor," Mrs Conti stated. "I thought it was about the English woman who called Gaetano earlier in the week."

"What English woman?" Adam probed as he and Tanya looked at each other. They edged forward on the sofa, pens poised above their notepads.

"I was clearing up in the kitchen when Gaetano received a call. He sounded upset about the person having his private number. He called her Miss Pinkston."

"Gaetano then called our nephew Dominic. From what I heard, I got the impression she was warning Gaetano about something, and I heard the words Gonzales and someone called Roberto. Gaetano said she was a copper and spoke with one of those posh English accents."

Adam looked at Tanya and mouthed, "Penny?"

After a few more general questions, Adam decided to wrap things up, given the situation. "Thank you so much for your help. You have been very brave, Mrs Conti, to help us. We'll do everything possible to catch your husband's and brother's killer. Unfortunately, there will be one requirement, which will be for you to identify the deceased bodies formally. We'll contact you tomorrow to arrange for the identification."

Adam sat with Tanya in his police car. "That scrap of paper beside Gaetano's body had the name Andrea Pinkston," Adam said. "Could our Penny Emmett-Jones be this Andrea Pinkston? Was it just a coincidence that she met with you? Is she a cop, and why is she here? Who is she working for? We better try and track her down, quick, smart."

*

"Tanya, the Channel 12 TV crew is setting up in the meeting room for the teleconference," said Adam. "I said they could have an exclusive, and they have arranged for Primrose Jackson from the Morning Show and the reporter from the crime scene, Vanessa Jeffries, to interview me. Whoever contacted Channel 12 meant to taunt us, and we need to find the arrogant bastard."

"What about the information regarding our English woman, Andrea Pinkston? Could she be our friend Penny Emmett-Jones?" Tanya questioned.

"During the interview, I want you to get onto our contacts within the DEA here in Sydney," Adam instructed. "Sandra Wong is their liaison with us, and request her help. We should also reach out to my contact in the Metropolitan Police in London, Chief Inspector Simon O'Reilly. Maybe either of them can help us with information on Andrea or Penny and see if there's a connection. Also, I think our Spanish-speaking friend may be associated with the Gonzales cartel, so mention that to them as well."

"On to it," said Tanya as she went straight to her desk and searched for the relevant contact numbers and email addresses.

"FYI, Adam, I've also got that APB (all-points bulletin) out on our friend Enrico Sanchez."

CHAPTER 19

"Good morning, viewers. This is your Morning Show host Primrose Jackson. This morning I am joined by our reporter Vanessa Jeffries at Australian Federal Police Headquarters in Sydney. We are talking to Detective Chief Inspector Adam Charles. Good morning, Vanessa and Adam."

"Yes, good morning, Primrose and viewers. Inspector Charles, what can you tell us about last night's terrible shootings in Sydney's west?" Vanessa asked, getting straight to the point.

"I am sorry to report that last evening two prominent Mount Willsmore businessmen, Gaetano Conti and Lorenzo Rossi, were gunned down in their warehouse," Adam replied. "We are currently checking CCTV footage in the vicinity, and we have tips that people with distinctive English and Spanish accents may be able to help us with our enquiries. There are also concerns for the safety of a family member Dominic Rossi. We ask anyone with information to come forward or call us on 1-800- CRIMESTOP. Confidentiality is assured."

*

"Agent Wong. This is DS Layton from the AFP."

"How can I help you?" Sandra replied as she signalled Penny to take a seat, putting her phone on speaker. "Please call me Sandra."

"Thanks, Sandra. Please call me Tanya. I presume you saw the media reports of the shootings in Sydney's west last night?"

"Yes, a terrible business," replied Sandra.

"After the shootings, we interviewed Mrs Conti, who provided some important information," said Tanya.

"Mrs Conti overhead her husband talking to her nephew Dominic. He mentioned Gonzales, which I see is where you can help us."

"Thanks for sharing that intel with us, Tanya. We at the DEA are keen to take out the Gonzales cartel and will do all we can to help you," replied Sandra.

"In addition, Mrs Conti said that her husband also received a call from a woman with a distinctive English accent earlier in the week. She heard the name Miss Pinkston," said Tanya. "At the crime scene, we found a piece of paper with Pinkston's telephone contact."

"It may be a coincidence, but I recently met a woman with a distinctive English accent. There was something about her. She came across as very efficient. The other day she was standing at my front door, claiming to have lost an earring. She said her name was Penny Emmett-Jones. Too many coincidences to my liking. We are going to track her down."

"Let me know whatever we need to do to help," Sandra replied as she mouthed the word *shit* towards Penny.

"DCI Charles has a contact with the London Metropolitan Police, and I'll email him to see if there's anything that they've got that may help us identify her. I'll get onto them this afternoon," noted Tanya. "I'm trying to track down where this Penny was staying and look at visiting her as she was supposedly returning to England to attend to a sick mother. "We are currently checking with city hotels for any with a registration for an Emmett-Jones."

"Let's keep in touch," said Sandra as she terminated the call with Tanya.

"I need to get back to the hotel," informed Penny. "I have all my equipment there. We better get moving in case they track me down. In the meantime, I will have to think about what to divulge to the AFP and when."

"OK," said Sandra as she stood and picked up her car keys. "I'll get one of my team to help you retrieve your equipment before our friends identify where you're staying."

*

The alarm sounded at 5 am, and Chris was up and going, starting the day with his usual routine in his Melbourne apartment. Firstly, there was a series of stretching exercises, followed by the journey down to his apartment's storage room to get his bicycle for the short ride to a local, open-air cycle track for a 45-minute workout, despite Melbourne's variable weather.

Returning to the apartment, Chris showered and switched on the TV to provide some company to his solo existence. He prepared a breakfast to provide the necessary energy for the busy morning at the gym, involving his popular HIIT class and a series of personal training sessions with his ever-growing female clientele.

Slicing avocado, cucumber, banana and blueberries with a squeeze of lime, he prepared a tasty thick shake. As the whirr of the juicer motor began to quieten, he heard the name Conti mentioned on the TV. Chris's eyes scanned the bench top for the remote and turned up the volume as he focused on the TV screen.

There was a face and a voice he knew – Adam Charles.

What! My Papa and Uncle Lorenzo dead? Where's Dominic? Mama, are you ok? Is Tanya involved? Is she ok? I can't call Mama; the phone may be bugged. I've got to get to Sydney, but who is this Latino-speaking person? It has to be a hitman from the Gonzales cartel. They are goin' to regret this. Wait till I get my hands on the bastard.

Thoughts tumbled through Chris's mind as he chugged down his thick shake before driving straight to the Powerhouse gym.

"Good morning Chris," came the welcoming chorus of the women stretching out on the gym floor in preparation for the morning HIIT class.

"G'day, ladies," Chris replied, trying to smile as he headed to Vera's office. He tapped on the door and entered, catching a red-faced Vera. She was sipping on a coffee and had extended her hand, reaching to pick up a sugar-coated donut sitting on top of a brown paper bag.

"What's up, Chris?" Vera asked as she withdrew her hand from the sugar-coated temptation and wiped her hand on the leg of her tracksuit pants.

"I'm sorry, but I've just received bad news, I'm afraid," replied Chris. "My

Mama is ill in Sydney, and I need to return straightaway. I want to hit the road now and drive straight through. It would be very helpful if you could take my classes for me until I return."

"That's terrible news. I totally understand," said Vera. "You better get going and take your time with the drive. We want you back safe and sound as soon as possible. I'll hold the fort until you get back. I hope your Mama is going to be OK. Keep us posted, and let me know if I can help."

A focused Chris walked past the waiting HITT class members without acknowledging their presence. As one, their heads turned as they stared open-mouthed, watching Chris head out the gym's exit. As Chris disappeared into the carpark, Vera stood with palms raised, attempting to placate the group of women who started to gather around her.

*

Sandra pulled up in front of Penny's hotel. With Penny accompanied by agent Sean Pham, she headed straight for the entrance. Penny turned back and called Sandra.

"Head to the laneway at the rear, and we'll come out the fire exit. Open the boot so we are ready to load my gear."

With Agent Pham's help, Penny loaded up the cricket equipment box with her larger pieces of weaponry and assisted him in moving the box over to the hotel room door.

"Once I've unloaded the contents of the room's safe, I'll help you to carry the box down the fire exit at the end of the hallway."

A screech of tyres drew Penny's attention to her window overlooking the driveway several floors below. There was the unmistakable activity generated by law enforcement with open car doors and bodies swarming towards the hotel entrance.

She grabbed her overnight bag and shovelled in the contents of the room's safe – travel documents, spare ammunition clips and electronic equipment. With the overnight bag on her shoulder, Penny helped Agent Pham to carry the heavy equipment box into the fire exit just as the sound of the ping of the opening elevator could be heard. With their heavy load, Penny and Sean started their way down the fire exit stairs to the waiting Agent Wong. Heavy footsteps thundered down the third-floor corridor, followed by pounding on her hotel room door.

"This is the police. Open up."

The boot of Sandra's vehicle was open, inviting Penny to lodge her equipment box. With the boot closed, Penny flung herself onto the back seat, where Agent Pham covered her in a black, woollen blanket. Sandra looked away as a car driven by DS Layton approached the rear entrance to the hotel. Sandra placed her car into DRIVE and, not wanting to draw any attention, slowly made her way down the laneway and out into the main street, disappearing into the busy CBD traffic.

"Hope you have a spare bed at home," called Penny from underneath the blanket. "I think I've just checked out of my hotel room."

*

"Fuck it. We must have just missed her," exclaimed Tanya as she punched the open cupboard door. She bent down and picked up the English Women's Cricket Team luggage tag.

"Who the hell is Penny Emmett-Jones? I hope the Metropolitan Police can shed some light on who she is."

Crestfallen at failing to intercept Penny, Tanya headed back to AFP HQ and sent an email to Adam's contact within the Metropolitan Police in London, Chief Inspector Simon O'Reilly

> *– Chief Inspector O'Reilly, DCI Adam Charles sends his regards and has asked whether you can assist with identifying a Miss Penny Emmett-Jones operating under the alias Andrea Pinkston...*

CHAPTER 20

Tanya was sitting at her desk when an email pinged into her INBOX.

"It's your mate, Simon O'Reilly, from London replying," she called across the office, loud enough for Adam to hear from inside his office. He gave her a thumbs up, quickly terminated the phone call, and pulled up a chair next to Tanya as she turned her computer screen towards Adam.

> *Hi Tanya, regarding your query concerning one Penny Emmett-Jones and using the alias Andrea Pinkston, I am sorry to say I have hit a brick wall. All the feedback I have received from various bodies has used wording such as TOP SECRET/ FILE NOT ACCESSIBLE/ A LEVEL CLEARANCE REQUIRED. I am sorry I cannot be of more assistance. Please pass on my best regards to Adam.*

"Bloody hell. Who is this woman, and why is she here?" said a frustrated Tanya as she swivelled in her office chair to make eye contact with Adam. "A level clearance required. Is she some super spy?"

"Penny or Andrea, whatever her name is, obviously moves in circles above our pay grade," mused Adam. "It's obvious she's here for a purpose, and I would bet her presence is linked to the Contis and the Gonzales cartel. I would guess we have similar aims but are tackling the solution differently. She seems to operate outside our legal framework, which could cause serious problems with our hierarchy if her activities come to light."

"I hope Penny makes contact and decides to work with us. Two heads are better than one," said Tanya. "There's something about her that says confidence and capability. I'd like to know her story. Hopefully, she is a friend and not a foe!"

*

"You should see what that animal did to Electra," said Gypsy as she dragged Dominic forcibly by the arm into the front office and closed the door.

"She's had to have treatment for what he did to her. Electra will be out of action for weeks and may need surgery to repair damage to her vagina. He was completely different from who was with her on that first occasion. He turned into some monster. What's the matter with him? He's psycho and needs fuckin' help!"

"I'm sorry, I had no idea he would turn into some sort of beast," mumbled Dominic as he shuffled his feet, unable to make eye contact with Gypsy. "Please reassure her that we'll look after her and cover her costs."

Before Gypsy could respond, the front door buzzed. She looked at the security camera screen and, with the habit of a lifetime, observed and evaluated a man of Pacific Islander appearance. Tall of athletic build, likely late twenties, or early thirties, he was wearing black slip-on Skechers™, denim jeans with slits above the knees and a tight-fitting, plain white T-shirt which enhanced his muscular chest.

"Can I help you sir?"

"Yes, Tiko Rokovou, to meet with Mister Enrico Sanchez," said Tiko using Roberto's fake name as a precaution.

Gypsy pressed the door release, and with the door buzzing, Tiko entered the corridor and waited outside the office door while his eyes adjusted to the light. Dominic gathered himself and stepped forward to greet Tiko.

"Dominic Rossi," he said as he extended his right hand. "Or, should I say bula," he added with a grin.

"Yes, bula. Great to meet you," replied Tiko with a bright smile revealing perfect white teeth. "I've come to meet with Enrico. Ah, here he is now," said Tiko looking over Dominic's shoulder.

"I need to speak with Tiko in private," said Roberto as he beckoned Tiko with a wave.

"Room 6 is free," said Dominic, pointing.

Dominic ushered the men into Room 6. In contrast to Room 14, it was a bright room with subdued lighting in a dark décor of reds, pinks and black. Room 6 was outfitted in whites and greys. To the side of the centrally located double bed were two lounge chairs on either side of the coffee table. It suggested a gentler ambience conducive to chatting, not just a wild sexual element. Possibly suitable for an older, regular client who wants to get to know his lady before any intimacy.

"Can I arrange some coffee for you guys?" Dominic asked.

Roberto looked at Tiko, who raised his hands and replied. "No thanks. I'm fine."

Dominic closed the door of Room 6 behind him and rapidly returned to the office and closed the door.

"Somethin's goin' on, Gypsy, and I get a bad feeling in my gut," said Dominic. "We need to listen in and see what they are on about."

Dominic accessed Room 6 on the computer screen and activated the hidden camera and audio.

He watched as Roberto opened the door and checked up and down the corridor. There was little activity in the HOP mid-morning, and Roberto closed the door, moving his chair to face Tiko.

"Thought I'd give you a bit of an update on events Tiko," began Roberto. "That dumbass Dominic delivered us his Uncle Gaetano and Papa Lorenzo on a plate. I explained that they had to sign over their warehouse in western Sydney and this building in Kings Cross to forgive the huge debt owed to Senor Gonzales. I told them they could rent the properties from the cartel and carry on business as usual. Once the fools signed the transfer papers prepared by their lawyer, I fuckin' blew their brains out right in front of that idiot. You should have seen his face. He nearly shat himself. Seeing the brain matter splatter on the wall was a beautiful sight."

"Wow," said Tiko appearing to shift uncomfortably in his chair with one leg starting to bob up and down nervously.

Dominic looked across at Gypsy with perspiration starting to form on his brow, which he wiped away with the back of his hand.

"Holy shit," was all he could manage as he continued to monitor the conversation.

"With you now set up in Fiji and ready to start receiving shipments for re-packing CH into the coffee pods, we have the making of a great operation," said a smug Roberto. "Next step will be to get the keys for the warehouse from the Contis lawyer. Once the police have cleared the crime scene, you and your gang can take over the premises."

"What about our friends Dominic and Carlo, the son who has disappeared, I've heard so much about?" Tiko queried.

"One of the reasons for taking out old man Conti was to try and draw out his son Carlo who is now within the Australian witness protection program. He knows a lot about our organisation, and Hernando wants him permanently silenced," detailed Roberto. "The death of his Papa will surely bring him out of seclusion, and I suspect he'll make tracks for his grieving Mama and maybe even look up that cop he had the hots for. We'll use that idiot Dominic to keep an eye on Mama, his Papa's sister. He can let us know when he turns up at the family home. Meanwhile, I'll aim to track down the cop. Once we eliminate Carlo, our friend Dominic will be next on the list, and you'll take control in Fiji and Sydney."

"Wow," was again all Tiko could manage, his head spinning with information overload.

Dominic spoke with Gypsy quietly, "Gypsy, we need to get out of here now! Call all the girls and tell them not to come in today, as we are closing for renovations. We will let them know when they can resume work. You also better make yourself scarce and forget everything you just heard if you know what's good for you."

"I'll call the girls, then hit the road," said Gypsy. "I have a sister up in Surfers Paradise. She'll put me up until the coast clears."

"Thanks, Gypsy. I owe you big time," replied Dominic. "I am just goin' to disappear as well. Let's get out of here."

Dominic placed his right index on his lips as Gypsy removed her heels, and the pair made their way quietly down the corridor, tip-toeing past Room 6. They reached the rear exit and gently closed the door, just as the door from Room 6 opened and a Latino voice called out.

"Dominic, come here."

*

"Where the fuck is he?" snapped Roberto as he entered the office.

"Holy shit," he roared as he saw the interior of room 6 displayed on the office computer screen.

"What's the matter?" Tiko asked as he followed Roberto into the office.

"That snivelling fuck Dominic and the old bitch heard everything we said. He was listening in. Where the fuck is he? Wait till I get my hands on him," snarled Roberto as he reached down to his ankle and drew a pistol from his ankle holster. "I'll check the rear stairs."

With the gun in hand, Roberto clambered down the stairs. His head turned in response to the screech of tyres and the loud honk of a car horn as a vehicle exited HOP's carpark.

"Fuck it. I can't let Hernando know the bastard got away. He'll have my balls."

Tiko joined Roberto. "What now?"

"I pretty sure he's shit scared and will go to the ground, and we'll not hear a squeak from him," replied Roberto. "However, arrange for your K-gang guys to keep an eye on Mama Conti's place in case he or Carlo turn up there. In the meantime, we can start work on taking over the warehouse and prepare to set it up before you head back to Fiji."

"You mentioned the cop that Carlo had the hots for. I can get some info for you," said Tiko as he moved to the office desk. "Let me at the computer. Here we go. Fiji Times archives. Conti Brothers Trial. Our star witness, Detective Tanya Layton, is based out of the AFP's headquarters in George Street. Looking like that, she would be difficult to miss in a crowd. No wonder Carlo had the hots for her."

"At least we have a starting point to track her down, should Carlo not turn up at his Mama's place. She's certainly easy on the eye. I wouldn't mind a night with her in Room 14," noted Roberto squeezing his crotch.

"As a suggestion, I reckon you should get out of here," said Tiko. "If Dominic gets nervous and dobs you into the cops, they will raid the joint. You can join me where we've been setting up for the K-gang in Sydney. We have rented an old warehouse not far from here, handy to the CBD and our customers."

"Yes, better to be safe," agreed Roberto. "Let me get my gear together from the storeroom. While I do that, park your car underneath so we can load up and get the fuck out of here."

*

Dominic dropped Gypsy off at her apartment in North Sydney and made his way to Mount Willsmore and the Conti family home. All the years ago, when Gaetano Conti built the house, he strategically located the house at the end of a cul-de-sac. This minimised the risk of drive-by shootings by deadly drug-dealing competitors. It also had a laneway that ran down the rear of the property. The laneway had provided the ability to leave the house undetected by prying law enforcement many times. A covered walkway hiding any movement to and from the laneway was accessed via the downstairs cellar in the Conti home.

As a precaution, Dominic drove around the neighbourhood and, not seeing any occupied vehicles sitting in the cul-de-sac, made his way to the local pizzeria. He slipped the proprietor Mario some cash, who then obliged Dominic by opening the garage door at the rear of the premises, which enabled Dominic to hide his car from any searching eyes. Dominic then made his way to the laneway and, punching in a PIN, could open the access to the covered walkway leading to the cellar door entry.

In the cellar, he called his Aunt's landline telephone number.

"Aunt Maria, it's Dominic. I'm in the cellar and coming up. I didn't want to scare you by arriving unannounced."

"Dominic, you are safe. Praise be to Jesus. I was so worried about you. I thought you might also have killed."

As soon as Dominic emerged from the cellar door, he was grabbed by his aunt, who smothered him in kisses as she began to weep.

Dominic put his arm around her, led her into the loungeroom, sat her into her favourite armchair, and walked over to the window. He pulled the curtain back slightly and peered into the street below. *Good, all quiet.* He closed the curtain and sat opposite his Aunt Maria.

Dominic sat forward on the edge of his seat, his right leg nervously twitching.

"Aunty, I have escaped from the man who killed Uncle Gaetano and Papa. He is a bad man and forced them to sign documents, enabling them to take over the family business premises."

"How could they do this thing?" Asked an astonished Maria as she dabbed at her eyes with a small, white hankie kept in her cardigan sleeve.

"The family owes these bad people from South America much money, and the takeover of the businesses was part of repaying the money," explained Dominic as he avoided relating the whole truth. "It appears they were still unhappy and killed them. They are after me now."

"We must go to the police," stated Maria. "Oh, I wish Carlo was here. He'd know what to do."

*

It was early evening as Carlo reached the outskirts of Sydney. He had pushed himself hard with a punishing, non-stop six-hour driving stretch from Melbourne to the Yass service centre. He pulled off onto the Melbourne to Sydney highway exit ramp, badly needing a toilet break, a coffee and something to eat. After re-fuelling, he parked in front of the adjacent Mcdonald's store and ordered a Big Mac Deal that he hungrily devoured. After a sip of Diet Coke, a large belch slipped out, which turned heads and caused a young boy in the next-door cubicle to laugh, bringing a rebuke from his mother.

After a toilet break, he was back in the car for the final three-hour stint to his Mama's place. He was looking forward to seeing his Mama after such a long time, albeit it had taken terrible circumstances to make such a visit possible.

Then there were the possible consequences of having to break the conditions of the witness protection program.

The traffic started to build as Carlo reached the outer western suburbs of Sydney. He was relieved to see the sign for the turn-off from the highway for the Mount Willsmore exit. Fatigue was starting to set in, and he was beginning to feel sleepy, so he cranked up the music on the car radio, wound down the driver's side window and slapped himself.

A tired, relieved man entered the family home's cul-de-sac entrance, where he noticed a vehicle parked up the street from home. The flash of his headlights revealed the silhouette of two heads with thick black, wiry hair sitting in the front seat.

Fijians, for sure. I'd recognise their hair anywhere. What are they doing parked in front of our house?

Carlo completed a three-point turn and then drove to the local pizzeria.

"Hey, Mario. Got a parkin' spot out back?" Carlo asked.

"Hey man, long time no fuckin' see," roared Mario. "What's goin' on? A raid by the cops or somethin'? Your cuz Dominic has already parked in the back. You can park in the laneway behind the garage door. It'll be ok there for tonight. I'll make sure the boys keep an eye on it."

"Cheers, Mario. Catch you later," said Carlo as he walked towards his family home, his heart racing with the expectation of seeing his Mama after such a long time. Tears in anticipation of seeing his Mama started to form in his eyes as he made his way down the laneway. He paused in front of the doorway leading from the laneway.

I hope they haven't changed the PIN.

The four digits opened the door, and he was headed towards the entry via the cellar door.

CHAPTER 21

Carlo quietly made his way up the stairs leading from the cellar. He paused at the top of the staircase, then pushed open the door leading to the living area. Muffled voices could be heard coming from the lounge room. Carlo crept to the entrance to the lounge room and cautiously peered around the corner. Tears began to form in his eyes as soon as he saw his beloved Mama and cousin Dominic.

Wiping away his tears, he stepped boldly into the lounge, opened his arms wide, and cried out, "Mama."

Mama slowly turned in her seat. Her mouth dropped open, and she slowly rose out of her chair. She began to sob, then rushed to Carlo, grabbing and smothering him in kisses.

"My son. My son. I have missed you so much."

"Mama. Mama," said Carlo as he tilted up his Mama's face, which had been buried into his chest and placed a lingering kiss on her forehead.

Sheepishly, Dominic approached Carlo and Maria, wrapped his arms around the pair, and then sobbed uncontrollably.

"Cuz, I've missed you so much. I've done some dumb stuff without you. I got too big for my boots, which cost the family."

"I'll get us some coffee and biscotti," said Maria as she made her way to the kitchen with a spring in her step.

"Cuz we need to talk down in the cellar asap," whispered Dominic as he turned his head towards the kitchen to check for Maria's return. "There's some heavy shit goin' on with the Gonzales gang, and I need to bring you up to speed."

"OK. I need to spend some time with Mama first. Then we'll talk business," Carlo replied. "For sure, I need to know what's happenin' with the Gonzales bastards."

With Mama's return, Carlo consumed several of her biscotti and sipped away on a sugary espresso while she talked about the murders of her beloved Gaetano and Lorenzo.

"I was so worried you would not know about the death of your Papa. At least you can now help me to arrange the funerals with Father Alessandro at Our Lady of Mercy Church once the police release the bodies."

"Officially, I'm not here, Mama. I'm in breach of the terms of the witness protection program by coming out to see you and Dominic," explained Carlo. "You can't mention me bein' here to anyone, got it," he added sternly, "not even Father Alessandro."

"But," started Mama before Carlo's raised hand to stop her speaking.

"No buts Mama, I'm not here," re-iterated Carlo. "I'll help, but no one can know about me, ok," he said, squeezing his Mama's hand. "Now I need to speak with Dominic about some business. We'll head down to the cellar for a glass of grappa while you tidy up and prepare some spaghetti with that red wine sauce. I've missed your cooking so much."

"I still don't understand all this witness business, but I'm sure we can work something out for the funeral," said Mama as she began to tidy up. "I want you to be able to carry your Papa's and Uncle's coffins at the funeral service."

Dominic and Carlo headed down to the cellar, where Carlo wiped clean two dusty glasses sitting upside down at the base of the grappa barrel. He filled them with two fingers of the fiery, golden liquid.

"Saluti," said Carlo as they clinked their glasses and drained the contents in one swallow. "Wow, that grappa has a kick. It's been a while since I had a shot," said Carlo with a shake of the head while he refilled the glasses. "Tell me what's fuckin' goin' on."

"Well," Dominic paused and took a deep breath before he continued, avoiding eye contact with Carlo. "Your Papa arranged a second shipment of CH from Hernando Gonzales to enable us to get back into business following what happened in Fiji. Unfortunately, there appeared to be a tip-off to the cops about the shipment, and we got raided by none other than your copper mate Detective Layton."

"Yes, I saw her on the TV news. I was worried she had been badly hurt when they reported she had gone to the hospital," said Carlo.

"In response, Hernando sent out a nasty fucker called Roberto Rodriguez," informed Dominic. "He came supposedly to broker a deal where our Papas would sign over the family business properties in return for forgiving the substantial debt owed to the Gonzales business. With the two lost shipments, the family was in debt to Gonzales for over five million dollars."

"You're fuckin' kiddin', five million bucks," stammered Carlo.

Roberto said the family could rent the properties back to enable us to keep operating," detailed Dominic. "In the circumstances, it seemed a fair deal, much better than the alternative of not paying. Of course, I wasn't involved in the business discussions, but from what I can gather, Roberto came to the warehouse to meet with Gaetano and Lorenzo and took them out after they signed over the properties."

"Where were you?" Carlo asked.

Dominic hesitated, again not making eye contact with Carlo, "I was back at the HOP in Kings Cross. I didn't hear about the hit until it was on the news the next morning. Roberto was at HOP and mentioned nothin' to me when this Fijian guy called Tiko turns up. I heard them talkin' about their plans that didn't include the family or me, so I figured I could be next on the hit list. I got out of there quickly and made my way here to make sure your Mama was ok."

"Somethin's up for sure. When I was turnin' into the street, I saw two guys sittin' in a car parked up the street. I reckon they were Fijians from the glimpse I saw of their heads in the headlights," said Carlo. "It would appear they are workin' for Gonzales and are lookin' for both of us. By taking out my Papa, they'd believe I would be compelled to come out of hiding and be tempted to provide much info on their operation to the cops."

"Shit. You're right," exclaimed Dominic. "What are we goin' to do?"

"As I see a summary of the situation, Hernando now owns the family business properties, killed our Papas, is after you and no doubt me too if I put my head up. It would also appear he's now in cahoots with some Fijians and, I suspect, could be trying to replicate what Guido and I began to set up in Fiji. He's a cunning, ruthless bastard, and the Fijians will need to watch out because soon enough, he won't need them either, and he'll then control the whole Trans-Pacific distribution network for his CH."

"Another thing that came up as a big surprise was a call your Papa received from an English bird. She told your Papa that she had info that a hit would likely be made on him," added Dominic. "Your Papa told her to piss off. Reckoned she was a cop. She said she wasn't a cop and was giving him a heads-up. Her words turned out to be true. We never knew where she came from."

"Dominic, from what you have described, I don't think I have any choice but to come out of witness protection and meet with Tanya to tell her and her bosses what's goin' on. I can't risk Mama or you bein' killed. It's a risk I'll have to take," said Carlo as he checked his watch.

"I know where Tanya lives over in Randwick and might visit her away from her office and that Inspector Charles. I'm goin' to tell her that I have no choice but to make the hard decision of comin' out of witness protection. Get a gun out of the safe and look after Mama. If any of those Fijians come to the house, no questions, take them out."

*

After showering and wearing fresh clothes, Carlo demolished a plate of Mama's spaghetti Bolognese. Feeling re-energised, Carlo went out into the laneway and headed back to the pizzeria to collect his car to make the long drive to Tanya's apartment. His head was spinning – the Gonzales gang, the killing of Papa and Uncle Lorenzo, Dominic likely on their hit list and the apparent developments in Fiji.

I don't think I have any choice. I'll have to come out to the cops, to Tanya and reveal what I know about the Gonzales cartel. Once I put my head up, Gonzales will want me taken out. It wouldn't surprise me if the bastard planned to draw me out all along, even though I kept quiet about his operation.

Carlo parked across the street from Tanya's apartment block. He smiled as he saw the familiar sight of her red Mini Clubman parked in front of the building. A low flickering light came from her balcony window, indicating she was probably watching television. After getting out of his car, Carlo paused, looked up and down the street, checked for any suspicious characters, and then went to the bottom of the staircase. He paused, then, with one final look back into the street, began to slowly ascend the staircase to the top floor landing, with his heart pounding.

Will she want to see me after so long?

At the top of the stairs, Carlo paused outside Tanya's door and listened. There was only the sound of inaudible voices coming from the television. Carlo took a deep breath, then raised his hand and pressed the doorbell, his heart beating rapidly. He heard footsteps come to the door.

"Who is it?"

Carlo was suddenly tongue-tied. He didn't know what to say.

"It's me, Carlo," he blurted out,

The light for landing came on, and Carlo heard the rattle of the security chain before the door was pulled open. Tanya just stood there, staring through the flywire door. She seemed lost for words.

"It is you, Carlo," she said in a trembling voice and continued to stare, seemingly unable to move.

Carlo reached forward, opened the screen door, and pulled Tanya towards him without hesitation. He looked longingly into her eyes before clutching her face and gently wiping away the tears starting to form in her eyes.

"Oh, Carlo, how I've longed for this day. I thought this day would never come, that I would never see you again. You know I have kept that note you left for me at the coffee shop next to my bed and looked at it every night."

Carlo closed the front door and, without a further word, picked Tanya up and carried her to the bedroom. They crashed onto the bed, igniting a frenzied unbuttoning and removing clothing, followed by an exchange of *Tanya, Carlo, Tanya, Carlo*..........

*

"Penny, the doorbell has rung at Tanya's apartment," said Sandra as she waved for Penny to join her where she had set up the speaker on the coffee table in her apartment.

"I distinctly heard her say, Carlo. It's him. He's at Tanya's apartment. He's turned up. From the sounds of things, they aim to make up for a lot of lost time. Luckily you didn't get to fit a device in her bedroom. Otherwise, it would have been a bit embarrassing."

"I'm sure after this moment of passion, reality will bite hard," said Penny. "A dead father, a dangerous Columbian ready to take him out, and now he's exposed himself outside of witness protection. I think it best we contact the AFP in the morning and indicate we can provide much assistance. I'll get you to arrange a meeting for us with Adam Charles. I believe it is time he meets Penny Emmett-Jones."

"Agreed, "acknowledged Sandra with a nod of her head. "We better keep listening just in case some unwanted visitors turn up, but keep the volume down."

*

Tanya and Carlo lay naked in each other's arms, not wanting the moment to end.

"You don't know how often I've thought about you," Carlo said. "Goin' into witness protection was the hardest thing I ever had to do, thinking I wouldn't ever get to see you or my family again. I've loved you since the first time I saw you in Fiji. I have survived livin' on the dreams of those times lyin' on the beach together. I am glad you've recovered from what my brother did to you. He nearly killed you."

"I'm all OK now," replied Tanya as she stroked Carlo's hair. "You know I will eventually have to put my cop's hat back on and tell my boss DCI Charles that you are out of witness protection and back in Sydney."

"Yes, I know. I had to make the call to come out. I thought I was protecting my family by disappearing and keeping information on the Gonzales cartel up my sleeve, but it did no good. They obviously didn't trust that I'd keep quiet. They've killed Papa, taken over the cocaine business in Aussie, and no doubt want me dead as well," said Carlo as he rolled onto his back. "I've got an idea to discuss with your boss in the morning. A plan to draw the Gonzales' hitman out of hiding. I want to nail the bastard and then maybe even take the whole Gonzales organisation down, once and for all. But that's tomorrow morning, so come here," he said, dragging Tanya towards him.

"Oh Carlo…." giggled Tanya. "You are a naughty boy."

*

"Tanya, you're up early this morning," Adam said as he sat in bed and looked at his bedside clock radio. "It's only 6 am, so the call must be urgent."

"Yes, boss, sorry to disturb you this early, but I've some news that will shock you." Tanya paused. "Carlo Conti turned up at my place last night."

"Holy shit!" Adam exclaimed as he started to fire off a string of questions. "He's come out of witness protection. How did he find you? What does he want? Will he speak with us? When can I speak with him?"

"Whoa, boss. Slow down," said Tanya as she tried calming the excited Adam. "The bottom line is that he's prepared to talk to us about the Gonzales gang, given what they have done to his family. He said it is time he finally disassociated the Conti family from the drug business forever."

"When can I speak with him?" Adam eagerly asked. He was now out of bed and headed straight to the kitchen, where he placed a double shot pod in his Nespresso machine with the mobile pressed to his ear.

"I'll bring him into the office by 8.30 and set him up in the main meeting room, ready to record the session," confirmed Tanya.

"OK, see you then," said Adam as he hummed happily and popped two pieces of whole meal bread into the toaster, grabbing a jar of peanut butter from the pantry.

It's going to be a good day.

CHAPTER 22

"Set to go?" Tanya asked Carlo as they sat in the AFP's carpark. "Ready for the first day of the rest of your life Carlo Conti. Adam is very keen to speak with you after I called him this morning and told him you were coming into the office. He wants to hear what you are prepared to share with the AFP and on what basis."

"Yes, hopefully, the first day of a very long life," Carlo responded as he reached across and squeezed Tanya's hand. "Let's go and meet DCI Charles. He'll finally get the information he wants from me, and I can take the first steps in ending the Conti family's era of crime."

Aware of security cameras, Tanya playfully slapped Carlo's hand away as he made to clutch her hand as they walked across the underground carpark on approach to the staff entrance to the building. "Sorry," whispered Carlo as he retracted his hand, bringing a smile to Tanya.

Tanya signed Carlo in at the service desk as his new identity, Chris Cerlik, given that he no longer carried an ID related to Carlo Conti. They made their way to the elevator, where Tanya scanned her ID and pressed the button for Level 3. After exiting, Tanya guided Carlo towards the main meeting room and invited him to sit at the board table.

"Whoever thought I'd come voluntarily to a cop shop and not wearing handcuffs," mused Carlo, prompting Tanya's arm punch.

"I'll get you a coffee, then round up DCI Charles to speak with us," said Tanya.

Tanya delivered Carlo a mug of instant coffee that caused his face to screw up in disgust after the first tentative sip.

"You call that coffee. Mama Mia," Carlo mocked. "You cops sure do it, tough."

"Just drink it," said Tanya sternly as she about turned and headed to Adam's office to let him know Carlo had arrived.

*

"DCI Charles, this is Agent Sandra Wong from the DEA."

"Hi, Sandra. I haven't got long as I have an important meeting just about to start," Adam stated.

"If your meeting has anything to do with the Contis and some recent murders, I think you'll be interested in speaking with Penny Emmett-Jones and me from the DEA," said Sandra. "We can be with you in 10 minutes from our HQ."

"What! Penny Emmett-Jones. Are you telling me she's a DEA agent?" Adam snapped. "We've raided her hotel room looking for her and have an APB out on her."

"I hope you have a good explanation for why the DEA has been running a parallel operation in my jurisdiction without keeping us informed," exclaimed Adam. "You and Emmett-Jones better get into my office to find out what is happening."

"We are on our way," replied Sandra as she quickly terminated the call.

"Not surprisingly, he didn't sound happy," noted Penny. "We better get over there."

*

Tanya tapped on his door and was about to speak when Adam said rhetorically, "you'll never guess who that was. None other than Agent Sandra Wong of the DEA, and she'll be in our office in 10 minutes with none other than Penny Emmett-Jones."

"Forgive the French, but what the fuck is going on?" exclaimed Tanya. "I'm intrigued to find out how the DEA and our mystery English woman appear to be working on the same case as we are?"

"Come on, let's go and speak with Carlo before our friends from the DEA arrive," said Adam as he made his way with Tanya to meet the waiting Carlo.

Carlo stood as Tanya and Adam entered the room. "Please sit down," said Adam. "I hope you forgive me, but we don't have time for pleasantries this morning as we have representatives from the DEA arriving shortly. They appear very keen to hear what you have to say and now seem to want to work with us regarding what happened to your father and the link with the Gonzales cartel."

"I know it's difficult to come out from witness protection, but after what happened to my Papa and Uncle Lorenzo, I had no choice. I am prepared to take the risk and end the Conti family's association with Hernando Gonzales and crime once and for all," explained Carlo. "I'll do what it takes, starting with catching the Gonzales hitman currently wandering the streets of Sydney. The family won't be safe until the bastard is arrested."

"That's certainly a different attitude from when we last met as you were about to head off into the witness protection," said Adam. "You were reluctant to tell us everything you knew about Hernando Gonzales and his organisation."

"I thought I could keep the threat of the Gonzales' away from my family by not telling you everything and keepin' somethin' up my sleeve," explained Carlo. "It obviously didn't work and cost me, my Papa and Uncle. I also understand from Dominic that they have taken over the family business properties through a Gonzales hitman who entered Australia as Enrico Sanchez but is, in reality, Roberto Rodriguez. He also told me that Roberto stopped in Fiji en route to Australia and met with Tiko Rokovou, head of the K-gang. All this indicates that they're likely to be set up to take over distribution in this world, creating a whole Trans-Pacific operation."

"What about Dominic?" Tanya asked. "Where is he? Is he safe?"

"He's hiding out with Mama and keepin' an eye on her in case Roberto shows up there," answered Carlo. "Interestingly, some men I recognised as

Fijians were sittin' in a car up the road from the house. They are undoubtedly part of what Gonzales is settin' up."

"We are aware of this Roberto's identity from CCTV of his arrival at Sydney Airport but subsequently lost his trail. We also have been advised that Tiko Rokovou has bought your Tradewinds Coffee company from the Fiji Government's forced sale of the business," informed Adam. "That adds weight to your thought that Gonzales is looking at setting up a Pacific-wide network."

"He's a crafty bastard that Hernando," sneered Carlo. "Tiko will have to watch out. Otherwise, he'll end up in a grave alongside my Papa and Uncle, with Gonzales ultimately wanting to control everything."

There was a tap at the door. "Sir, your visitors from the DEA have arrived. Shall I bring them in?" officer Gregson announced.

"Rod, they can wait until I'm ready," Adam said as he returned his focus to Carlo.

*

Adam looked at his watch. "I think keeping them waiting for 30 minutes was appropriate. Get Rod to show them in."

"Well, Agent Wong, glad you could spend the time to come and tell us what the DEA is up to here in Australia. You're not trying to capture all the newspaper headlines for the DEA," snapped DCI Charles.

"Well, if it isn't Penny Emmett-Jones," interjected an annoyed Tanya. "How's the world of cricket? Enjoying the tour of Australia with the team?"

"Yes, sorry about our initial contact Tanya," said Penny, "but we are here now and ready to work with you to make up for lost time and make amends for the poor communication. Maybe I can tell you more over a glass of wine sometime. I want to make it up to you."

"Please, everyone take a seat so we can get underway and start cooperating," instructed Adam. "Agent Wong, Sandra, let's start with you giving us an update on what the DEA is working on here in Australia and how we can finally work together?"

"I understand your annoyance at learning of the DEA acting in your jurisdiction without advising you, but I can assure you of our full support going forward."

"We are certainly very interested to hear what you've got to say, but first, let me introduce you and Penny to Mister Carlo Conti," responded Adam.

Sandra acknowledged Carlo with a nod of her head, then stated. "We received a tip-off from a source we had within the Gonzales organisation. The source informed us that the cartel planned to make a hit on Carlo. The aim was to stop him from being able to provide intel on the operation of the organisation in Columbia. Unfortunately, we believe our source has been discovered, and no further intel has been provided."

"It seems logical from what you say that Gonzales' man, Rodriguez, made the hit on Gaetano to draw Carlo out of hiding, then take him out", observed Adam.

"Yes," said Sandra. "That is where my colleague Penny enters the picture. Penny has been appointed by HQ in Washington to head up the operation. She has worked on various assignments, including a recent assignment in Columbia and has some excellent skills. We wanted to remove Rodriguez without drawing Carlo out of the WPP."

"I still think it would have been preferable to have included us in your plans," stated Adam.

"The DEA's focus was the Gonzales cartel which we saw fell outside your jurisdiction. I agree with hindsight and how things have escalated and become entwined since Roberto's arrival in Sydney. We are here today to work with you and offer our full co-operation," said Penny. "We have also been following what has occurred in Fiji with the K-gang and the acquisition of the Tradewinds Coffee company, which we believe is also linked to the Gonzales organisation."

"Well, you sound as though you are very well-informed and up-to-date," said Adam. "I suppose we need to discuss where we go from here. How best can we combine our resources to stop Gonzales in Australia and globally."

Carlo raised his arms and interjected, "I see two steps. Firstly, I want to ensure my family and I are safe in Sydney. I see that means taking out this hitman. Secondly, we need our DEA and the AFP to shut down the Gonzales operation in Columbia once and for all, which includes stopping the packing of drugs out of the Tradewinds factory in Fiji by taking out the K-gang."

Everyone started to speak at once, causing Carlo to stand. "Whoa. Hold up. Let me finish. If you haven't already done so, I suggest you take some AFP officers and raid the House of Pleasure in Kings Cross, the HOP as we call it and the family warehouse in Mount Willsmore in case our friends are holed up there."

Tanya and Adam exchanged glances before Adam left the room. There was an exchange of conversation outside the door before he entered, looking embarrassed.

"It's underway," he said, shrugging.

"Presumably, our friend will be long gone from those places, so we'll have to flush him out," declared Carlo. "I propose we call for a press conference in front of the AFP HQ tomorrow morning. We can advise the media that I will address them with Dominic regarding the slaying of my Papa and Uncle. What other chance will this Roberto see he has to get me? He'll expect us to be in protective custody after the presentation and will see this as maybe his only chance to kill me."

"Is that wise"?" Tanya asked. "It sounds like a high-risk plan to me."

"We have to draw him out," Carlo stated. "We can have plainclothes cops placed throughout the crowd and scan the crowd with CCTV. We know what he looks like, and we can be ready to swoop."

"I can also have some of Sandra's team placed in the crowd," Penny said. "We can coordinate via two-way if you provide us with your frequencies."

After a pause, Adam stood, "Carlo's idea, I see, is our best shot of luring him out into the open. I'll get our media department to work on a press release, and we can plan how we'll manage the operation."

*

This is Vanessa Jeffries from the Channel 12 newsroom. We have just received breaking news from the Australian Federal Police about the former Sydney crime figure Carlo Conti. He has broken his silence denouncing the recent slaying of his Father and Uncle by a suspected international crime gang and will hold a press conference tomorrow at 9 am. Along with his cousin Dominic, they'll convene on the steps of the Australian Federal Police Headquarters in Sydney to address the media.

I look forward to speaking to you live tomorrow morning on Primrose Jackson's Morning Show from AFP headquarters. Until then, I'm Vanessa Jeffries.

Thanks for that, Vanessa. We look forward to hearing from you in the morning. Now back to our regular program.

CHAPTER 23

Adam gathered the group around the meeting room's whiteboard and began to work out the plan for conducting the media conference. Adam had received confirmation the previous evening that the HOP was empty. There was no sign of Roberto. He was long gone.

It was agreed that Carlo and Dominic would stand at the top of the five steps leading into the HQ's entrance, backed by armed officers. The media would gather at the bottom of the steps enabling police to be able to look down on those in attendance and maintain a clear passage for pedestrians using the footpath.

Officers in plain clothes equipped with two-way capabilities would mingle in the street behind the media pack and at the head of the laneways running down either side of the main building. Security cameras would be monitored with facial recognition set for Roberto Rodriguez and Tiko Rokovou. It was also agreed that the police helicopter is available in the vicinity.

"Our DEA team will mix with the crowd and be synched into your radio frequency," added Penny.

"Let's assemble for coffee at 8 am to review the plan and check our equipment to ensure everything works. We can't afford any slip-ups," said Adam as he made eye contact with everyone. "Our targets will be armed and dangerous."

Penny raised her hand. "Given the situation with Roberto being armed, I want my DEA team to be armed. Not only for all our safety, but there may be the opportunity to take out Roberto."

Adam paused. "You raise a valid point, Penny. I know it is against protocol to carry weapons, but I will stick my neck out and allow you to carry weapons. Your DEA team being armed could save lives, and it will take too long to go through a formal approval process."

"Thanks, Adam," Penny replied.

*

With the formal meeting finished and the DEA visitors' departure, Adam gathered his team to prepare for the next morning's operation. Carlo was directed to Adam's office to enable him to make some personal calls.

"Dominic, it's Carlo. How's Mama?"

"She's OK but worried about you," replied Dominic. "She wants to see you at home so you're safe."

"Tell her I'm bein' looked after at police headquarters, and I'm safer here than at home. We are planning a media conference tomorrow at 9 am to denounce the murders of our Papas. I want you here to stand with me," said Carlo.

"Are you sure that's a good idea.?" Dominic asked. "It will provide Roberto with the perfect opportunity to target us."

"That's the whole idea. We want to draw the fucker out of hidin' and nail the bastard," said Carlo, his voice raising in anger. "The cops will have everything in place to catch him."

"Sounds a bit hairy to me, but I'll support you, cuz," replied Dominic nervously. "What time do you need me there?"

"Be here at AFP HQ by 8 in the morning to prepare, ok," said Carlo trying to sound positive. "We'll get the bastard if he dares to turn up."

*

Vera Mueller sat in the staffroom at the Powerhouse gym, enjoying a break before her evening Pilates class. She was munching on some celery and carrot sticks, not noticing the wall-mounted TV flickering away on the wall opposite the plain white formica-topped table. Another carrot stick was on its way to her mouth when Chris Cerlik's face appeared on the screen.

She reached for the remote, turned up the volume and was left open-mouthed, hearing words such as; Carlo Conti, Conti crime family, and media conference at 9 am tomorrow.

Who is Chris? Is he this Carlo Conti, a gangster, a drug dealer? I can't believe it. He's such a nice guy. The ladies will want to check this out tomorrow after the HIIT class. Vera reached for her mobile and began furiously tapping away.

Immediately Vera's Signal App on her mobile phone began to ping with messages from Ady, Anne and others. *Wow, it's Chris? I can't believe it. We have to watch it tomorrow morning.*

*

"I suggest we call it a day and put you up at a hotel tonight, with a guard outside your door. I would prefer you didn't return to the Mount Willsmore home," said Adam to Carlo. We will reconvene here at 8 am to double-check the plans for the press conference."

"It's ok, but I have a bed arranged for tonight. I'll be in safe hands," Carlo replied with a big smile as he looked at Tanya, who blushed and began to check her mobile phone for messages.

"I see," chuckled Adam. "You'll certainly be in very capable hands indeed. However, for peace of mind, I will arrange for some coverage in the street outside DS Layton's apartment."

*

"Heh, come and look at this, Roberto. We've got some urgent planning to do," said Tiko. "It's that fucker you're after, Carlo Conti, on the TV. He will speak at some press conference tomorrow morning at 9 in front of the cop's offices."

"What," said Roberto putting down his beer and standing beside Tiko. "It has to be a fuckin' set-up. They'll figure we'll want to take him out and be ready for us. I better talk to Hernando."

Roberto, Tiko and the Sydney members of the K-gang were housed in an old warehouse near the airport in a southern, inner Sydney industrial area. It was a plain brick-walled building, topped by a corrugated iron roof. It had a narrow frontage but ran well back from the street frontage of the building. The building had no fixtures apart from a dusty, partitioned wooden structure that once served as an office. There was a toilet and shower cubicle, which indicated that it hadn't been cleaned for some time from the smell. Parked inside were two black SUVs and two bright-red Ducati motorcycles. Several camp stretchers topped with sleeping bags provided the sleeping arrangements, and some old well-worn, single brown leather chairs were huddled around a small TV mounted on top of an inverted tea chest.

Roberto pointed to his mobile.

"We'll go and get some pizzas and beers while you make your call," said Tiko as he and the six other guys partially opened the screeching steel door to duck down and head to the local pub for refreshments.

Roberto called Hernando on the open line, with the door grinding to a squeaky close behind the K-gang members.

It was early morning in Columbia. "*Buenos dias,*" Hernando answered.

"This is a friend of yours," said Roberto cryptically.

"Ah, Mister Smith," said Hernando. "How are matters proceeding?"

"Our friend has returned from his travels and wants to make a big presentation tomorrow. I am sure he would like us to attend the meeting and welcome us," stated Roberto. "What do you want me to do?"

"I don't think you have much choice. I think you need to attend the gathering to say goodbye to him," said Hernando, equally as cryptic with his instructions. "With our new friends, I'm sure you can work something out to farewell our friend."

The steel door began to squeal open, "better go. The boys are back. I'll keep you updated. *Adios.*"

"Guys, we have some planning for tomorrow morning," Roberto said as he reached for a beer and a slice of pepperoni pizza. "Carlo Conti, as his fellow Italians would say, will be sleeping with the fishes tomorrow," Roberto laughed as he clinked bottles around the circle of burly, smiling Fijians.

"We don't have much time, so let's finish the pizzas and go for a drive to check out where tomorrow morning's action will take place. They'll be expecting us, so with some preparation, we can create chaos and enable us to take our target out."

After wolfing down the pizzas and beer, the group piled into the two SUVs and entered the CBD. They parked a block away from the AFP offices and broke into two groups to stroll past the building. Photos were taken from mobile phone cameras. With a nod from Roberto, the men returned to the cars and drove back to the warehouse.

Roberto booted up his laptop at the warehouse and zeroed in on the police building using Google maps. He also opened the photos he had taken on his mobile.

"Note the laneways on either side of the building. One goes to the underground staff carpark, the other to a loading dock. Neither laneway has an exit," observed Roberto. "At the entrance to each laneway is a large rubbish bin, so I want those incendiary devices we have placed in each bin. They'll make a good diversion for what I have in mind. I want a couple of you guys up early and into the city, well before sunrise, to set up. Now let's agree on the plan so everyone knows what they are doing before we get some sleep. It's going to be a busy day tomorrow, and I look forward to putting a bullet in that fucker Carlo's head."

*

Penny stirred early in Sandra's eastern suburbs apartment. It had been a restless night as her mind raced with possibilities for the tense day ahead.

It's a high-risk strategy, but I see little other chance to lure the Columbian hitman into the open and finally remove him as a threat.

Penny slid open the door and stepped onto the balcony to enjoy a view of the Australian and Aboriginal flags starting to flutter in the early morning puffs of wind atop the Sydney Harbour Bridge. The first pulses of sunlight were beginning to sparkle on the harbour waters.

There was a gentle tap at her bedroom door. "How did you sleep?" Sandra asked as she partially opened the bedroom door. "Come out when you are ready. The coffee's brewing."

Penny followed Sandra to the kitchen and extracted a stool from underneath the granite-topped kitchen bench. "I tossed and turned a bit. My mind was racing with the endless possibilities for how today may unfold. It's a very dangerous option," noted Penny. "I do not know whether Carlo is brave or stupid, but I owe it to Tanya to do my best to make sure he is ok."

"Hats off to him," said Sandra, pouring the black coffee into a mug. "We'll do all we can to protect him and catch our man."

"I do not like the venue. There are too many uncontrollable variables. A main street, traffic congestion and crowds of people," said Penny as she took a cautious sip of her coffee. "Our man could strike from any direction."

Sandra looked at the time on her mobile. "We better shower and get ready to be in the AFP's office by 8 am. The early morning traffic can get pretty heavy."

After her shower, Penny knelt beside her equipment box and extracted a pistol and ankle holster. She picked up Gertrude, hesitated, and then replaced the rifle in the equipment box.

I'll feel safer today, knowing I am armed, thanks to Adam.

Penny dressed in a grey pants suit and black, flat sole Colorados. She looked into the built-in robe's, sliding, full-length mirrored doors to see if she could detect any bulge from the firearm hugging her leg just above the ankle. Satisfied, she stepped out into the lounge dining area.

"I'm ready to go, Sandra."

"Like those dress runners," noted Sandra. "Looks like you're ready to chase our man down."

*

"Aunty, I've got to go now," said Dominic. "I must be at police headquarters by eight to prepare for the interview.

"I want to come too," stated Maria. "I want to be with Carlo."

"Carlo instructed that it is dangerous and you are not to come," explained

Dominic as he headed to the front door. "A police officer will remain with you to make sure you are safe."

On the slow drive into the city in the morning peak hour traffic, Dominic had much time to reflect on the recent chaos.

I've single-handily destroyed the family business. I've been responsible for the deaths of my Papa and Uncle, and I'm next on the Gonzales hit list along with Carlo. And, poor Electra, that evil bastard may have destroyed her. All of this because of my greed and fuckin' ego. How can I make amends for what I have done?

"OK, I'm movin'," called Dominic, accompanied by the middle finger salute, as the honk from the car behind brought him back to reality.

*

It was nearly eight as Penny and Sandra entered the APF headquarters and approached the security checkpoint. Tanya waved to the DEA agents and directed them around the metal detector, where they presented their IDs to the security officer.

There was frantic activity on the AFP's third-floor meeting floor as Penny and Sandra entered the room. Adam, Carlo and several AFP officers were standing around the whiteboard discussing the plans for the morning.

"Has Dominic arrived yet?" Adam asked as he checked his watch.

"He's passed through security and arrived at the reception," replied Tanya as she passed around mugs of coffee and donuts.

"Thanks. Please get reception to bring him to the meeting room," Adam requested. "We need to brief him."

"Hey, cuz, what's the matter?" Carlo asked as he double-hugged Dominic as he entered the room. "You look kinda sad. Is Mama OK?"

"I'm OK. It was just a slow drive in this morning," replied Dominic as he attempted a smile.

"Adam, Tanya, Sandra, Penny. This is my cousin Dominic."

"Hi Dominic, sorry, but we don't have much time for pleasantries," stated Adam. "We are going through the security arrangements for this morning.

We need to protect you guys and, at the same time, be able to capture our Columbian and his friends if they dare show their faces."

"If he knows about the media conference, I'm sure he'll puttin' his plan into place. He's no dummy, cuz," mumbled Dominic.

"You're right, Dominic. He's an experienced operator," agreed Tanya. "However, we have a good team and will be well prepared."

"Everyone take a seat," said Adam clapping his hands. "I need to go through the arrangements before we head down to the waiting media frenzy."

"From what I saw from out of the window, there's a big crowd assembling already," noted Tanya as she took her seat.

"OK, Carlo and Dominic, you'll address the media from a stand of microphones set up at the top of the stairs leading into the building's entrance," instructed Adam. "You'll be backed by a team of uniformed officers who'll scan the crowd for anyone moving towards the microphone stand."

"Also, the SWAT team will be broken into two groups on standby in the laneways, ready to be called into action on my command," Adam added.

Tanya or Penny, anything to add before we start heading down?"

"Thanks, Adam," said Tanya. "Uniformed officers will be positioned at the base of the steps leading up to the microphone stand. They'll scan the credentials of the assembled media and then corral them from the general public, who'll be kept well back."

"I know you are keen to draw out Roberto, but I see this as a high-risk plan, even with the AFP SWAT ready for action. There are too many people in the precinct. Any shooting will create a major panic that will be impossible to control. You should have restricted numbers in the area." Penny stated.

"I appreciate your comments Penny, but we see this as possibly the only opportunity for us to draw Roberto out from his hiding place," Adam replied.

"We will support you," Penny said. "Where do you want us deployed?"

"I would ask you and Sandra to mingle amongst the public at the rear of the media pack and call in any suspicious characters you deem attempting to access our speakers," indicated Adam.

"I'll give you the correct radio frequency," said Tanya as she picked up her two-way.

"Thanks, understood," Penny replied with a nod.

"As a final point before we get into position," said Adam, "plain-clothed officers would be stationed at each end of the building. Unmarked police vehicles will be positioned at each intersection surrounding the building. In addition, the police helicopter will patrol around the Sydney Harbour Bridge, ready to be called into action should it be necessary to track any people or pursue any vehicles fleeing the scene. Good luck, everyone, and be vigilant. We're dealing with some very dangerous characters."

*

Now we cross to Vanessa Jeffries outside the Australian Federal Police Sydney headquarters. Good morning to you, Vanessa.

Good morning to you, Primrose and Morning Show viewers around Australia. The tension is certainly building outside police headquarters this morning.

Are you expecting a big crowd for the 9 am media conference with Carlo Conti and Dominic Rossi, the alleged bosses of the Conti crime family? Primrose asked.

From the media and general public already assembled here, there is certainly going to be a big crowd to hear what Carlo Conti has to say about recent events," said Vanessa.

Thanks, Vanessa. We will return to you at nine for the start of the media conference, but it's over to Frankie J for the nation's weather.

*

"OK, everyone, let's get into position and hopefully grab this bastard if he's silly enough to show up," said Adam as he pounded his fist into his palm. "Good luck Carlo and Dominic."

"Ah, you sure you want to go through with this," Tanya asked Carlo, a quiver in her voice. "You say you know this Rodriguez is a dangerous character."

"We can't sleep and have a life together until we have him. I'll be fine," confirmed Carlo. He strode towards the door taking Dominic by the arm.

"What's the matter with you this mornin' cuz? Get your shit together, and let's do it for the family."

Dominic followed behind the group with his head down as they waited for the elevator.

All this because of me. I'm so sorry, Papa, Uncle, Electra. Carlo will never forgive me once he finds out.

CHAPTER 24

"Vera, I think we need to finish the Pilates session early this morning," said Ady as she caught her breath after the group completed a punishing 300 squats.

"Yes, we want to hear what our Chris or, should I say, what Carlo has to say on TV this morning at nine," chorused the rest of the class.

"OK, girls, we'll finish this morning's class early. Just another hundred squats," announced Vera to the group's groans. "That will allow you time to grab tea or coffee in the staffroom before the presentation."

"They say he was some big-time gangster," said Vicki to the rest of the class as they followed Vera into the staffroom. "A coke dealer and all that. Who would have thought that about our Chris."

"Come on, ladies. Another hundred squats," called out Vera.

*

Roberto sat in the front seat next to Malakai, who was driving the lead SUV. In the rear seat sat Osea and Timoci. Jioji drove the following SUV with Jo and Tui as his passengers. Tiko sat behind the convey on a Ducati as they approached a police officer manning a road barrier with a Temporary Road Closure sign.

"Keep calm," instructed Roberto as Malakai slowly pulled up at the barrier and wound down his window as the officer approached.

"Sorry guys, the road is closed today for a special event. You'll have to detour to the left if you want to get onto the Harbour Bridge," instructed the officer.

"Thanks, officer," responded Malakai as he wound up his window and led the K-gang convoy down the road to the left.

About 100 metres from the diversion, the cars and motorcycles pulled over and parked. The group gathered around Roberto and Tiko, who began to go over the plan, "Osea and Timoci, I want you stationed by the far rubbish bin, with Jo and Tui you positioned by the near bin," instructed Roberto.

"Time check, guys," stated Tiko. "I have 8.55."

"Check," chorused the group.

"The cops will be expecting us, and there will be plenty of them, so we need to cause maximum disruption to get people moving in panic, and that's when we'll strike. At 9.10, you are to set off the incendiary devices," directed Roberto. "Tiko, you'll be on the Ducati, and as soon as the distraction is underway, you'll come past the roadblock and pull up behind the media pack. I'll take the shots on Carlo and Dominic, jump straight onto the back of the bike, and we'll get out of there before the cops realise what hit them."

"Malakai and Jioji, you'll be ready in the SUVs to pick up the rest of the guys and make your way to the Cross City Tunnel," stated Tiko. "The helicopters won't be able to track us inside the tunnel."

"No crazy driving," said Roberto eye-balling the drivers. "We don't want to draw attention to ourselves. The element of surprise must be on our side."

"You'll park the SUVs in the emergency lane near the Randwick Road exit, where we'll drop the Ducati and jump into the cars," said Tiko. "By the time the cops check the tunnel CCTV we'll be long gone and safely back into the warehouse. Any questions?"

Roberto retrieved a backpack from the rear of the SUV and, shielded by the men, entered a narrow alleyway adjacent to the parked cars. In the alleyway, Roberto prepared for action by getting into his disguise. He wore a scruffy brown wig to hide his trim, black Hispanic hair and aviator sunglasses to mask his face. A heavy, dusty military-style trench coat was draped over his body. He placed his Air Pods into his ears, "testing," he called out.

"Everybody hear me, OK?"

With thumbs up from all in the group that the audio was working, Roberto removed two pistols from the backpack and checked the mechanisms. Satisfied the guns were ready for action, he placed one in each deep coat pocket and patted the pockets to ensure the weapons weren't protruding.

Osea and Jo checked the remotes for their respective incendiary devices, and with all in order, Roberto headed off with them towards the police HQ and the assembled media pack. The group merged with the excited, chattering crowd streaming past the traffic barrier towards the television cameras.

Malakai and Jioji remained seated within the vehicles, ready to start their engines and make their escape. Tiko stood with helmet in hand, ready for the signal to start the Ducati and go to retrieve Roberto.

Past the roadblock, the crowd began to slow as people decided on where was the best place to witness the proceedings. Osea, Timoci, Jo and Tui took the opportunity to break away from the crowd and make their way to their assigned locations. In position, they checked their watches. "We're ready. Confirm the devices are set to go."

*

"There's a hell of a crowd," observed Tanya to Adam as they stepped out of the building and led Carlo and Dominic towards the cache of microphones standing at the top of the steps.

"More than I expected," replied Adam. "It's going to be a lot riskier than I thought. I hope everyone is ready should our friends expose themselves."

"Testing, 1-2-3," came the call over the microphone from the technician, which caused the media pack to prepare their recording devices and check the focus on their cameras. Television camera lights were turned on as the entourage approached the top of the stairs and assembled behind the microphone dais.

"Good morning, everyone. I am Detective Chief Inspector Adam Charles of the Australia Federal Police. Mister Carlo Conti will address you in a moment with an important statement he has prepared. In the interest of security and safety, given the recent murder of his family members, there will not be time for any questions. I thank you in advance for your understanding."

Carlo stood behind Adam, waiting to be called to speak. He wiped his hands on his trousers as he felt the butterflies fluttering in his stomach and took a deep breath, trying to calm his pounding heart. *Remember, speak clearly and slowly.*

"Ladies and gentlemen, Mister Carlo Conti," announced Adam.

From behind DCI Charles, Carlo stepped up to the microphone, turning down the angle slightly. Carlo paused as he looked around the assembled media throng and to the crowd gathering behind the wall of police officers, then indicated to Dominic to join him.

"Thank you, ladies and gentlemen, for being here today. You may know that my family was involved in the illicit drug trade in Australia and overseas for many years. After coming to terms with the destruction my family's activities were causing in the community, I decided to provide evidence in court against my brother. As a consequence of giving this evidence, I was disowned by my own family and subject to death threats from an international drug cartel. To clear the family's name and disassociate the family from the drug trade forever, I intend to work with the AFP…….."

*

Penny and Sandra mingled amongst the crowd gathered on the footpath at the rear of the media pack, assembled at the bottom of the steps leading to the entrance of police headquarters.

I'll don't like this. There are too many people. It is a recipe for disaster if panic sets into the crowd. In his enthusiasm, Adam was too quick to agree to Carlo's plan. If they come, where will they strike from?

"I'll take the southern end of the crowd towards the traffic barrier, and you take the northern end," directed Penny.

Penny slowly moved through the crowd with a nod towards Sandra. Not distracted by the media lights or the voice coming over the loudspeaker, her eyes continually scanned backwards as she monitored for any potential threat.

"Team, I think I have something you need to be on the lookout for."

"Go ahead, Penny," replied Tanya from her vantage point at the top of the steps.

"There's a man. He looks like a vagrant. He's scruffily dressed in one of those old military-style heavy coats and has curly brown hair," said Penny. "He wandered in just before the start of the proceedings. The unusual thing was that he appeared to be wearing white Air Pods in his ears and had new Nike runners."

"I think I've made him," responded Sandra. "He has started to move more quickly towards the media pack. I reckon he's made me check him out."

"Roger that. Tanya and I will look out for him," responded Adam. "We're moving towards the top of the steps."

"SWAT team prepare for action. We have a possible sighting of our target. Male, dressed like a vagrant wearing an old military-style heavy coat with curly brown hair. He appears to be wearing white Air Pods and new Nike runners. Standby."

*

"Guys, urgent hit the devices now, don't wait," roared Roberto. "The tall bitch with the black ponytail and an Asian bird have seen me and started to move towards me."

Loud explosions shook the area. Smoke began to rise into the sky from both ends of the building. Heads turned, and a wave of panic swept through the crowd as people started to scream and surge in all directions. The police cordon became disorganized and could not control the panic-stricken media pack that moved like a herd of lemmings away from the building entrance.

Penny was pushed back from the building in the rush of people fleeing the scene.

"I can see the target, he's continuing to make his way towards the steps, but I cannot get to him," she shouted into her radio.

In the chaos, Roberto seized the moment. He threaded his way towards the bottom of the steps and saw his primary target. He reached into each deep coat pocket and began to line up his quarry with the guns he pulled out.

Dominic stood next to Carlo, facing the street as Tanya moved in to direct them towards the safety of the building's entrance. Dominic looked at the man striding towards the steps with his guns raised.

It's Roberto, and he's aiming. This is all my fault. Papa, Uncle, Electra. I've fucked up everything I've loved. I can't let this happen to Carlo and Tanya as well.

Both guns fired with a crack as Dominic stepped in front of Carlo and took two bullets in his chest. The force sent him crashing into the back of Carlo, driving them to the ground with a bleeding Dominic lying on top of Carlo.

"Police, do not move," yelled Adam with his weapon raised and pointed at the assailant.

Roberto fired shots into the air creating more panic amongst the screaming crowd, making it impossible with his training for Adam to take a shot. A red Ducati motorcycle pulled up next to the footpath and revved its engine.

Roberto surveyed the scene at the top of the steps and was about to move towards the fallen bodies when he saw the woman with the black ponytail draw a gun from an ankle holster. After hesitating, he rushed towards the throbbing motorcycle and leapt onto the pillion seat. "Let's get the fuck out of here."

Penny calmly raised her pistol and lined up her target, ready to take a shot, when she was joined by Sandra, who knelt beside Penny and began to draw her gun.

In the fraction of a second of distraction from Sandra, a gunshot rang out from Roberto's weapon, shattering the clavicle bone in Sandra's left arm and knocking her onto Penny, taking her off balance. Sandra clutched her arm and instinctively attempted to stem the flow of blood.

Penny supported Sandra in offering assistance and looked up in horror as Roberto took aim and fired another bullet into Sandra before she could raise her weapon. Sandra slammed into Penny, causing Penny to drop her gun.

"Take that bitch," said Roberto as he tucked the gun into the left pocket of his coat as the Ducati roared past the traffic barrier and rapidly accelerated away into the mayhem.

*

"Two suspects, one in black leathers on a red Ducati, headed south on George Street. He's just past the police barrier and made a right turn."

Penny sat on the footpath cradling Sandra's lifeless body that lay limp in her arms.

"Sandra, Sandra," called Penny as she looked down on her unresponsive colleague, with dried blood caking the entrance wound on the side of her head.

Leaving Carlo with Dominic, Tanya briskly approached Penny, knelt beside her and hugged her. Tanya removed her jacket, which she gently placed over Sandra. Tears started to stream down her face.

"Sandra. She saved me. She took the bullet for me," Penny glumly announced. "I will get them if it's the last thing I do."

"Officer down," called in Tanya.

Yes, we're going to get you... No matter how long it takes.

"Call in the chopper now," yelled Adam into his radio. "We need to track the bastard on the motorcycle before he gets to the tunnel entrance."

*

Carlo knelt beside Dominic with blood streaming from his chest.

"Medic. Quick. Please," called out Carlo. "Hold on. Helps coming, cuz. You saved me. Why did you do it?"

Blood began to seep from Dominic's mouth, causing him to cough. He struggled to talk after he coughed again.

"It's all my fault this shit happened. Me and my ideas of being the big boss."

"Save your energy, cuz. The medicos are on their way," said Carlo as he sat beside Dominic and stroked the cradled head in his lap.

"I told Hernando about the heist at the warehouse. It's my fault he sent out that bastard Roberto Rodriguez." Dominic coughed again with dark, red blood dribbling down his chin. "I was at the warehouse when he shot our Papas. I did nothing. You've got to get Hernando. I'm so sorry, cuz."

With a final cough, Dominic's head fell back as he took his last breath.

"Cuz! Cuz!" Carlo yelled as he hugged and then shook Dominic's lifeless form. "I promise you that on my Papa's grave, I make sure they get Hernando and Roberto once and for all.

CHAPTER 25

With Adam attempting to organise the chase down of the escapees, Tanya's priority was to focus on the crime scene. She surveyed the now deserted street surrounding the AFP headquarters entrance. Two ambulances pulled up, sirens sounding and red-blue lights flashing. Paramedics, bags in hand, ready for action, leapt from the vehicles.

Tanya left Penny with Sandra and returned to the top of the stairs, where Carlo was now weeping over the body of Dominic.

OMG. Adam will be in deep trouble for this debacle. They'll want a fall guy once this hits the media.

"Tanya, we've got to get to the control room and track the bastards down. Let's go," yelled a frantic Adam.

With police guards in place and medicos now attending to the fallen bodies, Tanya reluctantly moved to assist Adam. Tanya paused beside Carlo and placed a reassuring hand on his shoulder.

"Carlo, I've got to work with Adam on catching the bastards. So, I'll see you inside shortly. I've assigned an officer to be with you and get you anything you need."

"Chopper-1," called in Adam, "this is HQ-1 over. What's your position? Over."

"HQ-1, we are tracking a red Ducati motorcycle with a pillion passenger that has just entered the Chinatown entrance to the Cross City Tunnel. We have lost visual, and we can't cover all exits. We'll stand by and await further instructions. Out."

"Tanya get us hooked into the Toll Company's live camera feed asap," ordered Adam. "While Tanya co-ordinates the live feed, play me back the CCTV footage of the media conference," said Adam to the panel operator.

"I need you to enhance the images of the suspects and get an APB out," ordered Adam.

"I'll get straight on to it," confirmed the operator.

"It has to be the K-gang," snapped Adam as he pounded his fist into the bench top. "They are Fijians, for sure. The clever bastards created a diversion with the blasts that gave our man Roberto Rodriguez the opportunity to take the shot. I am going to be in deep shit with the Commander after this. Two dead bodies and one an American DEA agent. I will be back pounding the beat if I'm lucky."

"Boss, we've got access to the toll company's live CCTV," exclaimed Tanya. "Come on over. Let's find that bike."

*

The Ducati entered the tunnel and, unable to be tracked by the police chopper, sped towards the airport exit ramp. Taking the exit, Tiko merged with the airport-bound Harbour Tunnel traffic and roared to the agreed rendezvous at the Randwick Road exit. In the emergency lane sat the two SUVs, their hazard lights flashing. Roberto tapped Tiko on the shoulder and pointed towards the waiting vehicles.

With a thumbs up, Tiko pulled over and parked the bike behind the SUVs. Tiko and Roberto dismounted, quickly making their way into separate vehicles and were soon underway to the Randwick Road exit.

It was a short drive from the airport motorway exit to the Surry Hills warehouse. The black cars' engines revved as the drivers waited impatiently at the warehouse entrance, waiting for the heavy steel roller door to squeak and squeal to the top of its journey. With a click of the remote by Malakai, the squeaking and squealing recommenced as the door slowly close behind the cars, now safely housed within the warehouse.

"Get the beers," yelled a jubilant Tiko as he fist-pumped the air. "What a fuckin' rush."

"A fuckin' failure," snapped Roberto. "That fuck wit Dominic took the hit, and I've ended up shootin' a cop. They'll be after us now, so we must lay low. Put on the TV so we can monitor the news reports."

"I can hear a chopper," called Malakai from the front of the building from where he positioned himself to keep a watching eye on the street. "They are scouring the streets looking for us."

"They'll eventually track us down to this area once they start getting access to local toll road CCTV cameras, but it will take a while," noted Roberto. "I suggest we leave here as soon as it's dark. What are our options, Tiko?"

"The boys have plenty of family members here in Sydney to put them up, so they can lay low until things cool down," said Tiko. "For us, I reckon we sneak back into the HOP. With all the girls gone and no Dominic, they won't suspect we have the balls to sneak back in. We can hide out there until we decide what to do next. I'll get one of the guys to check it out for us when they head off tonight."

"Sounds like a plan," agreed Roberto. "I'll speak with Hernando later in the day, given the time difference and give him an update and see what he wants me to do."

*

"There they go," said Adam. "They've taken the airport exit in the tunnel and headed towards the airport. What's that? They are slowing and pulling up next to those two black SUVs. Wait, they are leaving the bike and jumping into the cars. Where's the chopper? Have we got patrols in the area?" Adam barked.

"Once they exited the freeway, we lost them, boss," said Tanya. "I'll get patrols to begin accessing local street CCTV cameras in the area. They must be holed up somewhere in the warehouse district, but hundreds of small facilities are in that area."

*

"Carlo, I think it's time you and Tanya call it a day," said Adam as he slumped into his office chair. "The bastards have gone to ground, and I've got the team working on reviewing CCTV from the warehouse/ factory district where they were last seen. You need to rest and begin afresh in the morning."

"Before we call it a night, I want to know when Papa and Uncle Lorenzo's bodies will be released for their funeral?" Carlo asked. "Mama is desperate to plan the funeral service with Father Alessandro, and I want to finish what I started this morning and show them I have no fear. In addition, I need to arrange a suitable time to speak with the DEA and that English woman. I want to tell them what I know about the Gonzales operation. It is time to revenge Papa's, Lorenzo's and Dominic's deaths and end the Conti name's association with crime."

"There is no way you'll be out speaking to the media in public again, Carlo," Adam stated firmly.

"I'll prepare a press statement if that is OK," said Carlo. "Then I'd ask you to contact the DEA to set up a meeting with them, maybe here in this office tomorrow morning, so you can also hear what I've got to say."

"Get your statement ready, and I'll check it out before you release it to the media. While you're doing that, I'll speak with Agent Sean Pham at the DEA. Given what happened with Agent Wong, I'll see when it will be ok for you to meet with him and Penny, the English lady, in our office tomorrow morning," said Adam as he started to calm down after a long, stress-filled day. "One more thing. I would be a lot happier if the both of you stayed in a hotel tonight, along with an armed guard in attendance."

"What about you, Adam? You should get some rest," noted Carlo. "It's been a tough day for you as well."

"A little bit longer before I call it a night," replied Adam. "I want to see if we can determine where those bastards have gone to ground."

*

"Andy, it's Penny. No doubt you have received the news about the death of Sandra. She was right next to me. I feel terrible as I couldn't get a shot off that may have saved her. She is a hero and deserves full recognition by the DEA."

"I agree, Penny," responded Andy. "How are you holding up in the circumstances?"

"Not too good at the moment, but I want to get my head together and track the cold-blooded killer down," replied Penny. "Carlo Conti has requested a meeting with me at AFP headquarters in the morning, along with Agent Pham. I was told he wants to do all he can to help us destroy the Gonzales organisation. We will attend the AFP's Sydney office meeting and hear what he has to say. I suggest I join you in Washington with Carlo's intel to develop an action plan. I do not want Sandra's life to have been lost in vain."

"OK, you get some rest tonight as best as possible, given the situation, and we'll speak again tomorrow," replied Andy. "I agree. We want to avenge Sandra's death and finish off Gonzales once and for all."

*

"Hernando, it's Roberto. I didn't want to wake you too early, but I wanted to update you on yesterday's events."

"Did you take him out?" Hernando immediately asked.

"His dumb cousin stepped in front of him and took two bullets in the chest. The gutless bastard turned out to be some great martyr," explained Roberto. "By the time I was lining up to take Carlo out, the cops were on to me, and I had to remove one of the scum while getting away."

"Fuck," snapped Hernando. "Taking out a cop, they'll be after you big time. You'll have to make a move to get out of Australia."

"Wait, Hernando. I'll call you back shortly. There's something about Carlo Conti coming up on the local TV news channel," said Roberto as he abruptly terminated the call.

*

Good evening viewers. This is Vanessa Jeffries from the newsroom. We have just received some breaking news from Carlo Conti, the person at the centre of this morning's shootings at the entrance to the AFP headquarters in Sydney.

Carlo Conti stated in a written statement that he was appalled by this morning's murder of his brave cousin Dominic Rossi and a senior agent with the American DEA, Sandra Wong. He says that his family will not be intimidated by this morning's action, and to respect his Mama's wishes, the funeral for his Papa and Uncle will occur in three days at the Our Lady of Mercy Church in Mount Willsmore. In the interest of security, attendance at the funeral will be by invitation only.

CHAPTER 26

At the end of Carlo's announcement, Roberto called Hernando back.

"Unbelievably, it looks like we may get another chance to get that traitorous fuck, Carlo, before I get out of here," said Roberto. "The idiot has announced a family funeral for Gaetano and Lorenzo in three days. That gives me plenty of time to arrange a nice surprise with our remaining explosives in the warehouse."

"No mistakes this time," said Hernando. "Get the job done, then get back home. We've got a business to run."

"They'll be looking for me at the airport and no doubt have the identity I used to enter the country in the system," informed Roberto. "I'll need your help to get out of here as I don't think with facial recognition technology, my other false passports will help in the circumstances."

"OK. I'll speak to Rafael Cortez, the Columbian Ambassador at the embassy in Canberra. We have assisted him with his retirement fund in the past, so he'll be cooperative and get you the passport you need to get out of the country."

"Adios," said Roberto as he terminated the call.

"Everything ok?" Tiko asked.

"I discussed with Senor Gonzales Carlo's announcement we just saw on TV," said Roberto. "He's given me the go-ahead to have another crack at taking out Carlo at the family funeral they just announced."

"We've got some powerful explosives we didn't use today," replied Tiko.

"Will you be OK setting off explosives in a church? Roberto asked.

"Are you kidding?" Tiko replied with a sneer. "I went to a Catholic boy's school, and how those lecherous priests fondled me was disgusting. I am no fan of religion."

Roberto smiled and responded with a thumbs-up.

"Let's get your guys out of here. Make sure you switch to the false number plates. Also, make sure they exit at different ends of the street."

"Ready to help you. Just let me know what I need to do," indicated Tiko as he moved to rustle up his team to get moving.

*

"Sir, I think I've located them," yelled the panel operator. "I've been working through the City Council's footage and have located their movements in the warehouse district."

"Great news," said Adam as he rushed across the room and pulled up a seat in front of the computer screen.

"You'll see from the City Council CCTV; we can follow the two black SUV's up to Philp Street, where they turn right. Philp Street is only short, and the camera at the other end of the street does not pick them up exiting the street," explained the operator. "I've checked the neighbourhood and noted one old warehouse with a To Let sign on the front. All the other buildings are occupied. I'll bet that has to be their hideout."

"Good work. Let's fire up the SWAT team," Adam said as he returned to his office to grab his Kevlar vest.

*

With the K-gang members gone, Tiko and Roberto were the only two cohort members remaining in the warehouse. Tiko's mobile rang, and they listened to a report from Jioji. Jioji confirmed that there was no cop presence at the HOP premises in Kings Cross.

"Jioji reports the HOP is all in darkness," said Tiko. "No cops are guarding the building, and there is just some blue and white checked tape stuck across the front door and fluttering around at the entrance to the carpark."

"Looks like we are good to go," said Roberto. "We better get out of here asap. Those cops will surely be trying to track us down, and CCTV is no friend of ours."

Tiko packed the saddle bags on the second Ducati with the remaining explosives, guns and ammunition. With a final check of the building, they roared out of the warehouse and were on their way to the HOP, the steel roller graunching its way to a close.

*

The police closed off each end of Philp Street, and the police chopper was hovering in the immediate vicinity with infra-red scanners in operation. An armoured SWAT vehicle entered each end of the street, and the squad of black-uniformed team members streamed out the rear of the vehicles with guns raised. The team began to move into pre-assigned locations at the front and rear of the warehouse.

"Are you in position?" Adam asked over two-way.

"Affirmative," came the quick reply from the SWAT's Sergeant Ray Collens. "Ready to go at your command, sir."

"Go! Go!" Adam roared, initiating an explosion that ripped the small door to the side of the roller door off its hinges.

Adam stood over the road from the entrance and watched as he heard voices yelling, the bang of concussion grenades and lights flashing in the building. After a few minutes, a voice came over the radio.

"Building, all clear. No one present."

After re-holstering his gun, Adam briskly stepped across the road and into the building. "Did you find anything helpful?" he asked.

Sergeant Collens indicated that at the warehouse's rear, they only found a pile of empty pizza boxes, bottles of beer, and some motor vehicle number plates. A small TV set was still warm.

"Fuck it. We must have just missed them, "exclaimed Adam as he kicked at a pizza box. "Better get the forensic team here to check for prints and DNA."

*

"Good morning Penny, Agent Pham. Sorry to meet you in such circumstances," greeted Adam as the guests entered the meeting room. "Ah, here's Tanya and Carlo."

"You look exhausted, Adam," stated a concerned Tanya as she entered the room.

"Yes, we located where the gang was hiding out and raided the place last night," explained Adam, ignoring Tanya's comment. "Unfortunately, we missed them but are still trying to track them down. Anyway, everyone, take a seat."

"Yesterday's events shattered us, and you have the full support of the DEA in helping to capture these guys," said Penny. "To that end, we want to dial-in Agent Andy Carter in Washington. Even though it is late at night, he's standing by for our call."

"Thanks for your support," noted Adam. "Please call him."

"Good evening Andy, I'm here at AFP HQ with DCI Adam Charles, DS Tanya Layton, Agent Sean Pham and Carlo Conti," greeted Penny.

After a recap of the previous day's events, including Dominic Rossi's and Agent Wong's deaths, Carlo got out of his seat.

"I want to revenge for the murder of my family members and Agent Wong. There's a lot I can share with you about the Gonzales operation in Columbia. I have visited their laboratories and can provide detailed descriptions of locations, security and the like."

"That's certainly well outside the AFP's jurisdiction," noted Adam.

"Rather than trying to arrange videoconferences across multiple time zones, I recommend we fly Carlo to Washington with me," Penny suggested. "We can keep Carlo in DC as long as necessary."

"I agree. We should get Carlo here immediately. Gonzales may start to relocate his facilities, with Carlo still alive and looking for revenge, so we need to plan to strike," stated Andy.

"All I need is a couple of days to help arrange and attend my Papa's and Uncle's funeral, then I'm all yours," said Carlo as he resumed his seat. "I'm committed to helping you get Hernando Gonzales."

"That would be perfect," replied Andy. "That will give me time to arrange to get you here safely and get a team together to meet with you."

"I saw that funeral plans for Gaetano and Lorenzo were announced on the news channel this morning. Was that wise?" Penny asked. "Won't that provide Roberto another chance to strike?"

"A valid observation Penny," replied Adam. "We have allowed three days before the funeral to plan the security arrangements. Access will be strictly limited, and we will have a massive police presence. Roberto will not be able to get anywhere near the church."

*

The exhaust on the Ducati rumbled as Tiko and Roberto slowly rode past the frontage of the HOP, cautiously scrutinising for any unwanted activity. There was no police presence as expected, apart from strips of the police's chequered tape flapping in the breeze. Tiko turned off the bike's headlight and rolled down into the carpark. He parked behind the rear staircase, hiding the motorcycle from anyone passing by in the street.

The men laden with the saddle bags quietly tip-toed up the stairs and slowly turned the door handle. It was locked, but the lock showed little resistance against Tiko's heavy riding boot. They stepped past the splintered door and into the corridor, partially illuminated by the streetlight from the small window located above the frosted front door of the building. They entered the office, closed the door and closed the curtains. Roberto flicked the switch with a nod to Tiko, and the fluorescent lighting flickered into life.

Papers were strewn everywhere, and furniture was overturned due to the police raid. Tiko commenced re-setting the furniture as Roberto moved to plug in his laptop computer, the absent office PC likely removed to scour for evidence.

"See if there are any beers in the storeroom fridge," said Roberto as he booted up his machine. "The cops may have left us a few."

"Not likely," laughed Tiko as he headed to the storeroom. "Don't ever get between a cop and a free beer."

Roberto began scanning the search engine for information, *Our Lady of*

Mercy Church, Mount Willsmore. Here we are, Church Street, Mount Willsmore. Parish Priest Father Alessandro Mancini. He made a note of the priest's mobile telephone number.

"You're right," said Tiko with a laugh. "The thievin' cops only left some bottles of water."

In one go, Roberto drained the contents of his 500ml bottle.

"I've found the church where Carlo indicated the funeral service would be held. We only stay here tonight in case of some curious passers-by, and then we head out to Mount Willsmore early in the morning. We can grab a couple of motel rooms out that way and visit the priest tomorrow. That will give us a couple of days to set something up before the cops start thinking about security for the funeral." Roberto looked at his watch, "it is a little late, but I'll get you to give the priest a call and ask to meet with him first thing in the morning."

Roberto showed Tiko the number he had written down, and he dialled the number. After several rings, an irritated-sounding voice answered just as Tiko was about to terminate the call.

"Father Alessandro. How can I help you?"

"Apologies Father, I know it is getting late. My name is Isikeli Waqa. My wife and I recently arrived to live in Australia from Fiji with our baby son. We plan to live in Mount Willsmore, close to some family and keen to have our son christened as soon as possible."

"Pray tell, why the urgency and for the call at this hour?" Father Alessandro asked.

"My mother and father are visiting from Fiji and have been called today about the death of a close relative and need to return to Fiji to attend the funeral. Would it be possible to meet with you in the morning to discuss what could be arranged at such short notice? I am sure we can help the church with a donation to help your work."

Tiko heard the rustle of some pages before Father Alessandro answered, sounding less irritated, "Yes, I can see you first thing at 9 am. I will be in the office located behind the altar. The main church doors will be unlocked."

"Father, very much appreciated. See you then."

CHAPTER 27

As the first rays of sunlight began to awaken the people of Sydney, Tiko and Roberto were on the road on the Ducati. They were making good time heading out to Sydney's western suburbs, travelling against the never-ending convoy of workers streaming towards the city. With fuel running low, they exited the main road and pulled into a service centre, offering a gas station and a Burger King next door.

Over their breakfast bacon and egg muffin, they re-checked the directions on their mobile's map application. "OK, this is where we are and here's the Mount Willsmore exit off the westbound M31. The Westward Ho Motel is five hundred metres from the exit, and the church is on the next street. The website indicated there are vacancies for tonight," detailed Roberto.

"Let's see if we can get an early check-in so we can drop off the saddle bags before I head off to the church to meet with the priest," suggested Tiko. "I think it best I go alone to keep the meeting simple and don't have to explain who's my friend with the Latino accent."

"Yes, that makes sense," replied Roberto. "Let's finish our breakfast and see if we can get an early check-in."

*

The throbbing engine of the Ducati caused the motel clerk to look up from his desk, where he was reading the newspaper and sipping on a coffee. He watched as the two men dismounted and removed their helmets.

They seem an odd pair.....one an islander, the other some European.

With helmets in hand, the pair stepped into the reception area. "Any chance for an early check-in?" Roberto asked. "We've got a meeting this morning, and it would be great to freshen up before the meeting."

"Let me see, I can do you an early check-in, but only one room is available," advised the motel clerk as he scanned his computer screen. "It has two separate double beds if that is ok."

Roberto looked at Tiko and nodded, and smiled. "We'll take it," said Roberto.

Tiko rode the motorcycle across the carpark to the allocated room and unloaded the saddlebags while Roberto opened the door, his nose detecting the scent of lavender air freshener.

"Pretty basic. Certainly not the Hilton," noted Roberto as he stood in the doorway and scanned the room.

As you entered, a luggage rack was immediately on the right wall, next to a small closet constructed of dark, lightweight laminated timber, with double sliding doors which seemed to stick when you tried to slide them. Continuing down the right-hand side wall was a bench top in matching timber that housed a small wicker tray, home to an electric jug and various sachets of tea and coffee. Underneath the bench was a small bar fridge that revealed a jug of water and some pods of long-life milk upon inspection.

The two double beds were covered in luminescent light green covers and sat on a dark-grey carpet. From the look of various spots and stains, the carpet hid a multitude of spillages and other indiscretions accumulated over some years.

"It should be only for one night if we get everything in place tonight," said Tiko as he joined Roberto in the room and placed the bags on the luggage rack.

*

As agreed, Tiko left Roberto at the motel and set off to meet with the priest, Father Alessandro. Exiting the motel, Tiko turned left and then turned into Church Street. Immediately to the left was Our Lady of Mercy Primary School. There was plenty of activity that morning, with parents dropping off their precious cargo in the ubiquitous SUVs. Tiko proceeded slowly past the school and entered the driveway leading up to the church's front door.

The church appeared to be relatively modern, constructed in granite-coloured bricks. Above the wide, mahogany, double entrance doors was a towering steeple featuring multi-coloured glass panels, topped off by a black metal crucifix. Tiko parked the Ducati in front of the doors and removed his helmet, placing it under his left arm as he walked towards the entrance. He pushed against the left door, which swung easily open.

The bright morning sun streamed into the building through a large stained-glass window of the Last Supper at the far end of the church. A central aisle ran between 20 rows of pews on either side, leading up to several stairs where communion was served in front of the altar. Tiko walked down the aisle towards the sign OFFICE but paused at the end of the aisle to perform the sign of the cross.

I better do the old knee bend if the priest is watching me.

The door was ajar, so Tiko could see Father Alessandro making handwritten notes on a document on his desk. He tapped on the door, causing Father Alessandro to look up.

"Isikeli, I presume," said Father Alessandro as he greeted his visitor.

Tiko froze when the Father called him Isikeli and then gathered himself.

"Yes, sorry, Father."

Focus, you idiot.

"Take a seat and tell me how can I help you," said the Father.

"As I mentioned last night, my family has recently moved to Australia, and we had originally planned to come with the whole family and meet you after mass one Sunday," explained Tiko. "Last night, we had an unexpected call from Fiji. Due to a family bereavement, the call makes it necessary for my parents to return home immediately. We want to hold the christening before they go home."

"I have a fairly business schedule over the next few days, regrettably with a large double funeral. When were you thinking of having the christening?" Father Alessandro asked.

"Our hope would be in two days, at around 10 am," said Tomasi. "After the ceremony, I will arrange to take my parents to the airport for their flight to Fiji."

"I am so sorry, but I have a clash with the funeral I mentioned at that time and day. I could squeeze a christening in tomorrow morning, then I would need the afternoon to prepare for the funeral," offered Father.

"I'll check with the family, but I am afraid with other family commitments before they depart, tomorrow may not be suitable," said Tiko. "My parents will have to miss out as I don't think they'll be able to afford to return for some time. I'll get back to you by this afternoon to see if we can move some things around."

"Either way, I look forward to welcoming you and your family to the parish in the not-too-distant future, along with a future student for the primary school," said Father Alessandro with a smile.

*

An eager Roberto greeted Tiko when he returned to the motel room.

"Were you able to confirm the funeral is on?"

"Day after tomorrow for 10 am," confirmed Tiko, nodding. "We should be able to get in and out of the church relatively easily, as the front door has basic locks, and there was no security system I could detect. In this close community, there are not too many problems with break-ins in the local parish church. The front row pews where the family would sit are very close to the steps leading up to the altar where the coffins would be placed."

"We could place the explosives under the steps, factoring the blast to discharge towards the front row seats," added Roberto. 'We can get in and out tonight before they consider engaging security for the funeral. We can be long gone with the timers set for 10.15 on the day. You'll be flying back to Fiji, and me in Canberra at the Columbian Embassy. I am getting a hard-on just thinking about the splattered bodies."

"OK then," said Tiko. "Let's put out the *Do Not Disturb* sign and prepare the devices."

*

After enjoying the *All, You Can Eat Buffet* at the nearby New Peking Chinese Restaurant. It was late evening before Tiko and Roberto returned to their motel room, their hunger sated. They checked for other motel guests wandering around the grounds, loaded the saddlebags onto the Ducati and set off to the church.

The church was in darkness as they made several passes up and down the street. With no police presence evident, Roberto gave Tiko a thumbs up as the motorcycle crunched its way up the gravelly driveway. They stopped in front of the doors, where Roberto unloaded. Without speaking, Roberto indicated for Tiko to move the bike into some bushes to the right of the building.

By the time Tiko rejoined Roberto, the door was open, and they were inside, locking the door behind them. They stopped and listened carefully for any activity within the building. With a nod, they switched on their torches, proceeded to the altar steps, and began unpacking.

"Shit," exclaimed Roberto as headlights shone through the side windows. The music pulsing from the vehicle that pulled up in front of the church entrance stopped as the engine was turned off.

"Over there into the confessionals," whispered Roberto as they gathered their load and scuttled in behind the curtained booth.

"I left my torch on the step," whispered Tiko.

"Shhh," indicated Roberto, placing his finger on his lips.

"I won't be long, Mildred," someone called out as the main church lights began to glow. "I left my wallet on my desk. I want to pay you for the floral displays you prepared for the funeral so I can invoice the Conti family."

"It's the fucking priest," Tiko whispered.

The metal-plated torch stuck like a sore thumb on the red-carpeted step. However, with the Father's focus on quickly retrieving his wallet, he was in and out of the building, unaware of the danger lurking in the confessional. With the music fired up in the car and the crunch of the tyres on the driveway, the assassins re-emerged to complete their handiwork.

With a knife, Roberto removed the carpet at each end of the small staircase and prepared the devices. He set the timers for a countdown of 36 hours, culminating in detonation at 10.15 on the morning of the funeral. With the carpet carefully replaced, they packed up, then hurriedly exited the building and re-locked the door after a quick check for anything left behind.

"After that, I think we deserve a drink," said Roberto as Tiko hit the electronic starter on the bike, and they headed to the local bottle shop for a six-pack of beer.

"You reckon explosives is the way to go?" Tiko asked as he clinked his bottle next to Roberto's. "Cheers!"

"I didn't see we had much of an option without a rifle," replied Roberto. "With the likelihood of beefed-up heavy security, there is no way we would get anywhere near the funeral service to enable me to take a shot with a handgun. Using explosives was the best option without a sniper rifle. The bombs will take out both front rows and whoever stands on the stairs. Carlo Conti will join his Papa, leaving no more fuckin' Contis."

"After finishing the beers, we better get some sleep as we have a big day tomorrow," noted Roberto. "We'll book an Uber to get you to the airport for the flight to Fiji, and I'll ride the bike down to Canberra and leave it at the embassy. The ambassador can arrange to dump it."

With the food and beers consumed, Roberto and Tiko slept soundly, awakened by the alarm on Tiko's mobile. Tiko boiled the jug and made a couple of instant coffees.

"My God, that is awful shit." Roberto grimaced after taking a sip. "Do people drink this shit? You better hurry up, shower and get ready for your Uber pick-up, Tiko."

"I've got nothing to check in at the airport," said a freshened Tiko after emerging from the bathroom. "I'll get the Uber to stop at the local shops on the way to the airport and pick up a small carry-on bag with a few bits and pieces, so I don't look out of place. Working with you, Roberto has been pretty scary, but wow, what a ride it has been. I look forward to welcoming you back to Fiji to start this business and continue working together."

"Yes, it has been great working with you, man, and I am sure Hernando will contact you shortly regarding the next steps. I look forward to watching the explosion on the TV tomorrow morning. I will give you a call to detail the body count."

A horn blast heralded the arrival of the Uber, and with a bear hug, Tiko was on his way to the airport. Roberto settled the room account, and while they were a little large for him, he donned Tiko's black leathers for the three-hour ride to the capital Canberra and the Columbian Embassy haven.

*

"Father Alessandro, this is Detective Layton from the Australian Federal Police," Carlo introduced Tanya with a smile. "She's lookin' after me, given the trouble the other day."

"Pleased to meet you, Tanya," Father said as he grasped her right hand in both hands. "Look after him. I've known him since he was a boy. I suppose you want to make arrangements for the funeral service tomorrow."

"Yes, Father," answered Carlo. "With the planned security, we have to restrict the service to guests only, and there will be a heavy police presence around the church."

"We nearly had a conflict for tomorrow," laughed Father. "Had some Fijian man I hadn't met before, wanting to arrange a christening at short notice. Some sort of family emergency back in Fiji. He's not called me back, so I presume he no longer wants the christening to be held."

"A Fijian man, you say," said Tanya. "Excuse me, Father. I need to make an urgent call." Tanya left Carlo to talk to Father Alessandro about the arrangements and stepped to the front of the church to call Adam.

"Adam, it's Tanya. I'm out at the church in Mount Willsmore with Carlo," said a concerned Tanya. "The priest mentioned that some Fijian man turned up at the church yesterday. Sounds like too big a coincidence to me."

"Get Carlo back into protective custody as a priority, and given the information you've received, we can discuss alternatives to tomorrow's arrangements with him," ordered Adam. "We can't afford a repeat of the media conference. I'm in deep shit as it is with the Commissioner. I hear he will order an enquiry in what he described as embarrassing to the force."

CHAPTER 28

"It appears our Roberto Rodriguez has gone to ground along with his Fijian mates," observed Adam as he sat in his office with Tanya. "What about those four Fijians who activated the explosions at the rubbish bins? Any ID on them, or the guy on Ducati?"

"The rider of the Ducati was pretty well covered up in his riding gear; helmet, gloves and leathers. Couldn't identify him," replied Tanya. "The other news from the Kings Cross station's patrol was that people had been in the House of Pleasure overnight. The rear door kicked in, and a light was left on inside."

"Shit," exclaimed Adam. "We should've had someone observing the place. The Super is not going to be happy."

"Who would've thought they were brazen enough to go back there," noted Tanya. "We now need to be on the lookout for Roberto at all exit points, as he'll no doubt want to get out of the country with us on his trail."

"You're right. I'll give Sam Rogers at Border Force a call," said Adam as he began to check his phone contacts and dialled the number.

"Senior Inspector Sam Rogers," came the quick answer.

"Sam, Adam Charles from AFP. I need your help."

"No problem. What can I do for you?" Sam answered.

"You helped us track that person who entered the country under Enrico Sanchez. We now know he is a Columbian Roberto Rodriguez and believe he'll be trying to flee the country after being involved in a couple of killings, including an American DEA agent," explained Adam.

"Yes, he's been all over the news," noted Sam. "Everything will be set up at our end to nail him. We have his image in our facial recognition system, and I'll keep you informed of any developments."

"Thanks, Sam. I appreciate your help."

*

"Andy, sorry it's late," said Penny, "but I thought I would update you, as we have the Conti family funeral later today."

"Good morning Penny," answered Andy. "It was terrible news about the shootings. It is good you can attend the funeral service."

"As we discussed, Andy, I want to get Carlo to Washington as soon as possible after the funeral and as safely as possible," noted Penny. "To that end, Agent Sean Pham has come up with an idea for us to get a US Air Force flight into Australia's Richmond Air Force Base near Sydney. Then we can safely fly him to the US rather than risk using commercial airlines."

"A good suggestion," said Andy. "I'm sure I can arrange something out of Hawaii or Guam and get you both to DC."

"I will speak with Carlo straight after the service and get the AFP to continue to ensure his safety while you and Sean firm up the travel arrangements," said Penny.

I can hardly wait to see you again, Andy. Maybe we can have a little one-on-one time?

*

Roberto smiled as he throttled back on the Ducati on approach to the sentry guarding the driveway entrance to the Columbian Embassy. The large Embassy building had been easy to find with his Map App, tucked behind the Australian Federal Parliament House.

High white painted stucco walls surrounded the embassy compound. The walls protected a central, two-level complex, also constructed in white stucco style walls and topped by distinctive orange terracotta tiles. A broad verandah ran around each level of the building.

"Buenos Dias," said Roberto as he greeted the security guard and handed him his Columbian passport. "I am Senor Roberto Rodriguez, and I have an appointment to meet with Ambassador Cortez."

"Un memento," said the guard as he turned and entered his tinted, bullet-proof glass enclosed watch-house. After exchanging words on his telephone, he returned with the heavy steel door slowly rolling open behind him. "Follow the driveway around to the rear of the building where the Ambassador's PA, Senor Ramos, will meet you."

Roberto rode slowly to the rear of the building and dismounted. He removed his helmet and unzipped the leathers. A tallish man, immaculately presented with slicked back hair, wearing a black suit, white shirt, thin black tie and polished, pointy black shoes approached.

"Buenos Dias, Senor Rodriguez," I am Senor Ramos, Mister Ambassador's PA. If you follow me, I will take you to your room. After your journey, I am sure you would like to freshen up before you meet Ambassador Cortez. In the wardrobe in your assigned room, there is a range of clothes for you to choose from. You should find something suitable in your size."

"Muchos gracias, Senor Ramos," replied Roberto as he stepped in behind his host and followed him to his room.

The room was housed in the staff accommodation wing of the embassy and decorated in a basic Spanish hacienda style. Entry was via a thick, heavy dark-timbered door, opening into a relatively plain room with a grey tiled floor. On the far wall was a double bed, and to its right, a partially opened door exposed a wash basin, above which sat a small mirrored cupboard. To the left was a sliding glass door leading out onto the verandah that wrapped around the entire first-floor level of the building. Next to the balcony door was a massive timber wardrobe with a central mirrored-glass panel.

"I will call back in 30 minutes, Senor and take you to meet the Ambassador," said the PA as he turned and left the room, gently closing the door behind him.

Roberto noticed towels and washcloths on the end of the bed, then wandered over to the wardrobe. The right-hand side had a series of drawers containing underwear, shorts, T-shirts and the like, with the left-hand side had a range of shirts, trousers on coat hangers and footwear propped up and a rack at the base of the wardrobe. Roberto selected a semi-formal look with a white long-sleeve shirt, dress jeans and a pair of pointy, black lace-up shoes. Precisely 30 minutes later, after a tap on the door, Roberto was escorted to Ambassador Cortez's office.

Senor Ramos knocked on the office door and ushered Roberto inside, leaving him alone with the Ambassador.

"Greetings Senor Rodriguez. You come highly recommended by my good friend Hernando," said the Ambassador as he stood and walked over. "Take a seat," he said, directing Roberto to a dark Chesterfield-style sofa. "Help yourself to some water or coffee."

"Thank you, Mister Ambassador," said Roberto as he sat and looked around the traditional office. Fawn-coloured carpet, with a classic glossy, dark wooden desk, home to the Columbian coat of arms on the front. Behind the high-backed leather, matching Chesterfield-style chair sat a tall, glass-fronted bookcase with various Spanish and English titles.

After some informal chit-chat about family and what was happening back home in Columbia, Senor Cortez got down to business.

"I understand from Senor Hernando that you have been working on some important business for him here in Australia and may have encountered some issues with the authorities that could make it difficult for you to leave the country."

"That is an excellent summary of the situation Senor," observed Roberto, not adding any additional information.

"I further understand you entered the country under a different name, and there is the likelihood that officials will be looking for someone using that identity wanting to leave Australia," added the Ambassador.

"You are well informed, Senor," answered Roberto. "How can you help me to get back home?"

"What we will do, is issue you with a Columbian Diplomatic Passport under a new name. We will avoid using your real name in case officials have tracked down your real identity," stated Senor Cortez. "I am heading up to Sydney at 11 am tomorrow for dinner with the Australian Trade Minister tomorrow night, and you can travel in the embassy car with me. We have booked you on a QANTAS flight to Santiago, Chile, that departs at 4 pm. I will come to the airport with you and stay with you until they board the flight to ensure there are no problems with any officials at the airport."

"I am indebted to you, Senor," said Roberto.

"Glad to be of assistance," responded Cortez. "Hernando has been very good to my family and me over the years, and I am very happy to help. I now need to get back to work and will leave you in the hands of Senor Ramos until tomorrow morning."

Ambassador Cortez crossed to his desk and pressed a buzzer, bringing Senor Ramos back into the office. "Ramos, please take Senor Rodriguez with you and complete the formalities for his new diplomatic passport, including registration with the Australian Department of Foreign Affairs, as Julio Martinez."

Ramos introduced Roberto to an official who prepared him for his passport photo. The official with a make-up kit slightly changed Roberto's appearance, giving him an older look. Grey streaks were incorporated into the hairline around the ears, and a caterpillar-like moustache was affixed to the top lip. Roberto looked into a hand-held mirror with a smile on his face.

"I like it."

On the way to his room, Ramos led Roberto to a small lounge area, a wide, narrow room enclosed by two large frosted glass sliding doors. To the right-hand end were four small square wooden tables with two wooden chairs at the end table. Against the wall was a large matching buffet, home to an espresso machine with utensils and condiments suitable for meal service. The left-hand end had two large three-seater couches around a low glass-topped coffee table with a shelf, home to a range of Spanish language magazines and newspapers. A large 65-inch Samsung TV was wall-mounted above a cabinet, housing a DVD player and a selection of DVDs.

"This is the guests' lounge," informed Senor Ramos. "Dinner will be served here at 6 pm and breakfast tomorrow morning from 7 am. A TV and a DVD player with some recent Spanish language films are in the corner."

With everyone else apparently on important diplomatic duties, Roberto was left to his own devices and had a quiet evening in the lounge. A range of tapas was enjoyed with a bottle of Argentinian Malbec, followed by a popular Spanish television crime series, *Hierro*. After finishing the bottle of wine, he retired for the night, full of expectation for the explosion timed at 10.15 the next morning.

Hasta la vista Carlo.

*

After calling housekeeping, Roberto rose early and discovered an in-house gym in the basement. The standard gym equipment – treadmill, cycle, cross-trainer, a barbell with an assortment of weights and some hand weights, all looked relatively new.

It doesn't look like the place is used very much. Roberto started his routine by warming up on the rowing machine.

Warmed up, Roberto pounded away at a brisk pace on the treadmill and worked up a good sweat. After cooling down, he returned to his room and showered. Refreshed, he packed some clothes and toiletries into the small carry-on bag provided by Senor Ramos, ready to depart Sydney Airport with Ambassador Cortez. After packing, Roberto headed to the lounge area, ready for breakfast.

He devoured a fresh, cut fruit and freshly squeezed orange juice plate, then ordered Spanish-style scrambled eggs. Eggs sprinkled with shaved Manchego cheese served on rustic bread. Roberto checked his watch and noted it was just after 10 am and, full of anticipation, poured himself a coffee and headed over to the lounge section. He sat down, retrieved the coffee table remote, and selected the Channel 12 news channel.

Roberto noted it was 10.20 with the regular morning variety program screening. Agitated and waiting for news of the explosion, he stood to go and refill his coffee when he heard an urgent bulletin.

This is Vanessa Jeffries from the Channel 12 newsroom. We have just received breaking news that a suspected bomb blast has occurred in The Our Lady of Mercy Catholic Church in Western Sydney's suburb of Mount Willsmore. Channel 12 has been advised that the church was to have been the venue for the Conti Family's funerals this morning. Due to a security alert, the funeral service was changed overnight to Sydney's Ryde Cemetery chapel. Regrettably, church officials have confirmed that a parishioner cleaning the church was killed in the blast. Her name will be released after the family has been informed.

"Fuck, fuck" screamed Roberto in rage as he stood and hurled the remote at the screen, then slumped into a lounge chair.

"Is everything OK?" Senor Ramos asked as he entered the lounge.

"What time do we head to the airport?" said Roberto as he stood and stormed past Ramos on the way back to his room.

"Wait, Senor," called out a surprised Ramos. "Your new passport and flight tickets are on your bed. I will check your appearance to ensure everything is ok before you head down to the car."

Roberto stopped and turned.

"Apologies for being so rude, Senor Ramos. I had just received some bad news. My boss will not be happy."

*

"Another body to add to the death toll of that bloody Columbian," snapped Adam. "The Chief Super is going ape-shit. He's had the Minister of Justice berating him, and the press coverage is looking for blood. He's certainly looking for a scapegoat, and you know who it will be."

"Don't worry. We'll get him. He's still in the country," responded Tanya. "At least the last of the Conti men is safe with the venue change. They have to give you credit for that. You saved many lives. Your gut instincts were correct about the coincidence of a Fijian turning up to the church."

"Might buy me a little time with the boss," said Adam. "We have got to keep Carlo safe until we can get him on to that flight to the US, and we have to catch that blasted Columbian before he causes any more chaos."

*

The Ambassador was waiting for Roberto in the car as he wheeled his bag up to the waiting black Mercedes sedan and handed the piece of luggage over to the driver. Roberto joined the Ambassador in the back seat, and the driver closed the door.

"I hear you were upset this morning Roberto," probed Ambassador Cortez.

"Yes, I am sorry, but I received some bad news from back home, so it will be good if I am on my way back this evening," replied Roberto. "Thank you again for your hospitality which is very much appreciated."

"I see you have a new look," said the Ambassador with a smile.

"Senor Ramos has done an excellent job," replied Roberto.

The rest of the drive to Sydney was in relative silence, with the Ambassador busy on various calls and studying a pile of documents he had extracted from his briefcase. Roberto amused himself by reading The Australian newspaper he retrieved from the pocket behind the driver's seat.

With the Ambassador busy reviewing his documents, there was little conversation, inducing Roberto to doze. He was suddenly awakened when the driver announced they would arrive at the International Airport in approximately 15 minutes. His heart rate began to increase in anticipation of what awaited him at the airport. He looked at the Ambassador, who smiled, nodding reassuringly as he reached across to squeeze Roberto's arm.

CHAPTER 29

The Mercedes pulled up before the QANTAS international check-in counters entrance just after 2 pm. The driver reached the curbside and opened the Ambassador's door. Roberto slid across the back seat and stood beside the Ambassador on the curb while the driver retrieved his small carry-on bag from the car's boot.

Roberto followed Ambassador Cortez up to the First-Class check-in counter, where the Ambassador presented his credentials to the female staff member. "My colleague will be flying Business-Class today to Santiago, and I would like to take him into the Chairman's Lounge before departure. We have some important matters to discuss."

"Just a moment, Mister Ambassador, while I make arrangements," the woman replied and then began to make some calls to gain the necessary authorisations for the non-travelling VIP Ambassador to access the air-side of the airport.

The normally calm Roberto started to fidget, invoking a stern look from Senor Cortez.

"Sorry, Senor," said Roberto trying to relax.

"That will be fine, Mister Ambassador. The Senior Immigration Officer will meet you just before the security checkpoint and take you both through. Is there any luggage to check, Mister Martinez?"

"No, thank you, I only have my carry-on bag."

The QANTAS staff member handed Roberto his boarding pass, and with the

Ambassador headed to clear immigration formalities. The Senior Immigration Officer greeted the Ambassador with a nod and then personally escorted the duo through the clearance process.

"I am sure you know how to get to the lounge Mister Ambassador," said the Officer. "When you are ready to leave, just ask for me at the Service Desk, and I will escort you back to your car."

Roberto began to relax in the lounge with a coffee. "Thank you, Ambassador Cortez, for your assistance. I am certain to mention to Senor Hernando the help you have provided. I expect he will convey his gratitude to you in the usual way."

"A pleasure to help Roberto. I see the flight is starting to board, so let me escort you to your gate, and then I will leave. Please pass my best wishes to Hernando and let him know I will catch up with him for dinner when I am next in Bogota," said the Ambassador.

*

"Hey Sam, take a look at this," said the security officer.

"What is it, Stefan?" asked Sam Rogers, the senior Border Force officer on duty, as he wandered over to Stefan's CCTV screen.

"I have about a 60 to 70 per cent hit on facial recognition with that guy talking to the Senior Immigration Office (SIO). It's with the person the AFP has asked us to be on the lookout for with the names of Enrico Sanchez or Roberto Rodriguez."

"The SIO has escorted him and his associate straight through the barrier and bypassed security," noted Sam. "Who's the older guy with him? He must be a VIP. I better speak to the SIO."

"Colin speaking," answered the SIO on his two-way.

"Colin, it's Sam Rogers. Those two men you ushered passed security, who were they?"

"That Sam was the Columbian Ambassador Cortez and one of his senior staff members, a Senor Martinez. The fellow Martinez is flying out to Santiago, and the flight is now being called for boarding. Is there a problem?"

"Thanks, Colin, I'll get back to you," replied Sam as he terminated the call and began to scroll through his contacts for Adam Charles.

"Get onto QANTAS and get them to hold the flight until we give them the all-clear."

*

"Adam, it's Sam Rogers at the airport. We have a partial match for your Enrico Sanchez or Roberto Rodriguez. His appearance is slightly different. He has grey hair and a thick moustache, making me think he may have altered his appearance."

"Are you sure?" Adam asked.

"It's about a 60 to 70 per cent hit on facial recognition, which is enough for us to investigate further," Sam answered.

"Can you hold him?" Adam queried. "I can be at the airport in half an hour."

"We have a big problem and a potential major diplomatic issue if we try to detain him. The man is travelling as a Julio Martinez with a Columbian diplomatic passport. The Columbian Ambassador is with him. We would have to get approval from the Department of Foreign Affairs."

"Is there anything we can do?" Adam pressed.

"We've had QANTAS delay the flight, and they are not happy because after 15 minutes, they incur penalties, and we don't have 100 per cent surety on the ID," replied Sam. "Without anything more concrete, I will have to let him go."

Sam watched as Roberto presented his boarding pass to the flight attendant, who greeted his VIP passenger with a smile and welcomed him aboard. The Ambassador gave a final wave and returned to the Service Desk to be escorted out of the building.

"Sam, can you send me his photo and passport details?" Adam requested. "I'll see what I can do with Foreign Affairs about getting the Chilean Government to check him out on arrival in Santiago and detain him."

"I don't like your chances without a positive ID and him holding a diplomatic passport," replied Sam. "Anyway, I'll get the info straight away."

*

When the flight attendant re-opened the cabin door, Roberto finally relaxed in his business class seat with a pre-takeoff glass of Veuve Clicquot. His mind began to race.

Are they coming for me now that the Ambassador has gone? What are my options? He retrieved his mobile phone from his shirt pocket and started to boot it up, ready to call the Ambassador.

A Border Force officer stepped into the cabin, spoke with the flight attendant, and handed her a document.

"Would Mister Dimotsos please press your call button?" the flight attendant announced. "You left your passport in the departure lounge."

The officer turned and exited the aircraft as the flight attendant headed down the aircraft with a passport in hand for the errant traveller.

Roberto drained his glass of champagne and signalled to the attendant for a refill. With the aircraft now on pushback, Roberto eased back into the seat and thought,

"Carlo Conti, I will still get you for as long as it takes."

*

Adam's phone rang on his desk, and he noted the number.

Just what I need, Chief Superintendent (CS) Norton calling me. This can't be good news.

"Adam, it's James. Please come up to my office."

The Chief Super's office was on the top floor of the AFP's headquarters, next to the Chief Commissioner's office and other senior officials, including the Chief Legal Officer and Media Liaison Officer. The floor was bathed in sunlight from the glass-panelled office's floor-to-ceiling windows surrounding a central reception desk.

Adam made his way to the receptionist. "DCI Charles for CS Norton."

"He's expecting you, so please go straight in," she directed.

Adam tapped on the door and then entered. The CS was focused on some paperwork and, without looking up, pointed to the chair on the opposite side of his desk, pen in hand. Adam felt uncomfortable in the silence as a bead of sweat slowly trickled down his spine. *Come on, get it over with.*

Finally, the CS placed his pen down and looked at Adam with the intense look of someone who had been in the police force for over 20 years.

"I'll get straight to the point, Adam. The Chief Commissioner (CC) has been under intense media pressure given the loss of three lives with the Carlo Conti fiasco, including an American agent. It has caused a major diplomatic issue with the US Government."

Adam sat silently under the CS's scrutiny and started to shake his right leg. He started to speak, but the CS raised his hand, cutting off Adam's attempt to say anything.

"The CC wants heads to roll, and unfortunately, given your operational control, it is your head on the chopping block," stated the CS. "You have been a long-serving officer and, until recently, had an excellent track record. As such, you will be transferred from the media spotlight to the Darwin office for 2-3 years. Hopefully, the storm would have blown over by then, and we can consider a re-posting back to Sydney headquarters."

"It has been a regrettable situation, and I understand your position, sir, but I need just a bit of time before I get shipped out," said Adam. "If you can give me a month to co-ordinate important interrelated matters with the Fijian Police Force, the DEA and on the local front to stamp out the emerging K-gang. We don't have the luxury of time to bring another senior officer up to speed, and I have all the contacts. We must act now to shut down the Gonzales empire once and for all. Time is not on our side, and we must act now."

The CS paused and turned to look out the window as he brought his fingertips to his chin. He turned back to Adam.

"You are right. It will take too long to bring another senior officer up to speed, so I'll give you a month, but no more stuff-ups or speaking to the media. Otherwise, I'll be joining you in the outback."

"Thank you, sir," Adam said as he stood and left the office. "I won't let you down."

"Close the door behind you. I need to sell this to the Chief," stated the CS as he reached for his phone.

*

Time was now his enemy, so Adam immediately returned to his office, signalling Tanya to join him as he raced past her desk.

"Close the door and sit, " he told Tanya. "I've just been with the CS upstairs, and what I'm sharing with you is highly confidential. The hierarchy is shipping me out to Darwin. Not unexpectedly, it's my head that rolls after what has happened with the killings in front of the office and the explosion in the church."

"They can't do that," stammered Tanya. "There's so much we need to do with all the intelligence we have gathered. We want to put an end to the Gonzales cartel. Carlo has risked so much coming out of the WPP to help us. I don't want to let him down."

"I have bought some time, and the CS has given me a month to wrap things up. How's Carlo fairing?" Adam asked.

"He's left my place and back out with his Mama," Tanya replied. "He needs time with her following all the deaths. We've arranged 24-hour security at the front and rear of the property.

"I know the Americans will want to take him off to Washington shortly and start to gather his intelligence on the Gonzales operation so that they can develop a plan of action," stated Adam. "Let's get Sean Pham on the line now."

"Agent Pham speaking."

"Sean, it's Adam Charles. Can we speak?"

"Give me five minutes, and I'll arrange for Penny to join us. I'll also see if I can get Andy Carter in Washington on the line. He is getting used to the late-night calls," replied Sean. "Speak soon."

*

"OK, Adam, I've got Penny Emmett-Jones with me here in Sydney and Andy on the line in Washington," introduced Sean.

"Thanks, Sean," replied Adam. "I've got Tanya Layton with me. Let me start by saying again how sorry we are at the loss of Agent Sandra Wong and how determined we are to work with you to bring Hernando Gonzales to account."

"Appreciated," said Andy. "Now, where to from here?"

"OK, as an update, we tracked down our man Roberto Rodriguez. We believe he left Australia using a Columbian diplomatic passport under the name Julio Martinez," informed Adam. "He's currently on his way to Chile on a commercial flight. We believe there is little we can do to arrest him with his use of diplomatic credentials, but we are working on it. Our Department of Foreign Affairs is currently working with their counterparts in Chile to detain him on arrival in Santiago. We'll keep you informed."

"OK, that's good, Adam. From our end, we want Penny and Sean to escort Carlo to Washington as soon as possible," stated Andy. "To that end, we are arranging a US Air Force flight out of your Richmond Air Force Base. With him here in DC for a de-briefing, we can plan on taking out the Gonzales operation in Columbia. We want to move before they decide to make any changes to their operation, knowing Carlo is still alive and likely wanting to exact revenge for the murder of his father, uncle and cousin."

"I see we have a huge opportunity to stop him once and for all," said Adam, with his voice rising. "We will speak with SS Viliame Naqima in Fiji about the proposed Fijian distribution hub and with DS Layton locally. We'll aim to takeout the K-gang setting up in Sydney."

"We need this all coordinated, so we take out all the centres on the same day and time across the multiple time zones," stressed Andy. "As soon as we have finished interviewing Carlo, we re-convene and agree on timelines for the combined operations in Columbia, Fiji and Australia, designated Operation Coffee Pod."

"I believe we have all agreed to proceed with Operation Coffee Pod," Adam laughed. "Let's get Penny, Sean and Carlo off to Washington."

Adam did not mention the time pressure he was under from his superiors.

I need to get it done, he mused as he terminated the call.

*

The QANTAS flight arrived on time at Santiago's Arturo Merino Benitez International Airport. Roberto peered out his aircraft window, unsure of what awaited him when he stepped off the flight. The aircraft rumbled across the tarmac and pulled up with a jerk at the gate.

Welcome to Santiago International Airport. The local time is.........

Roberto ignored the rest of the announcement as he fired up his mobile, ready just in case he needed to fire off a call to Hernando.

He stepped off the aircraft and felt as though people were staring at him as they seemed to look up from their clipboards as he passed by. However, he felt relieved when he saw a small white signboard headed Columbian Embassy and his name Julio Martinez, in large black letters.

A relieved Roberto quickly strode up the sign holder.

"Greetings, Senor Martinez. I am here to ensure no problems with your connecting flight to Bogota."

With a smile, Roberto dutifully fell in behind the Columbian embassy official, who took his single carry-on bag and led him to the Bogota flight gate.

Gracias, Ambassador Cortez, for what you have done.

Roberto started to prepare a text message for Hernando Gonzales and advise him that all was well.

CHAPTER 30

After a couple of days of completing the diplomatic red tape and waiting for the flight to be arranged, Carlo was at Richmond Air Force base, ready to board the USAF plane bound for Washington, DC. His Mama and Tanya had granted permission to access the base to bid him farewell.

"I'll leave you to say your goodbyes and make sure my equipment box gets loaded," said Penny as she and Agent Pham headed up the stairs to board the 737 painted in matt green.

"Bye, Mama," said Carlo as he bent over to envelop her in an all-embracing hug. "I'll be fine, and Tanya will look after you while I'm away."

"She's a wonderful girl, and you better come back in a hurry and marry her," Mama whispered. "I'm running out of years for bambinos to look after."

A shocked Carlo smiled at his Mama as he held her at arm's length, then turned to Tanya.

"Look after Mama, ok," said Carlo emotionally. He kissed Tanya, then turned and headed up the stairs. He stopped and called out, "I love you, T."

"Love you too," whispered Tanya as she put her arm around Mama's shoulders.

"He's a good boy," Mama said to Tanya. "Look after him."

"I will," she replied as she squeezed Mama, pulling her close.

Mama and Tanya stood waving beside the runway as the aircraft slowly gathered speed. The beast rumbled down the runway, accompanied by the roar of the Pratt and Whitney turbofan engines. It seemed the plane was going to run out of runaway, but then it began to rise off the tarmac slowly like a pelican rising out of a lake, appearing to just miss the white gums lining the end of the air base.

"My boy, he's doing a good thing," noted a pensive Mama.

"Yes, Mama, he's doing a good thing to help stop the gang that killed your Gaetano and Lorenzo," agreed Tanya as she took Mama's hand and headed towards the carpark.

*

As Carlo, Penny and Sean became airborne, it was early morning in the jungles of Columbia. Roberto was being driven up to the gates at the entrance to Gonzales hacienda in the jungles of Columbia. After a cursory look into the vehicle, the guard with a rifle slung over his shoulder signalled for the driver to carry on.

There were no pleasantries as Roberto stepped onto the verandah, where Hernando sat in his rocking chair, sipping on an espresso coffee.

"What the fuck happened in Australia?" Hernando snapped. "It was a complete disaster and cost me big time. I had to draw on many favours to get you out of Australia and Chile. The Chilean Government was under extreme pressure to give you up to the Americanos when you landed in Chile."

"I don't know what to say apart from saying I'm sorry," replied Roberto. "I had Carlo lined up, and his stupid cousin Dominic stepped in front of him as I took the shot. I couldn't get another chance, as these two-women cops were coming at me. I took one of the bitches out, then had to get away, thanks to our Fijian friend Tiko."

"You also set off a fuckin' bomb in a church," roared Hernando, causing some men in the courtyard, tending to the gardens, to look up. "The amount of pressure I received from the Cardinal in Bogota Cathedral after it was reported in the local press, who said we were involved.

Hernando shook his head at Roberto, who had the sense to keep quiet.

"Anyway, what's done is done. We now need to rectify the situation, so let's go and talk to our new Fijian associate Tiko."

Hernando and Roberto made their way inside the hacienda.

"I see our friend Pedro is no longer around," observed Roberto as they entered the hacienda.

"He has been taken care of," a curt Hernando replied.

The thick stucco walls and relatively small windows made it quite dark with the lack of natural light. Hernando flicked the light switch inside the front door, and a battery of ceiling-mounted LEDs lit up the large open-plan living area. Several cream-coloured, hand-woven hemp and wool rugs were strewn across the glossy pine-timbered floors.

To the left-hand of the entry was a long, black antique Spanish Baroque farm-style trestle table with seating for twelve, with matching high-backed, black wooden chairs. By contrast, to the right-hand side was a large 7-seater cream-coloured lounge suite set around a massive, low dark-timbered coffee table.

The men walked past the centrally located kitchen with an island granite-topped bench and a double sink. Several wooden stools were parked by the kitchen bench. They continued to a back office and asked the man managing a vast array of electronic equipment to leave the room and close the door.

Roberto sent Tiko a text message to get ready for a VPN session. After Tiko replied in the affirmative, Roberto initiated the call moments later.

"Greetings, Tiko. I have Senor Gonzales with me."

"Wow, the big boss," replied Tiko. "To what do I owe the honour?"

"As you know, we had a setback in Australia and missed the opportunity to take out Carlo Conti," said Roberto.

"That dude has more lives than a cat," replied Tiko. "Where do we go from here?"

"That's the reason for the call," interjected Hernando. "We need your help and fast."

"Ok, what do you want from me?"

"With your men still laying low in Sydney, we need them to track Carlo down and take him out once and for all," stated Roberto. "Your guys know where his mother lives, having staked out the place. He is bound to show up there, and then your guys can strike."

Tiko hesitated before saying, "Sounds like a plan, but the cops will protect the place, and it won't be easy to make the hit."

"We'll leave that to you and your guys. I'm sure they'll get the chance if they're patient and watchful," said Roberto. "In the meantime, we need to get rolling with your production line to start generating some cash. Given what went down in Australia, we've had several large expenses recently."

"Now you're talking," said Tiko. "The production line has been tested, and most of the original staff from the nearby village are ready and keen to start work. We need the gear to feed into the filling line."

"With the closure of the Acapulco hub, we have been able to establish a new location for a delivery chain, starting off the coast of Peru. We have some New Zealand yachties who are currently on the way to Fiji with 100kg of CH," said Hernando. "They should be with you in 2-3 weeks to drop off the consignment."

"Great news," replied Tiko. "I'll wait for your instructions about the delivery and get on to the boys in Sydney to work on a plan to take out our Sydney-based problem."

*

After what seemed to take forever, an exhausted Carlo, Penny and Sean arrived at Andrews Air Force Base outside Washington DC.

"Military aircraft are certainly not built for comfort. My back is killing me," said Carlo stretching. The group made their way down the aircraft stairs.

"I can't believe it. Look there," Carlo pointed. "Isn't that Air Force One preparing for take-off? Amazing."

Agent Andy Carter stood next to a Ford SUV with dark window tinting, waiting to greet the new arrivals. Carlo noticed what seemed to be a lingering hug Andy gave Penny.

There appeared to be a bit of sparkle between their eyes. Maybe a bit of history there.

"I'll get you all to your hotel as I know you'll be exhausted and will want to rest up. We can start our de-briefing session tomorrow morning," said Andy as he raised the rear hatch of his SUV to load the array of luggage.

The two men took the back seat of Andy's vehicle, and Penny sat up front next to Andy. Again, Carlo noticed some chemistry between the pair as they continually looked at each other.

Something goin' on there, Carlo chuckled to himself.

"What are you laughing about?" Andy asked as he looked at Carlo in his rear mirror.

"Nothin'. Just thinkin' I hope we get to return home via a regular commercial flight. I don't think my back and backside would handle another military flight. I'll never complain about having to fly economy ever again," replied Carlo, which brought applause and laughter from Penny and Sean.

*

"Bula Jioji," greeted Tiko. "How are the rest of the guys going?"

"All good, bosso. We've just been waiting for your instructions on what we should do next," replied Jioji. "I have arranged to meet the boys today for lunch and a couple of drinks."

"You better take it easy on the drinks, as plenty is about to happen," noted Tiko. "The big bosso in South America wants us to track down that nuisance Carlo Conti and take him out. The most likely place we expect he'll show up is his family home, which you guys have previously staked out."

"Pretty risky, bosso," observed Jioji. "The cops will be all over the place. He'll be hard to get to with them swarming around the place."

"You'll have to be patient and monitor his movements. The cops can't be next to him 24-7, so you'll need to bide your time and not be too obvious that you are watching the house," directed Tiko. "When you get together with the other guys, you can work out a plan to monitor the house. Keep me informed," said Tiko as he terminated the call.

*

Jioji, Malakai, Osea, Tui, Timoci and Jo met at the Penrith Rugby Leagues Club near the Conti Mount Willsmore family home and warehouse. Jioji, the designated lieutenant for the K-gang in Sydney, had reserved a table in the club's bistro. Double-decker burgers with a large serving of fries were washed down with jugs of lager to the cacophony of sounds and flickering of lights from the banks of poker machines located next to where the men sat.

With the men fed and feeling relaxed, Jioji spoke to the group.

"I've spoken with the bosso in Fiji this morning, and he wants us to take out Carlo Conti once and for all."

"That won't be easy, Jioji," spoke up Tui. "After two attempts, the cops will keep him safe, wrapped up like a baby. It will be very risky."

"Agreed, it won't be easy, so we have to be patient," stated Jioji as he eyed each group member. "We think the most likely place to find him will be his mother's place in Mount Willsmore. We know the area's layout and only need him and the cops to be off-guard for a second and then strike. Maybe we can hit him when he goes shopping. He can't be locked inside with his Mama forever. Over time, he will get careless."

"Won't the cops recognise us after the hit at AFP headquarters," queried Jo. "Us Fijians will always stick out if we hang around the neighbourhood."

"I have an idea," said Jioji, who paused before continuing, "I reckon we get a few tools together and approach some of the nearby houses to do some gardening or general maintenance. That way, we can keep a close eye on the place and appear to be working, not just sitting in a car."

"It could work," said Jo. "At least we won't be targets sitting in a car parked in the street with the cops on patrol."

*

"DS Layton, DSC Rob Gregson is calling in from Mrs Conti's place."

"Yes, Rob," answered Tanya.

"In a house down the street, I have noticed a couple of guys of Fijian or Pacific Islander appearance. They're in the front yard with what looks like gardening equipment," noted Rob. "It may be a coincidence, but I should report the matter."

"Good work," replied Tanya. "I agree it is too much of a coincidence, given what happened at HQ a few days ago. Get Mrs Conti to call her neighbour and see what she can find out about the men. Are they regulars, or have they just turned up recently? Also, see if you can get some discreet photos of the men during your shift change. We can then check for facial recognition overnight to see if we get any hits on their ID. Also, ask the local police to see if they can find any Black Ford SUVs parked nearby and check the plates."

*

"Bingo," exclaimed an excited Tanya to DSC Gregson. "It's the men linked to the explosions at HQ. We've got a very close ID match with the facial recognition, and the plates are reported as stolen."

"Mrs Conti's neighbour confirmed that the guys had door knocked looking for work and were charging an attractive rate for gardening and general maintenance. Do you want us to move in and arrest them?" Rob asked as he peered out from behind the curtains.

"I don't want them to know we are on to them," stated Tanya. "As a first step, I'll arrange for extra coverage inside the house if they attempt to kidnap Mrs Conti or make some other attack on the house. We'll get the local police patrol to put a tracker on their vehicle. I want to find out where they're hold-up. DCI Charles will arrange for us to be part of a massive operation, including rounding up these K-gang members in Sydney."

"I'll get straight on to the local police patrol and arrange for the trackers to be placed on their vehicle and keep a close eye on them in case they move towards the house," confirmed Rob. "Mrs Conti is not happy at not being allowed out of the house, apart from going into the garden. Also, we've arranged for groceries to be delivered to the house. I need some exercise on my days off, as I'm putting on weight with the cakes and coffees she is churning out."

"Good work Rob. Keep me informed of any developments with the local boys and their tracking of our gardeners," said Tanya. "Gotta go. DCI Charles has just called for me."

*

"Hi, Tanya, come on in. I'm going to call SS Naqima in Fiji," said Adam indicating for Tanya to take a seat as he started to call Viliame.

"Hey, Viliame. It's me, Adam. I've got DS Tanya Layton with me."

"Who else would it be calling me just as I'm about to finish for the day," said Viliame with a chuckle. "Hi, Tanya."

"Yes, sorry about that," replied Adam. "Just wanted to update you on the K-gang here in Sydney. We've identified some of the guys involved in the diversionary explosions near headquarters on the day of the shootings. Two of them are posing as gardeners working nearby the Conti's Sydney house. We've identified six men in total, all of Fijian appearance, who participated in the attack, with one unidentified male who rode the escaping motorcycle. He was dressed in leathers and wearing a helmet."

"I think it could have been our friend Tiko Rokovou," noted Viliame. "Through Fiji Immigration, we discovered he departed Nadi International Airport for Sydney a couple of days before the incident and returned soon after the attack."

"That could well be our additional unidentified culprit," added Adam. "However, the main reason for the call is to update you on an operation we are putting together called Operation Coffee Pod."

"Sounds interesting. How can we help over here?" Viliame asked.

"This is highly confidential and on a need-to-know basis only," Adam stated.

"I understand," responded Viliame. "I will keep the info very tightly held amongst my team."

"In the next few weeks, we are aiming to undertake a major multi-national operation to stop the Trans-Pacific Gonzales drug cartel once and for all," Adam said. "Tanya will target the K-gang cohort that is starting up in Sydney. They appear to be aiming to fill the void left by the demise of the Contis. On your end, we have received intel from Interpol that a New Zealand-registered yacht, *Waitomo*, has allegedly picked up Gonzales's product off the coast of Peru, near the capital Lima. On their departure card from Lima, they designated Savusavu in Fiji as their next port of call."

"With our friend Tiko and Tradewinds Coffee, that doesn't sound a coincidence," observed Viliame. "I'll get DS Chand on the job to have Tiko under observation and keep an eye out for the arrival of the Kiwi yacht *Waitomo*. It will take the yacht a couple of weeks to reach Fiji, so the timing should provide plenty of time to prepare for their arrival."

"The other highly confidential piece of information is that we have Carlo Conti meeting with the DEA in Washington DC as we speak," stated Adam. "That will be the final piece of the puzzle to be put into place. We want to be able to hit them in Sydney, Savusavu and Columbia simultaneously. The key element is getting the significant DEA resources that will be required to be put in place for a major strike operation at the home of the Gonzales operation. It will need to be a military-scale operation."

"You have my 100 per cent support," said Viliame. "I'll let you know when the yachties have arrived in Savusavu."

CHAPTER 31

"DCI Charles, it's DSC Gregson. I have an update on our gardening friends. We were able to track them to the former Conti warehouse in Mount Willsmore."

"Of course," roared Adam as he thumped his forehead with the palm of his right hand. "According to Gaetano's lawyer, the property transfer was done as part of some debt forgiveness. Please get him on the line for me straightaway, Tanya?"

"Mr Russo, it's DS Layton from the AFP. I need some info from you on the transfer you completed on the Conti and Rossi properties before the deaths of Gaetano and Lorenzo."

"I have it right in front of me. I am in the process of completing the transaction with the Registrar of Titles," Mr Russo replied. "The transferee is Tiko Rokovou."

"Thank you so much. You've been a great help," answered Tanya as she concealed the excitement in her voice.

"Shit," exclaimed Adam. "No wonder they're sending me to Darwin. I'm losing it with so much happening. How could I not have thought of the bleedin' obvious?"

"Surely they can't possibly transfer you to Darwin after all you've achieved?" Tanya pressed as she leaned forward in her seat and stared at Adam.

"While I'm still operational, I need to get everything in place with us, the Fiji Police and the DEA, to complete Operation Coffee Pod," said Adam. "As

I told you yesterday, this information does not leave this office. "Now, let's get on with the job."

*

All the chatter in the room stopped as Carlo, led by Andy, walked into the DEA meeting room. Carlo noted a mix of women and men dressed in various uniforms and plain clothes.

"Team, this is Carlo Conti," stated Penny. "Despite the recent death of his father and uncle, he has agreed to join us today to help plan and implement Operation Coffee Pod."

"G'day, everyone," responded Carlo. "My motivation is to end the Gonzales' drug empire once and for all. I no longer want the Conti name associated with drugs and crime."

"As you can see here at DEA HQ, we have assembled a high-powered team this morning keen to hear what you have to say," said Andy looking around the room. "They want to hear what you can share with us about the Gonzales organisation so we can implement Operation Coffee Pod as soon as possible."

"Thanks, Andy. I look forward to working with you and your team to make Operation Coffee Pod happen."

"We have been advised that planning is underway to take out the growing Sydney and Fijian-based operations as part of Operation Coffee Pod. So over to you, Carlo."

Carlo stepped up to a large whiteboard and picked up a black marking pen. "I am not proud to say my family has long associated with Senor Hernando Gonzales. During that time, I had the opportunity to visit his operation in Columbia. Hopefully, I can give you enough info to enable you to make a successful strike at the heart of his organisation. If you have any questions during the presentation, please stop me."

Carlo started his presentation with a description and drawings on the whiteboard of the location and layout of the operation. He described how the Gonzales facilities were located about 20 kilometres East of Cali, a principal western Columbian rural city. The stucco-walled hacienda compound was secluded and well-protected by natural elements. It was approachable from the West by one road, making it difficult for a casual passerby to pass unnoticed a series of manned observation posts. The compound was protected from the North by a steep, rugged hillside, on the East by a wide, fast-flowing river and from the South by dense jungle and a banana plantation.

"That would only give Hernando one escape route by road," observed Penny.

"That's correct, Penny. However, Hernando maintains two helicopters within the compound with pilots permanently on standby," responded Carlo. "Given the isolation, he has plenty of notice from the various guard posts and electronic warning systems of any imminent attacks by rival gangs or raids by the Federales. He can disappear in minutes."

"That adds a degree of difficulty in getting to him before he could take off in one of his helicopters," noted Andy. "We'll have to think about how best to take him out. What about his drug manufacturing operations?"

"Nothing is visible from the air by drones or satellites," explained Carlo. "There appears to be a series of horse stables at the north wall. Underneath the stables is where the cocaine labs are located, secured within a large concrete bunker so difficult to access and destroy. It's a very professional operation. Hernando employs a large staff who live on the property. He seems well protected from the local police, whom no doubt have their meagre salaries topped up by Hernando."

Carlo answered several questions from the group clarifying the layout and what weapons the guards were using.

"If no one has any further questions for Carlo, I'll need to excuse him from being involved in our secret discussions on operational matters," said Andy. "Thanks for the information, Carlo. You've been most helpful. I'll arrange a room for you nearby. We can call you if we have further questions or need clarification."

"Happy to have helped and wish you the best of luck in takin' the bastard out," said Carlo as he placed his marking pen down and was led from the meeting room to an adjacent vacant office.

"From what Carlo has described, I recommend an airborne assault," stated Andy. "Commander Teese, can we get one of your helicopter carriers in position off the coast of Columbia within the next two weeks?"

"We have the USS *Neil Armstrong* based in San Diego," replied Commander Teese. "We can have the vessel in position loaded with assault helicopters within your time frame. The vessel maintains a position in international waters off the coast of Columbia, but the airborne assault will require entry into Columbian airspace. The raid will require the State Department's authorisation."

"Commander, you are correct," Andy replied. "I'll get onto the State Department and brief them. It will be vital that they restrict their contact for the raid approval to the Columbian military, the natural enemies of the drug cartels in that country. Gonzales will have friends in high places within the government, and we can't risk a leak." said Andy.

Andy stepped to the whiteboard, "The task force will be in position to attack just before dawn. A squadron of helicopters would arrive unseen, under cover of the northern hillside. Once the escape helicopters are taken out, we can land our choppers and disperse our team into the compound to arrest Gonzales and destroy the lab facilities."

"I want to be there," stated Penny. "I know what this Roberto Rodriguez looks like and want to make sure we nail him."

"One hundred per cent Penny," affirmed Andy with a nod towards Penny. "You and your friend Gertrude could come in very useful. From DCI Charles in Sydney, we have also been advised of a suspected drug shipment on the way to Fiji from Peru via a New Zealander-owned yacht. Once the shipment has arrived in Fiji and is in the hands of the K-gang, we will coordinate for Operation Coffee Pod to strike simultaneously in Sydney, Fiji and Columbia, subject to State Department authorisation. I'll give DCI Charles a call while you're all here."

Andy checked his watch, did a quick mental calculation of the time in Sydney, and noted it was around midnight. Despite the time in Sydney, he decided to call Adam. A sleepy-sounding Andy answered the call with a croaky voice, "DCI Charles."

"Andy Carter here, Adam. Sorry to call you so late. I've got Penny and a room full of key people planning the strike on Gonzales HQ for Operation Coffee Pod. Can you give us an update from your end?"

"Sure, Andy. I've spoken with our colleagues in Fiji, and they'll watch our friends in Savusavu and let us know when the yachties have arrived with the shipment. We've identified the hideout for the Sydney-based members of the K-gang, so we'll be ready to mount raids in both Fiji and Sydney once you confirm the strike time."

"OK, that's great news," said Andy. "We'll work on putting everything in place here with the State Department, DEA and the US Navy and be ready to press the button as soon as the shipment arrives in Fiji. Better let you get back to sleep."

*

Andy entered the office, where Carlo sat in an office chair, looking out the window.

"I still can't believe I'm lookin' at the Pentagon. "Who'd have believed it," said Carlo.

Andy smiled. "Carlo, your information proved invaluable. We'll get you back in the morning to clarify a few points, and then we've got you booked to fly back to Sydney via commercial flights. You'll leave DC's Dulles airport tomorrow afternoon. You'll connect with an evening QANTAS flight out of LAX for Sydney. Just in case, an unidentified, armed Marshall will be on the flight. Penny will remain here in Washington to assist with Operation Coffee Pod."

"In that case, I'd like to do some shopping. Maybe get something to take home for Mama and Tanya. Could you drop me off at the centre near the hotel?" Carlo asked.

"No problem," replied Andy. "I'm just about to take Penny back to your hotel and can easily head back via the local shopping mall. Give me five minutes to wrap everything up with Commander Teese and his team, and we'll get out of here."

*

"Here we are, Carlo. I'll pick you up in the morning at the hotel at eight to give you time for breakfast before coming into the office for a final de-brief," said Andy as he pulled up in front of the mall entrance.

"Thanks, Andy. See you in the morning. Maybe we could have breakfast together before Andy arrives, Penny?" Carlo suggested.

"For sure. How about 7 am?"

"See you in the restaurant," said Carlo as he quickly jumped out of Andy's vehicle after an impatient taxi driver honked from behind.

"He's made a massive transformation from being a drug lord," observed Andy as he drove away. "You free for dinner, Penny?"

"Yes, he's made a massive transition, and I like him," said Penny. "Now, for dinner, I was thinking about a quiet in-room meal with a nice bottle of Californian Chardonnay. Care to join me?" Penny posed with a cheeky grin.

Andy looked at Penny and smiled as he hit the accelerator, causing Penny's head to jerk back. "I was thinking, with budgetary constraints, that you may like to move into my apartment for the rest of your stay in DC."

"Why, Agent Carter. I do declare you are very forward. I suppose I can see my way to help with budgetary issues, especially with sending Carlo back to Sydney in Business Class. I can see why the big boss may want to minimise expenses."

"I haven't told him about Business Class. It should be a nice surprise. He deserved it after the information he made available," said Andy.

*

Carlo entered the mall entrance foyer, stepped up to the store directory, and began scanning under the heading *Gifts & Jewellery*.

Here we are, Souk's Gold and Jewellery Store, Level 2.

CHAPTER 32

Carlo had thought about the future on the long 14-hour flight from Los Angeles to Sydney. In the subsequent days since his return to Australia, he had been kept away from the family home despite his Mama's protestations.

Now in Melbourne, Carlo felt nervous as he walked into the Powerhouse Gym to meet with the proprietor Vera Mueller. Unexpectedly, his fob security device still worked as he pressed against the turnstile gate and entered the gym floor area.

"Good morning, ladies," he loudly called out to the members of the 9 am HIIT class working out on the gym floor under the instruction of Vera. Nena's 99 Red Balloons, a favourite song, pulsed away over the stereo system as the class turned in unison.

"It's Chris. It's Chris," they screamed.

Vera turned down the volume and stepped over to greet Carlo, with class members pressing from close behind.

"From the media coverage, I suppose we no longer call you Chris. I presume it's the famous Carlo from now on," said Vera harshly. "Who would've thought our much-liked Chris was a crime baron in a former life."

"Can we speak in private in your office?" Carlo asked, smiling at the class members. "I have somethin' I'd like to run past you."

Without a word, Vera turned and strode towards her office. She called back towards the group.

"Beverley, would you please take charge and finish the class."

Carlo followed Vera into the office and closed the door behind him. Vera pointed to a chair next to her paper-covered desk.

"What can I do for you?" Vera asked, her eyes fixed on Carlo's.

"Firstly, I wanted to apologise for you not knowing who I was, but that was not possible under the terms of the witness protection program," explained Carlo. "I had given evidence against some very unsavoury characters keen to see my body in the morgue."

"Oh," said Vera, looking guilty. "I didn't know about the witness protection business. It must have been very difficult for you, especially with the murder of your father and uncle."

"It has been a very trying time for the family and my Mama. In a relatively short time frame, she has lost my brother Guido, my Papa and my Uncle Lorenzo, her brother," said Carlo as he wiped his eyes with the back of his right hand. "She's strong, my Mama, and will get through the tragedies. To help support Mama, I'll be returning to Sydney, which is why I wanted to discuss somethin' with you."

"What's that," said Vera, unsure how to handle Carlo.

"I've got a business proposition for you," Carlo began. He paused and drew a deep breath, "I would like to open a franchise of the Powerhouse Gym in Sydney. I like the name and the types of programs you offer."

"Wow," said an enthused Vera, leaning forward in her seat. "That sounds like an intriguing proposal - an opportunity to expand the business." A smile began to form on her face. "I like the idea in principle."

"In confidential discussions between the family lawyer Mister Russo and the authorities, I understand that there is a strong likelihood that a warehouse that was extorted from the family by an international crime gang may be returned to the family," detailed Carlo. "It's located in the heart of Sydney's western suburbs, and I propose converting it into a gym like you have set up the Powerhouse Gym here in Camberwell."

"Wow, that was unexpected, and I like where you are going," said an enthusiastic Vera. She picked up a pen and began to make notes on a notepad. "I could come up to Sydney and help with the outfit of the premises and the recruitment and training of the team. We can work out a franchisee or partnership arrangement between our respective lawyers."

"That's fantastic. Thanks for the support," said Carlo extending his right hand towards Vera to shake on the arrangement. "I'll let you know once Mister Russo has confirmed the matter has been settled and get back to you. We can then arrange for you to visit Sydney to check the place out. In the meantime, let me have your lawyer's details, and I'll pass the info on to Mister Russo."

Carlo stepped out of Vera's office to be greeted by the class members. Bodies clustered around Carlo, and arms extended, holding mobile phones that flashed for what seemed to be an unending demand for selfies.

An Uber pulling up in front of the gym brought an end to the barrage of questions that were fired at Carlo. With a final wave, an excited Carlo was out of the door and on his way to the airport for the return flight to Sydney. One job had been ticked off, and now for a very important next step.

*

With all the activity surrounding Operation Coffee Pod, an exhausted Tanya had been putting in long hours at AFP headquarters with Adam, her fellow officers and Agent Sean Pham on his return from DC. Following a call from Carlo to Adam Charles, Tanya had been given a rare day off.

"It'll be great having tomorrow off. You must have put the heat on Adam," said Tanya as she slumped into the lounge chair in her apartment and rested her head on Carlo's shoulder. "Maybe we can go for a walk along the beach at Bondi in the afternoon and order some Indian curries to watch with a movie."

"Better than that," said Carlo, which caused Tanya to lift her head and look at Carlo. "I've booked that Fijian restaurant in Newton, Kana Levu, for 7 pm. Given that we first met in Fiji, I thought a Fijian restaurant was appropriate. You can rest in the afternoon and recharge the batteries, ready for the big night out."

"I've got nothing to wear," said an excited Tanya as she stood and rushed to the bedroom, rummaging through her wardrobe. "Clothes shopping tomorrow morning. I need a new dress and some shoes. I haven't been out to dinner for ages. Thanks so much for organising a night out. I loved the food in Fiji, especially the seafood."

*

While Carlo watched a soccer match on television, Melbourne Victory versus Sydney City, Tanya headed to the bathroom and filled the bathtub. She added some bath salts, and once the tub was around three-quarters full, she tentatively dipped a toe into the steaming water. Tanya added some cold water, and after stirring the bath salts with her hand, she gently lowered herself into the water and closed her eyes.

Finally, Tanya had some time to think, a rare luxury given all the recent chaos brought about by the return of Carlo, the killings and now Operation Coffee Pod.

It has been so wonderful to see Carlo and be in his arms. Ever since falling in love with him in Fiji, I dreamed about a moment like this. I was shattered when he had to go into the witness protection program and thought I would never see him again. That day I saw him standing at my door and the explosion of passion with him. Him inside me for the first time, our insatiable desire.

Tanya sat upright in the bathtub, staring at the tap.

OMG, I haven't had a period this month. We didn't have any protection on those first few crazy nights. I'm going to have to sneak off to the pharmacy.

*

"Bula," greeted the host of the Kana Levu Restaurant. "My name is Lemani."

"Bula Lemani. Conti, table for two," responded Carlo with a smile and a nod.

"Yes sir," replied Lemani with his broad Fijian grin as he picked up menus and directed the couple towards their table. "We have a nice quiet booth for you towards the rear. Celebrating anything special?" Lemani asked.

"Just a quiet night to enjoy some good Fijian food," answered Tanya.

Kana Levu was situated on the main strip of shops in Newtown. It was a long narrow restaurant with lightly timbered booths on either side of a central corridor leading to a bar and open kitchen at the rear. Each booth was seated for four people, two on either side of the table. The restaurant walls were lined with tapa cloth, hand-printed with Fijian tribal motifs and on the wall above each booth were blackened, crossed Fijian timber warrior clubs. Being early, it was quiet, and only one other couple was studying their menus.

Lemani lit the candle in the clamshell adjacent to the wall amongst a selection of condiments.

"Would you like to order a drink while you look at the menus?" He asked, placing the menus on the table and highlighting the list of specials pinned to the front of the menu.

"I'll start with a Fiji Bitter," said Carlo licking his lips in anticipation.

"For you, madam?"

"Just a soda, lime and bitters to start," chose Tanya. "I might have some wine with the meal."

"Are you sure, just a soft drink?" queried Carlo with a frown on his brow.

"That'll be fine to start," replied Tanya as she picked up her menu.

After a few minutes, Lemani returned with the drinks and hovered with his pen poised on his pad. "I thought we'd both start with the kokoda. Then my good lady would like the grilled dory with a side salad and a small serving of dalo chips. I'll have the boneless chicken curry with rice," said Carlo as he returned the menus to Lemani.

"The entrees will be out shortly," confirmed Lemani. "Any more drinks?"

"Yes, please. A bottle of the Mumm Champagne," Carlo requested, noting the shock on Tanya's face as she mouthed the words, Mumm, wow!

Lemani returned with the ice bucket and popped the cork on the champagne. He began to pour a glass for Tanya, who raised her hand when her glass was half full. "Come on. You'll have to drink up if we're goin' to finish the bottle. Cheers," cried Carlo as he clinked his glass with Tanya's.

"Carlo, there's something…." Tanya was cut-off mid-sentence as the servings of kokoda were placed in front of them, served in a half coconut shell.

"Entrée is served," beamed Lemani as he stood expectantly beside the table.

"Thank you, Lemani," replied Carlo, causing the host to retreat to the kitchen area and begin to chatter to the chef and a waitress, with looks back towards the table.

Tanya picked up her fork and searched for a nice chunky piece of fish. She was looking forward to the acidic tang from the lemon juice and the bite from the finely chopped pieces of chill and onion. Her fork paused above the coconut shell as something sparkling caught her eye. She leaned forward to take a look, her mouth dropping open as she looked up at a smiling Carlo.

"Will you marry me, Tanya Layton?"

"Yesss," stammered Tanya as Carlo half-stood and leant across the table to kiss her, accompanied by cheers and claps from the staff assembled at the bar.

Tanya extracted the ring from the shell and, after wiping it on her serviette, placed it on her left ring finger. She moved her hand around and smiled as the large diamond sparkled in the lighting.

"We better drop in on Mama and give her the news tomorrow morning," said Carlo as he grasped Tanya's hands. "I interrupted you earlier when you had somethin' you wanted to tell me."

"Well, this engagement is very timely as you're going to be a Papa," beamed Tanya. "Carlo Conti will no longer be the last of the Contis!"

"When? How?" Carlo asked with a stunned look on his face.

"Well, it does take two people, and I think you know what happened when you turned up on my doorstep," replied Tanya. "It wasn't like I'd been on the dating scene and needed to be on protection, wondering about Carlo Conti and whether I would ever see him again."

"Mama will be so happy. Father Alessandro will find a large donation in the collection plate this Sunday with her prayers answered," said Carlo. "I think this is a night of big announcements."

"You've something else to share?" Tanya asked.

"Now that I'm out of the witness protection program and us officially engaged, I'll be returnin' to Sydney as soon as possible and need to start makin' a livin'," replied Carlo. "When I went to Melbourne recently to tidy up all my affairs, I spoke to the owner of the Powerhouse Gymnasium where I was workin'. She has agreed to work with me to set up a Powerhouse Sydney franchise. Her name is Vera Mueller, and she has a great concept with a mix of classes with instructors and the usual gym equipment."

"Where would you set up?" Tanya asked.

"I understand from Mister Russo, the family lawyer, that it's highly likely the warehouse in Mount Willsmore will be returned to the ownership of the family business once all the business with the AFP and the Gonzales' is completed," answered Carlo.

"In my position, I can't comment on that, but it sounds like a great opportunity," stated Tanya.

"Maybe once we're married and the bambino enters the world, you could join me operating the gym," probed Carlo. "We could even set up a chain of gyms over time."

"Sounds good to me, especially with Adam being shipped out after we complete matters with Hernando Gonzales," said Tanya as she squeezed Carlo's hands. "I can't see myself working in the AFP without Adam."

"What's happenin' to Adam?" Carlo queried.

"From his description, the bigwigs are making him fully responsible for what occurred with the mayhem at police headquarters and the church. They are shipping him out to Darwin for a few years until things quieten down," explained Tanya. "That's highly confidential information."

"Of course," said Carlo. "I think you and I need to get back to your place and do a bit of celebratin' after the main course."

"Celebrating, is that what you call it?" Tanya teased as she started to bring the first morsel of fish to her mouth.

*

"Tea or coffee?" Andy asked Penny as he swung naked out of bed and retrieved his LA Dodgers boxer shorts lying beside the bed.

"I will stick with the coffee. I am not too partial to your tea-making skills," said Penny as she reached down the side of the bed to gather her bathrobe from the floor.

"That's a bit harsh," replied Andy with a laugh as he headed to the kitchen and fired up his coffee percolator.

Penny was sitting in bed when Andy returned with two mugs of steaming black coffee.

"Andy, Operation Coffee Pod will be my last mission. I want to avenge the death of Agent Wong by shutting down the Gonzales cartel once and for all. Then I want to return to my village of Melbourne and resume my life as Fiona Irvine. I cannot go on making excuses as to why I can't see my family and friends."

"With this shoulder of mine giving me hell, I believe it's time to retire from active duty. Maybe a desk job in London could be the go, and it's not too long on the train to Melbourne. So, is there any room for a crazy American to help you to return to your life as Fiona Irvine in England?" posed Andy as he turned to look at Penny.

"Is that some sort of proposal?" Penny questioned as she placed her coffee down on the bedside table

"There must be some sort of compromise, as I don't reckon I could handle the English weather permanently."

"You are so romantic," Penny said, gently placing her hands on Andy's cheeks and drawing him towards her.

"Oh, Miss Emmett-Jones, or should I say, Miss Irvine, you are very forward," responded Andy as they slid down under the bedding.

"Be careful where you place your hands. They're probably hot after holding that mug of coffee."

CHAPTER 33

After showering, the duo had time for a light breakfast of orange juice and Granola™ before heading to DEA HQ. Confirmation had been received from the State Department to proceed with Operation Coffee Pod. They were meeting with the officials from the US Navy, the Captain of the *USS Neil Armstrong* and key DEA personnel to prepare for the armed assault on the Gonzales facilities in Columbia.

"Ladies and gentlemen, yesterday I spoke with DCI Adam Charles from the Australian Federal Police," said Andy as he stood in the DEA meeting room to commence the planning session. "DCI Charles has confirmed that the AFP has identified the hideout of the Sydney arm of what is known as the K-gang. The K-gang is building a base in Australia to work with the Gonzales gang. In addition, he has spoken with police colleagues in the Fiji Islands and confirmed the K-gang's operation in Fiji is also under close watch."

"We are now just awaiting confirmation that the latest Gonzales shipment has been delivered to Fiji, then we are set from an Aussie and Fijian perspective to launch Operation Coffee Pod," added Penny.

"In the meantime, we need to get the *USS Neil Armstrong* ready to set sail from San Diego and have the vessel stationed in international waters off the coast of Columbia with our helicopter assault team ready to strike," said Andy. "I'll lead the strike on the Gonzales facilities."

"Mr Conti, who was here with us last week in DC, was able to give us valuable information on the layout of the Gonzales facility," explained

Penny as she stood to address the group. "We have information on the security systems, accessibility, location of the manufacturing laboratories and the presence of two helicopters set for emergency take-off on a 24/7 basis."

"We'll have one of our agents in place on the hillside overlooking the property to ensure that Hernando Gonzales is at the location before we give the go signal to initiate the raid," confirmed Andy. "Commander Teese over to you to explain in more detail how the operation will proceed from a navy perspective."

*

"SS Naqima, this is DS Chand in Savusavu. We have just received confirmation from Fiji Customs that a New Zealand-registered yacht, *Waitomo,* has left Tongan waters and has indicated the vessel will be entering the port of Savusavu to clear Fijian Customs formalities in approximately two days."

"Thanks for the update, DS Chand. What are your plans for monitoring the arrival of the shipment?" SS Naqima asked.

"We have men issued with infrared equipment and will watch the yacht from when it arrives in Fijian waters. We'll also monitor the Tradewinds Winds Coffee business for any signs of delivery activity," replied DS Chan. "We suspect they'll use the same procedure the Contis used when moving the drugs into Fiji. They'll likely arrange to access the sunken cargo at night using the Tradewinds Coffee's boat, the *Coffee Queen*. We'll have men posing as fishermen around the harbour entrance area to monitor the yacht. I'll confirm with you as soon as we detect they have retrieved the consignment and stowed it at the company's warehouse."

"Thanks, DS Chand. I'll call DCI Charles in Sydney and update him."

*

The two Fijian fishermen sat quietly in their long, narrow punt with hand-lines dropped over the side, waiting patiently for a bite. The sun was rapidly sinking over the hills to the west of Savusavu Bay as the white-hulled, 40-foot teak-decked sloop *Waitomo* approached the tall, white beacon marking the entrance to the harbour.

The fishermen watched as the two crew members of the yacht were busy dropping the mainsail and turning the sloop windward in preparation to drop anchor adjacent to the beacon. As the yacht hove to, the beacon's light started to flash, indicating the approaching night. The crew member at the stern began to raise the Blue Peter Ensign to the top of the mast in line with customs protocols.

"Bula," came the traditional Fijian greeting, accompanied by a wave from the fishermen in their punt to the crew members as they watched the *Waitomo* drop anchor.

"You boys doing some fishing?" responded the crew member standing on the foredeck, testing the anchor's holding. "Catch anything?"

"Nothing seems to be biting, so we'll leave you guys in peace and head home before it gets too dark," replied the fisherman who stood in the stern and prepared to pull the starter chord of the outboard. "Have a good visit to Fiji, and as a tip, the beer at the yacht club is good."

"We are looking forward to our first cold beer," came the reply from the yachtie with a thumb's up. "Unfortunately, we arrived too late to clear customs today, so a beer at the yacht club will have to wait until the morning after we complete arrival formalities. Cheers, guys, or should I say bula!" The yachtie added with a grin and a wave as the fisherman powered away towards the township.

*

"DS Chand, it's Sgt Nailatikau. The yacht *Waitomo* has dropped anchor at the harbour entrance beacon. My men confirmed they'll anchor overnight and head into port to clear customs in the morning."

"As soon as they up anchor in the morning and head into town, I want divers to confirm that they have dropped their drug consignment in the water next to the beacon," ordered DS Chand. "With a consignment confirmed, we'll then set up to monitor for the collection of the drugs by our Tiko, mostly likely tomorrow night. I'll coordinate with DC Dreketi to ensure the infra-red viewing equipment is near the beacon and at the Tradewinds Coffee Company."

*

Tiko sat nervously in the office at Tradewinds Coffee, his fingers tapping away on his desk. He had been advised the previous evening that the Kiwis, Rob Moody and Barry Van Horn, had anchored the *Waitomo* in Savusavu Bay. He now waited for the call from the crew on their satellite phone that they'd cleared Fiji Customs. His mobile phone vibrated on his desktop.

"Tiko," he blurted out.

"Rob," came the heavily Kiwi-accented voice. "Barry and I are sitting in a very nice café at the Copra Shed, enjoying our first decent meal and coffee for a few weeks. Are you going to join us?"

A relieved Tiko quickly made the short journey into Savusavu town and pulled up in front of the Copra Shed. He stood at the entrance and scanned the tables on the walkway, jutting out over the water, looking for the new arrivals. It was easy to spot the arrivals sitting contentedly in their seats with empty plates and coffee cups in their hands.

The yachties were tallish, broad-shouldered, with well-tanned, wiry bodies, exposed by board shorts and open-necked polo shirts. Sunglasses were pushed back on top of their heads.

"Bula, Rob and Barry," greeted Tiko.

"Bula bro," chorused the men. "Coffee?"

"No, I'm fine, thanks," replied Tiko. "No problems with your arrival?"

"All went pretty smoothly," answered Rob. "We had favourable Tradewinds across the Pacific and found the anchorage you described at the harbour entrance without any problems. Everything is sitting there waiting for collection, presumably tonight."

"Yes, we'll head out tonight in my boat, moored at the jetty in front of the property on the other side of town," said Tiko. "You guys can stay with me until you set sail for home and be a bit more comfortable."

"Fantastic," said Barry. "You can probably tell we need a hot shower after three weeks at sea. We are looking forward to a couple of your famous Fiji beers."

"Get your gear together, and we'll head out to my place," said Tiko. "I've got a few beers chilling down ready for you guys to get into once I confirm your arrival with our friends in South America."

*

"DS Chand, I can confirm that our divers have identified eight large, screw-cap, plastic canisters attached to lead weights in the water near the beacon," advised Sgt Nailatikau.

"Thanks, Sergeant," said DS Chand. "DC Dreketi has everything in place to monitor the activities of Tiko and the visitors. We'll have teams in a fishing boat stationed near the beacon tonight and at Tradewinds Coffee, ready to confirm the landing of the consignment after pickup. I'll now call SS Naqima in Suva to give him an update."

"Naqima," came the clipped answer to DS Chand's call.

"Sir, our Kiwi friends have arrived in Savusavu and, as suspected, have sunk their cargo near the Savusavu beacon," informed DS Chand. "We have everything in place to monitor their retrieval of the drugs and the unloading at Tradewinds Coffee."

"Good work DS Chand," said SS Naqima. "Remember, we don't want them to have any inkling they are being watched. We must be patient and wait until we get the OK from the Aussies before we strike and arrest them."

"Yes sir, I'll keep you informed of any developments," advised DS Chand. "We'll be ready to arrest Tiko and his K-gang members, along with the Kiwis, as soon as you give us the word."

*

"After you guys freshen up, I'll give you a tour of the production facilities, and then my housekeeper Mereoni has organised some lunch, which we can enjoy with a couple of beers," informed Tiko as they pulled up at the homestead. "In the meantime, I'll contact our friends and let them know everything is going to plan."

"I'm really looking forward to that hot shower. Hope you've got plenty of hot water," said Barry as he sniffed his armpit and pulled back his head.

With the men shown their rooms and directed to the bathroom location, Tiko retreated to his office and closed the door. He checked his watch and noted it was early evening in Columbia. He booted up his computer to access the VPN, and after a brief delay, the call was answered.

"H, here."

I miss having Pedro answer these calls. Why didn't he tell me about the problem with his son? It will take me some time to find someone I can trust again.

"H, it's T. I can confirm that our Kiwi friends have arrived, and tonight, we'll retrieve the shipment."

"That's great," answered Hernando. "I needed some good news. I was hoping you could accelerate the production of the pods and have them shipped out as quickly as possible to Australia. I want to start generating some cash with your boys in Sydney."

"The line has been tested, and production is all set to go as soon as the product is in hand," replied Tiko. "My boys are setting up in Sydney in your former friend's warehouse and will be ready to receive the finished goods within the next few weeks. In the meantime, they are watching for our friend, but there's no sign of him anywhere, including the family home."

"Keep me informed," said Hernando, terminating the call.

*

"Bula Adam, it's Viliame. I've got an update for you."

"Hey, bula Viliame," responded Adam. "What's the news?"

"Our Kiwi friends have arrived in Savusavu, and we have them under close surveillance," answered Viliame. "They've followed the same routine used by the Contis by sinking the consignment at the entrance to the bay. We reckon they'll be ready to move to collect the drugs tonight."

"Good work Viliame. I'll update our friends in the US," informed Adam. "Let me know when the drugs are off-loaded into Tradewinds Coffee. That will trigger our DEA friends to give us the go-ahead to raid the properties in Fiji and Sydney. I'll contact Agent Carter and give him the news. It's not too late in DC," said Adam looking at his watch.

*

"Andy's phone," the call answered by a female English voice over a very crackly line.

"Well, if it isn't Miss Penny Emmett-Jones," teased Adam. "We've got a terrible line."

"DCI Charles, I do declare," responded Penny in an attempt at a Southern US accent. "We are currently steaming down the west coast of Mexico, ready to be in position off the Columbian coast in the next 24 hours. Here's Andy."

"Hi, Adam," said Andy as he took his phone from Penny. "You've got an update for me? Hopefully, good news."

"Yes, Viliame from the Fiji Police has informed me that the New Zealand yacht has arrived, and the Gonzales's shipment should be picked up in the next few hours. They are under close watch, and I'll confirm with you as soon as the consignment has been retrieved and is in hand with the K-gang."

"We're making good time and should be ready to launch our raid within the next 24 hours, as Penny indicated."

"OK, we'll await your go command in Sydney and Fiji. Best of luck, and make sure you get Hernando and the evil bastard Roberto," said Adam.

"Roberto is high on our target list," responded Andy. "We want him to answer for what he did to Agent Wong and many others over the years. Speak soon."

*

DS Chand nervously paced in the communications centre at the Savusavu Police Station. The sun had set, and no movement had been reported from the lookouts at Tradewinds Coffee. Suddenly, words crackled over the two-way radio.

"They're on the move."

DS Chand's heart began to race as he dashed over to the radio console and took his seat, ready to direct operations.

"DC Dreketi, they're on the move. Be ready to monitor them from your position on the point. Let me know when they reach the beacon. Sergeant Nailatikau, don't get too close to them. Keep a discreet distance from them in your punt. I don't want to spook them from making the pickup."

"I can see the navigation lights of their boat coming out into the bay from the Tradewinds Coffee jetty," reported Sgt Nailatikau. "I'll keep well back and watch for their lights."

After an anxious 30-minute wait DC Dreketi called in from his position.

"I've picked them up via my infrared binoculars. They appear to be stationary next to the beacon. I'll let you know when they're on the move, and I'll send the divers down to check that the retrieval of the consignment has been made."

*

"You guys want a beer?" Tiko asked as the deckhand dropped the anchor of the *Coffee Queen* next to the flashing harbour beacon.

"Wait till we get the containers onboard. Then we can relax with a beer," replied Rob. "Don't like to dive with alcohol in the system, even if it is Fiji Bitter."

"You can dive, Rob and I'll look after the beers with Tiko," teased Barry.

Rob didn't need a wetsuit in warm tropical waters and was soon in the water with only a waterproof torch. He retrieved the lines attached to the canisters, passing them to Tiko and his deckhand, who quickly had the canisters aboard.

Happy with their efforts, they soon returned to the Tradewinds jetty.

*

An hour had passed since DC Dreketi's call, and an agitated DS Chand began to return to his pacing around the police station. Finally, DC Dreketi's crackling voice broke the silence.

"Confirm they're on the move. I'll prepare the divers with torches to check that the drugs have been retrieved."

"I can pick up the vessel lights heading back towards Tradewinds," confirmed Sgt Nailatikau.

253

After another nerve testing wait for DS Chand, DC Dreketi confirmed that the divers could not find the submerged plastic canisters in the waters near the beacon.

"DC Dreketi, I now want you to move to the Tradewinds Coffee premises and monitor the unloading of the cargo. You can park in Wailailai village next door to Tradewinds Coffee and go to the guys who've been staking out the jetty and production shed."

"Yes, sir. On my way," replied DC Dreketi.

The clock ticked another 30 minutes before Sgt Nailatikau reported that the targets were approaching the jetty at Tradewinds. They hadn't appeared to detect they were being watched and had maintained a steady cruising speed.

"Dreketi here," came a whispered voice. "I can see the boat arriving at the Tradewinds jetty. They've tied up and seem to be in good spirits from what I can see from under the jetty lights. They're laughing and joking. Ah, they're now unloading the large plastic canisters from the launch's stern. I can see them carrying the canisters to the packing shed."

"Good work, team," said an exuberant DS Chand. "When this is all over, the drinks are on me."

The arrival of the drugs at Tradewinds Coffee instigated a chain of communications across the Pacific Ocean. DS Chand to SS Naqima in Suva Police Headquarters. SS Naqima to DCI Charles in Sydney at AFP HQ and then to Agent Carter onboard the *USS Neil Armstrong* approaching Columbian territorial waters.

All now awaited the DEA assault team arriving in position on their helicopter transport vessel, ready to launch the assault on the Gonzales compound. The plan was for an order to be issued to all strike teams to get into position, coinciding with the launch of the helicopters at 4 am local Columbian time. The final order was planned for 6 am, when the helicopters were in position, just on sunrise.

Simultaneous raids would occur at local times in Sydney at 9 pm and Savusavu at 11 pm local time.

CHAPTER 34

Squads of police had assembled at the Sydney and Savusavu dispatch points, awaiting the green light from Agent Carter to get into position at their respective strike locations.

On the other side of the Pacific Ocean, the helicopter transport, the *USS Neil Armstrong*, was positioned off the coast of Columbia, at the closest geographical position to access the town of Cali.

Four choppers were set for take-off on the ship's deck. In the early hours, a gentle offshore breeze maintained a relatively calm sea, ideal conditions for the operation. Six DEA agents were assigned to each craft, and there was a hive of activity as the teams loaded – side arms, M-16 rifles, flares, concussion grenades, grenade launchers and an array of small explosive devices. Agent Carter with Penny, would be aboard the lead helicopter. With the distance required to reach the target and return to the ship, Andy knew they would only have a safety factor of around 10 to 15 minutes to return. It would be tight, with the possible risk of a chopper going down on the return journey if the wind direction changed.

Andy checked his watch. It was five minutes to the mission launch.

"I see you have Gertrude in hand, Penny," he said, trying to sound calm.

"Would not travel anywhere without her," Penny replied as she placed the trusted firearm in its holder under her seat.

With a final check of the lead agents on the other three craft, Andy gave the order to begin the operation.

There was a flurry of activity as the DEA agents piled aboard their helicopters and strapped themselves in. As the second hand reached the hour, the attack teams lifted off the gently rocking deck in unison and headed towards the darkened Columbian coastline and their unexpecting quarry.

The signal was received in Sydney and Savusavu. It was all systems go to get into position and await the signal. SS Naqima had joined DS Chand in Savusavu to prepare for the strike on Tradewinds Coffee, and in Sydney, Adam with Tanya were preparing for the hit on the Mount Willsmore warehouse.

*

"Looks like all six of our boys have settled in for the night," informed DSC Rob Gregson, sitting in his unmarked police vehicle, parked on the far side of the deserted, dimly lit Mount Willsmore industrial estate. "I can see one of the Fijian guys has arrived with a carton of beer, and another has returned with a mountain of pizza boxes. I don't think they're going anywhere tonight."

Arriving with headlights extinguished, Adam and Tanya pulled up next to DSC Gregson's position just as Sergeant Collens, head of the SWAT team, arrived. Adam signalled for the group to meet out of sight of the warehouse behind a nearby closed daytime coffee and donut dispensing caravan.

"We've identified all of our K-gang friends are inside the warehouse. They are currently enjoying beer and pizza," Adam spoke softly. "I don't think they'll be too vigilant at nine with what they'll be consuming."

*

A crackly voice came over Adam's satellite phone.

"This is Attack one. We are ten minutes from our ETA. Assume positions and await the command to strike."

"We'll be ready to blast open the entry door next to the roller door at precisely nine," informed Sgt Collens. "The team will be equipped with body armour and shields in readiness for any hostile response. Adam, your team can follow behind us, ready to make the arrests."

Adam illuminated his watch dial, "Thanks, Sergeant. Time check is ten minutes to the hour…..now, let's get into position."

The SWAT team looked threatening, dressed in black uniforms and night vision goggles, sitting over the top of black ski masks. With their thick rubber-soled boots, they stealthily made their way into a position at the entry door. Explosive devices were placed next to the door handle and at each of the three large hinges of the thick steel door. The explosives would be activated by a radio-controlled device held by Sergeant Rob Collens on receipt of the go signal.

The SWAT team retreated to a distance of 30 metres on either side of the door and hugged the wall to await the signal to detonate the devices.

Again Adam's satellite phone crackled into life, "Attack two and attack three. This is attack one. The command is for GO!"

"Go, go, go," Adam roared into his two-way. "Blow the door."

*

Inside the warehouse, the unsuspecting Sydney K-gang members sat in the warehouse office watching a game of rugby league on a small TV screen. They had set the warehouse up as a base, bringing in inflatable mattresses and some cheap furniture – fold-up tables and chairs, second-hand sofas, a small two-burner gas stove and a refrigerator. Upon receipt of the first shipment from Fiji, a forklift would be brought in, ready to stack the shelves.

"I'm goin' for a piss," said Tui as he stepped off the office bench with half-time approaching. "I'll grab another round of beers ready for the second half."

Tui stood relieving himself in the bathroom when the building suddenly shook with loud explosions.

"Get down on your belly, get down on your belly and don't move," screaming voices yelled. "Hands behind your backs."

Tui zipped up his pants and tentatively peeked out of a narrow crack in the bathroom door, revealing the swarming black uniformed SWAT team, appearing through a smoky haze. His fellow K-gang members offered little resistance and lay flat on their stomachs with hands placed as ordered, ready to be restrained with black cable ties.

Tui tip-toed to the toilet cistern, removed the lid, and extracted a Ziplock bag containing a Smith and Wesson, snub-nosed 640 handgun. He removed the gun from the bag, retrieved his mobile from his back pocket, and dialled Tiko's number in Fiji.

Adam, Tanya and Rob stood with their backs to the bathroom, guns pointed at the prostrate gang members when Adam suddenly spoke up after a headcount check.

"Wait a minute. There are only five. Where's the sixth guy?"

As one, they started to turn towards the creaking bathroom door. Tui burst out with his gun raised and yelling into his mobile.

"Tiko, Tiko, the cops are here." With the police frozen in surprise, Tui shoved his mobile into his jeans back pocket and grabbed Tanya around the neck. He held the gun to Tanya's head and shuffled back towards the front door, hanging off its hinges after the entry blast.

"Put your fuckin' guns down, or I'll blow her fuckin' head off. Get your car keys out bitch. Come on, you guys, get up. Let's get the fuck out of here."

As Tui continued to edge backwards with his arm around Tanya, she reached into her trouser pocket and extracted her car keys which she held at head height with her arm outstretched. As the K-gang members started to get onto their feet, Tanya could sense Tui was being distracted, so she dropped her keys and attempted to grab the gun. She drove backwards with her legs, causing Tui to stumble, and their bodies crashed to the floor. A shot discharged from Tui's gun, and a SWAT member rushed forward to disarm Tui by kicking the gun.

"Back on the floor, you prick," ordered Sgt Collens as Tanya was lifted off Tui. "Shit, she's been hit. Call an ambulance."

"Fuck," cried out Adam as he raced to Tanya's side. "Gregson, get on to SS Naqima in Fiji and tell him about the call. I hope he hasn't been able to alert the gang in Fiji. Is the ambulance on its way?"

Adam removed his jacket and used it to apply pressure to the wound, slowly oozing blood from the right side of Tanya's stomach region. "Let Carlo know. I hope the baby's going to be ok," whispered Tanya as she fell unconscious.

"Holy shit. Where's that fuckin' ambulance," said Adam as he cradled Tanya's head. "A baby! OMG! What's Carlo going to say?"

*

The time was approaching 11 pm local time as a string of barking dogs greeted the Fijian police team as they entered Wailailai village, located next door to the Tradewinds Coffee property. SS Naqima scanned the Tradewinds property with his infra-red binoculars and noted that the main house, where Tiko, his Kiwi visitors and gang members were holed up, was in darkness.

Security lights were illuminated on the jetty where the company's vessel, the *Coffee Queen,* was moored. A security guard could be seen making regular circuits of the two operational sheds before returning to the security hut located to the left of the jetty.

"DS Chand, I'd like you to brief the team. Your experience with the property during the arrest of the Conti brothers will be invaluable," stated SS Viliame Naqima.

"Right team, you'll note the security guard returned to the hut on the left of the jetty. It is where the security office is located and where the guard can access the CCTV," detailed DS Chand. "The CCTV covers the entrance from the main road, the jetty area, the homestead's front door, and the grounds surrounding the coffee packing and roasting sheds."

"With the CCTV, it'll be difficult to approach the main house without alerting the security guard," observed Viliame.

"I propose we cut off the power to the property and get to the guard before the backup generator kicks in," DS Chand proposed. "We'll encourage him not to make any warnings to the homestead. Ah, here's DC Dreketi with Miss Mereoni, the housekeeper."

"Yes sir, Miss Mereoni can help us with the house's layout," responded DC Dreketi.

Mereoni explained that there were two doors providing access to the house.

The main door leads in from the front verandah, and a rear door exits from the kitchen to the laundry area. The doors were constructed with heavy, local hardwood timber. From the front door, a passageway opened immediately on the right to the lounge area, and three bedrooms were further down the hall on the left. The first bedroom housed the two Kiwi visitors. In the second bedroom slept, four Fijian friends of Mister Tiko and Mister Tiko occupied the main bedroom. Directly opposite Mister Tiko's room was the bathroom. At the rear of the house were an extra toilet, an office and the kitchen. Each bedroom had a large, curtained window.

"Thank you, Mereoni, you have been very helpful. Constable Whippy will take you back to your bure and stay with you," said DC Dreketi.

"Based on Mereoni's feedback, our targets will be scattered throughout the house, including the bathroom, lounge and office. We'll take out the power five minutes to the hour and then move on the guard to avoid him waking up anyone in the house. We'll then place men outside each bedroom window and simultaneously crash in the front and rear doors with sledgehammers," instructed SS Naqima. "Prime target is Tiko in the main and second bedrooms with his fellow gang members. I don't expect the Kiwis to put up too much resistance. Make sure we also check the bathroom, lounge, office and toilet. They may be armed, so I don't want anyone surprising us."

At five minutes to the hour, the power was cut, and two constables raced into the security office as the guard turned on his flashlight and began to check the controls on his console. They presented their IDs and got him to sit quietly in the office. Three rapid flashes of torchlight indicated all was quiet in the security office, signalling the rest of the police team to get into position.

SS Naqima was poised at the bottom of the two steps leading up to the front verandah and the main door. He watched as the second hand on his watch's luminous dial crept towards the hour. At 11 pm, the GO command crackled over his satellite phone from the other side of the Pacific Ocean.

As the front door was caved in with the heavy blows from the sledgehammer, the faint ring of a mobile phone could be heard from down the hallway.

"Quick, quick. The main bedroom," roared SS Naqima.

As the policemen burst into Tiko's room, he had just picked up the flashing mobile phone from the bedside table. A voice could be heard coming from the speaker.

"Tiko, Tiko, the cops are here."

"Put that down," demanded SS Naqima as he marched across and snatched the phone from Tiko. " You won't be needing that for some time. Especially with what you have in your sheds."

CHAPTER 35

"Those Argentinians sure make a great Malbec," said Hernando as he sniffed at his glass of inky, dark-red wine. "Here's to the next stage in the growth of the Gonzales empire. With the K-gang, we'll finally take over the Western Pacific and, who knows, eventually force our way into the lucrative Asian markets from our new Sydney base."

"Now that the consignment has arrived in Fiji, we can call Tiko tomorrow afternoon. I'll send him a message that we'll call," said Roberto. "It will be good to discuss his plans for getting production fired up and stock into the Sydney warehouse as soon as possible."

"I'll also ask him for an update on whether they have tracked down our man Carlo yet," noted Hernando. "I need to speak to the Kiwis as well. I want them back here as quickly as possible. Ideally, I'd like to get another shipment into Fiji before the hurricane season starts later in the year."

"We'll probably need to check out other means of getting bigger volumes of product into Fiji once production gets underway," said Roberto. "We'll need to develop a system to supply CH all year-round to the packing facility."

"Once I finish this wine, I'm off to bed," said Hernando. "We have a big day tomorrow with more coca leaves to arrive for the labs to get production underway for a big order into the US. I managed to finalise a deal with our Italian friends in New York. Also, our friends in Cuba have been doing a great job of getting CH in via family connections in Miami. We'll very quickly make up the loss, courtesy of the Contis."

"I'll head off to bed as well," said Roberto. "The lovely Carmen awaits me. I haven't had a good fuck since my one in Sydney after killing Gaetano and Lorenzo. Electra was her name. I still get a hard-on just thinking about her."

"No more of your crazy stuff, OK," added a concerned Hernando. "Madame Carlotta doesn't like the way you treat her girls. None of them wants to come out here, despite the big money you are paying."

"They certainly don't complain about the money, and I've helped Carlotta out with the pesky town sheriff, who's always got his hand out to her," responded Roberto as he stood and made his way to his room. "I'll be good to Carmen. Promise," he called back to Hernando.

*

"Attack One, this is Black Dog," came the call over Andy's headset as the choppers skimmed across the top of the dense, dark Amazon jungle. "The drone check indicates all our targets are present, and all is quiet, apart from some activity in the kitchen area at the rear of the compound."

"Black Dog, our ETA is 5 minutes. All proceeding to plan."

Black Dog sat in his post in the hills above the Gonzales compound, intently focused on his laptop screen. He continued to scan the inside of the walled fortress with his drone, monitoring for any potential threats to the rapidly approaching assault craft.

The throbbing pulse of the helicopters could be heard as they approached Black Dog's hilltop position. Black Dog covered his keyboard and held tightly onto his equipment as the massive downdraft from the low-level chopper engines hit his post, gradually rescinding as the craft roared down the hill towards their unsuspecting targets.

"Sydney, Savusavu, you've got the all clear. Go," roared Andy as the choppers began to swoop down on their unsuspecting target like falcons hunting their prey.

*

After a long, torrid night, a weeping, Carmen had roused Roberto from sleep. She fled from his bedroom as the first dim light of the new day started to flicker through his bedroom curtains.

"Ungrateful bitch," Roberto mumbled as he got out of bed to relieve himself in his ensuite.

What's that rumbling noise? Roberto peered out of his ensuite window with the unidentified noise gradually increasing in volume, causing his toiletries to rattle on the shelf in front of his mirror.

"Helicopters. Shit," he yelled. "Hernando! Hernando!" He pulled on his pants and a t-shirt and ran to Hernando's room, pounding on the closed door.

Hernando sleepily opened his door in a shiny, silky, crimson bathrobe. "What is it? It's not even sun up. What's that fuckin' noise?"

"Fuckin' helicopters. It must be the Federales," said Roberto as the first explosions hit the compound surrounding the hacienda. "Why weren't we warned the bastards were coming."

"Shit, let's get moving. Alert the pilots and get them to start up the choppers," said Hernando as he discarded his robe, grabbed a pre-packed bag next to his door and slipped on some runners. He started to head for the front door, with Roberto following close behind, with a bag in one hand and a handgun in the other.

As Hernando opened the front door, he watched in horror as missiles slammed into the two waiting helicopters, sending blackened balls of flame into the sky and leaving a tangled mess of metal intertwined with the bloodied bodies of the pilots.

Looking skywards, Roberto could see unmarked, camouflaged helicopters beginning to descend into the compound. Armed troops in unidentified clothing were rapidly pouring from the craft as soon as they landed. Dust and grit were thrown around, causing Roberto and Hernando to shield their eyes as the invader's engines continued to roar.

Roberto's mind was racing as he heard the accents of the raiders' voices, *"Fuckin' Americanos. It must be the DEA. No wonder we didn't know about the raid. The bastards have knocked out our choppers, and no one can get in from the outside gate to save us."* He grabbed Hernando by the arm and started to head with him towards the stables where the vehicles were parked.

"Let's vamos," yelled Roberto as he accelerated the Ford Explorer out of the garage and headed for the hacienda gates just as explosions from the underground laboratories rocked the ground and sent plumes of smoke into the air.

*

Amongst all the mayhem created in the compound by smoke bombs and exploding grenades, the Gonzales staff squatted on the ground with their arms raised. Some movement towards the stables at the rear property caught Andy's attention.

"It's Roberto and Hernando," said Andy directly into Penny's ear, pointing towards the two men about to jump into a vehicle. Penny instinctively retrieved Gertrude from the rifle bag on her back and fell some distance behind Andy as he headed towards the garage.

A black SUV suddenly burst out of the stable garage and motored rapidly towards the gate. Andy raised his handgun and fired off several rounds, which caused the vehicle to pick up speed, bullets ricocheting off the armoured windscreen. The vehicle swerved and headed directly at Andy, smashing into the left side of Andy's body and flinging him away from the vehicle's path.

Penny took a depth breath and calmly raised Gertrude. She fired shots into the driver's front tyres. The SUV only started to slow slightly as it ploughed into the partially opened gate.

A shot from the vehicle raised dust next to Penny. She instinctively dropped to the ground and set up Gertrude towards the direction of the shot. A smiling Roberto began to aim his weapon towards Penny.

Deep breath, slowly exhales, squeeze gently.

With a surprised look, Roberto dropped his gun and clutched his chest. He looked down as blood began to ooze through his fingers as he slowly crumpled.

"In the vehicle over by the gate, grab the guy in the passenger seat. That's Hernando, our primary target," ordered Penny to an officer coming to her side.

Penny rushed over to Andy's limp body.

"Are you ok?" Penny asked as she quickly checked over his lifeless body, noting blood oozing from his chest.

Oh, God. This is not good. He's unresponsive.

Penny bent over and checked his pulse. Not feeling anything, she placed her hands under Andy's armpits and dragged him towards the waiting helicopter. She signalled to a fellow agent who rushed over and helped Penny carefully place the unresponsive Andy onboard the chopper.

"Come on. Get Hernando onboard. We need to get Andy back on the ship," she shouted.

The officer directed to seize Hernando cautiously approached the crumpled vehicle with steam pouring out from under the bonnet. He opened the passenger side door with gun drawn and saw the passenger slumped over the console with blood seeping from a deep head wound. Another DEA officer arrived and helped carry the unconscious Hernando to the command chopper.

Onboard the chopper, the pilot informed Penny that the local Federales were on their way.

Assuming command, she ordered, "This is Attack One. Let's get out of here."

As the chopper began to rise, Penny could take in the scene onboard. An unconscious Hernando was strapped into his seat with his head slumped forward. Andy lay face down on the floor with a pool of congealed blood, having blackened the back of his shirt.

Penny knelt beside Andy's lifeless form and turned over his body. There was the sudden realisation that he was dead. She just sat and stared at the scene below as the fleet of choppers began to rise and head back towards the coast and the safety of the awaiting *USS Neil Armstrong*. In the distance, she noted the headlights from a fleet of vehicles raising dust on the dirt road as they rapidly made their way down the access road towards the main gates of the compound.

In the chopper, Penny sat motionless, staring at the compound below. The hacienda was burning, and smoke was billowing from the bombs set off in the underground laboratories.

Hernando is under arrest, and Roberto is dead. But Andy is also dead! Was it all worth it?

Penny reached for some binoculars in her backpack and scoured the scene below.

I am sure another organisation will quickly fill the void to meet the world's insatiable demand for the devilish white powder.

She looked at the devastated scene as the choppers rose above the surrounding hills. There was a flash of light from the jungle below.

"Attack One, this is Black Dog. Safe travels; I'm outta here. Over and out."

*

The time was approaching 8.15 am as the DEA fleet, airborne for nearly two and quarter hours, equipped with long-range fuel tanks, reached the coast of Columbia. ETA for the *USS Neil Armstrong* was five minutes.

Hernando looked across at Tanya with dried blood caked on the bandage wrapped around his forehead.

"Your government is two-faced. You used my organisation to get rid of President Torres and get your man Casillas elected, and then you do this to me. May you all rot in fucking hell."

Penny looked up from the lifeless form of Andy Carter cradled in her lap and glared at Hernando as the chopper descended onto the carrier's deck.

Why did I go for the tyres? Why didn't I shoot to kill? We didn't need to take Hernando alive. It has cost me the only man I've loved.

I'm done with this life.

*

Carlo sat anxiously in the waiting room of Sydney's St Vincent's Hospital. It had been 12 hours since the completion of Tanya's surgery, complicated by her being in the early stages of pregnancy.

"Mr Conti, I'm Mister Estros, Miss Layton's surgeon. It was a very difficult surgery, but I can be reasonably confident she will recover fully, given adequate rest and rehabilitation."

"Thank sir. Can I see her?" Carlo asked.

"Yes, she is still sleepy but keen to speak with you. The nurse will direct you to Room 327."

Carlo followed the nurse to Tanya's room and was relieved to see her sitting up in bed, sipping on some water through a straw. He wanted to rush over and hug her but knew that was impossible.

"How are you, my darlin," said Carlo as he wiped away the tears rolling down his cheeks. He sat on the chair next to Tanya's bed and clasped her left hand, avoiding the right hand with its protruding cannula and tubing, dripping fluids into her body.

"I'm a bit tired but starting to feel better. The surgeon said the procedure went well and repaired the damage to my right side. Most importantly, all is good with the baby. You won't be the last Conti for much longer. I was told we are having a boy."

"You're retiring from the police force for sure," said Carlo. "You'll join me in the gym along with junior Conti."

"Yes, I'll be joining you at Sydney's Powerhouse gym. No worries."

—

THE END

OTHER BOOKS IN
THE CONTI TRILOGY

CRY IN YOUR SLEEP

The legend goes that a princess escaping an arranged marriage sought refuge underneath a tree, beside a remote mountain lake on the Fijian island of Taveuni.

In her sadness, she cries in her sleep, the tears becoming the red flowers of the *Tagimoucia* plant, which the villagers use for its medicinal properties.

Adrian Nicholls, an ambitious rising star in the global pharmaceutical industry, will do anything to succeed.

Jacob Bryant, a talented Australian scientist, is a champion for the ethical development of medicines. They are both in pursuit of developing a pain-relieving product from the Tagimoucia's beautiful red flowers.

In the Sydney underworld, the Conti brothers see an opportunity to expand their growing drug empire. Will a growing relationship with Fijian scientist Dr Mere Koroi distract Jacob from achieving his aims? How will all their paths cross in the picturesque islands of Fiji in their race for success?

Cry In Your Sleep is the gripping debut novel in the *Conti Trilogy* pharmacrime drama series, by Australian author Bruce Hewett.

Available now in paperback and on Kindle® from Amazon.

THE BULA TRAIL

Free after three years imprisonment in Sydney's notorious Long Bay Prison, the Conti brothers want to make up for lost time and get back into the drug business. But where?

Could the paradise islands of Fiji lying in the tropical mid-Pacific Ocean provide the answer? Could Fiji become the hub to distribute Columbian Heaven to Australia and beyond?

Guido Conti is angry at the time lost in prison. He wants revenge. He wants the big bucks. He wants a drug empire and wants nothing to stand in his way.

Guido's twin brother Carlo is more of a thinker. Could there be an opportunity outside the illicit drug business that makes money but without the ever-present risk of prison or even death?

Detectives Adam Charles and Tanya Layton are angry at what they see as the early release of the Conti brothers from prison. They suspect the Conti's will not sit idly around and want to stop them becoming a danger to the community again. Will their paths cross in the picturesque islands of Fiji?

The Bula Trail is second the thrilling installment in the *Conti Trilogy* pharmacrime drama series, by Australian author Bruce Hewett.

Available now in paperback and on Kindle® from Amazon.

ACKNOWLEDGEMENTS

When I sat down to start writing my first book, *Cry In Your Sleep*, I never thought there would be a sequel, let alone a trilogy. It has been a wonderful journey and helped me transition from full-time work with something to keep the mind busy.

None of this journey would have been possible without my publisher Roderic Grigson. Rod challenged the storyline, questioned the plausibility of my characters, fact-checked the content and invited me to take risks with the characters created. Each book demonstrated my progression as a writer with Rod's invaluable input.

Three books in three years have been demanding on myself and my time, and I must acknowledge my wife, Bev, for being so tolerant of the hours I spent locked away writing. I promised her that I would now take a break from writing.

Bruce Hewett

ABOUT THE AUTHOR

After graduating as a pharmacist in Perth, Western Australia, Bruce set off to see the world but fell in love with his first stop in the Fiji Islands. During the next ten years in Fiji, he managed a community pharmacy in Suva, established his own community pharmacy in the township of Lami and represented Fiji in the 1984 Los Angeles Olympic Games in yachting.

Bruce married a local Fiji gal Beverley, and following the birth of their first child, the family made the difficult decision to leave behind family and friends in Fiji to commence a new life in Sydney, Australia. In Sydney, Bruce joined the pharmaceutical industry, where he spent the next 35 years in a variety of senior management roles in Australia, New Zealand and the UK, as well as establishing his own successful consulting business.

Now living in Melbourne, Australia, Bruce, besides writing, spends his time as a non-executive director of a publicly listed healthcare company. He also enjoys keeping fit, voluntary work with a charity and spending time with his two children, Vanessa and Sean and their families.

This is Bruce's final book in the trilogy of his novels *Cry In Your Sleep* and *The Bula Trail* sequel. He has also published two short stories in *The Scribe Tribe, Volume Two, and* collected short stories and poems from the writers of Balla Balla.

To discover more about Bruce and his writing, please visit:

hewettwrites.com